DARK QUEEN

A MAFIA ROMANCE

BY KER DUKEY

DEDICATION.

For Christian,
my Babydaddy, husband, best friend, and my fierce, strong,
delicious King.
I'm honored to be your Queen.

A queen will always turn pain into power
~ Author Unknown

CHAPTER ONE

Alyssa

PAIN, sharp and pulsing, explodes within my flesh, spreading like a wildfire up my back and abdomen.

The shocked eyes of the man who promised me safety will be the last thing I ever see.

The intensity steals my breath.

My mouth opens, but only a squeaked, inhuman noise exits.

My sight becomes cloudy, tears welling and falling to my cheeks.

Is this how Mom felt?

Cold...the darkness closing in...

I'm going to die here.

My chest aches as the pounding slows.

Thud.

Thud.

Thud.

The world spins, fading...

How can it end like this? I was a queen—*his* queen—and it will be his kingdom that kills me.

CHAPTER TWO

A COUPLE OF MONTHS BEFORE…

Alyssa

BURYING my mother left me with a sense of freedom. I could finally breathe, and that opened a pocket of guilt inside my chest.

I need to get out of here.

She was ill for such a prolonged period, I came to terms with the fact that she was dying a long time ago, but I didn't think it would be so slow, so degrading.

She withered away painfully, lost herself day by day, until all that was left was a pathetic carcass unable to even relieve her bladder on her own terms.

I'm so glad she's gone.

Those thoughts fill out that pocket, expanding within me.

Guilt. Guilt. Guilt.

I'm drowning in it.

"Is it wrong to feel like she died well before she stopped breathing?" I wonder aloud, the memory of her ragged breathing and coughing rattling her chest bone lingering within me.

She sounded like a spluttering generator out of gas. The noise still haunts my dreams.

Clint, my best friend for over a decade, looks at me. "No. Her battle was long and hard on you both," he reassures, like a good friend should.

Though, I'm not sure if he means hard on me and Mom or me and Dad.

My dad will be fine. They practically became strangers over the years, two ships docking at the same port but completely separate entities.

Sometimes I wonder if they only stayed together because of some messed up sense of duty they thought they owed me...or themselves...or the world.

The truth is, Mom resented Dad for ruining her chance to take her dance career to the next level.

Resentment is corrosive. It rotted away inside her until all that remained was a bitter, angry woman.

She channeled all that poison into me, molding me into what she wanted for herself.

"Make a wish," Clint says, pointing up at a shooting star.

We lay in the field at the back of my house under the inky night sky, the humming of crickets all around us, night animals coming awake in the woods at the border of our property.

Clint's hand nudges mine, hoping I'll take it, but I won't. No matter how hard I wish I had those feelings for him, I don't.

If anything, he bores me. But it would crush him to know I hate these nights with him. I only used to come out here to escape the sounds of mom's death rattle.

It would be easier if my heart wanted him—hell, even my body—but neither are drawn to him.

"So, when do you think you'll be back?"

Never.

I tilt my head toward him, taking him in, memorizing his features to keep me company on lonely days in the big city.

He's handsome in a typical kind of way.

His wavy blond hair casually falls over his forehead, making it hard not to notice his pretty blue eyes with flecks of lighter shades throughout the irises.

Playing lacrosse has given him an athletic physique most girls get giddy over.

He's well-liked, popular, and could have any girl he chooses, but he'd rather hang out with me.

I don't see why he even likes me—I don't even like me half the time.

We don't have a lot in common. I dedicate most of my time to dance, and he just slots himself in my life wherever he can.

He's lived across the small lake from me since I can remember, always joking we're the real-life Dawson and Joey from Dawson's Creek, a show we watched re-runs of with Mom while she slowly faded away.

I'm no Joey, though. There's no deep-seated crush, no good girl virgin waiting for him to notice me.

He did notice me.

The looks he thought were subtle, the brush of his hands against my body at any opportunity, the anger toward anyone who would flirt with me.

I've known for a long time he's wanted more, but the very thought of settling here, living the same life my mother did, cripples me with dread.

Guilt. Guilt. Guilt filling me up.

"Ally." He nudges me, his brow furrowed, and I realize I'm still staring at him.

Turning away, I say, "It'll depend on if I get in." Smiling wistfully, I think to myself, *I have to get in.*

Sighing, he pulls at the blades of grass. "You'll get in. You're the best dancer I know, and they invited you, right?"

Wrong.

"I'm the only dancer you know." I snort.

The truth is, I should have applied two years ago, but Dad was useless, so Mom needed me here, and now I'm two years older.

To anyone else, a couple years is nothing, but to a dancer, it can mean everything.

Swan Academy of Dance is for the elite and costs a fortune. They're selective—especially with girls my age.

You have to be in the best health, have the right physique and structure suited to the demands.

This open audition was like winning the lottery.

They're offering five students the chance to train with them for a year in a special scholarship program, and I need one of those spots.

A year of studying at their academy, and you have a golden ticket to any ballet production company you want, *anywhere* you want.

Freedom.

The breeze ripples through the trees, lifting the scent of fresh-cut grass, filling the air with it.

Tonight feels like the end of an era, like this will be the last time I have to fake it while I lay here with my "best friend," safe, secure, with only the dreams of venturing out into the real world.

It's juvenile. Normal. I can't wait for it to be over.

"It's getting late," I muse, getting myself into a sitting position, brushing out the creases in my plain black dress.

I don't get why people wear black for funerals.

It's so formal.

Boring.

Mom was a colorful person. We should have worn shades of

the rainbow. Purple was her favorite color, and no one wore it. There weren't even purple flowers on her coffin.

A chill races up my spine. Her purple face. Bloodshot eyes staring up at the yellow ceiling above her bed in her musky room.

Dad rushing in after hearing my screams.

There was no look of horror on his face, no sorrow or shock.

He didn't cry, check her pulse—nothing.

He didn't even ask why her mouth was agape, bed rumpled, why my arms were bleeding from being scratched so badly.

He wasn't there while her body jolted like a fish being plucked from water, but the evidence was.

Flop. Flop. Flop...

While I held the pillow over her face, clutched so tight in my hands, my nails punctured the skin on my palms through the fabric. Tears coursed down my cheeks as she clawed at my arms, wanting air.

Flop...flop...flop...

Nothing.

She just stopped. Stopped moving—breathing—living.

Silence.

I gave her mercy.

It's an easy lie I tell myself. It was me I gave mercy to.

"I'm cold. I'm going inside." I push the words out, rubbing up my arms to ward off the non-existent wind.

"Wait," Clint begs. His brow furrows as he seems to struggle to form words. His mouth opens and closes three times before he finally says, "I'm not ready to say goodbye."

He covers his face with his palms, scrubbing downward.

Poking his rib, I roll my eyes. "I'm not going off to war."

He's always been dramatic, a little immature. The trouble with growing up in a small town: there's no rush to grow up and nothing exciting to experience. It's a slow way to die. "You can come visit." I shrug.

Please don't visit.

His body jolts with a burst of laughter. "I know that."

Getting to his knees, he chews on his lip and swipes a hand through his blond locks.

"There's something I want you to know before you go and get swept off your feet by some city guy." He shakes his head, and I squirm at his awkwardness.

"What is it?" I scoot forward, annoyed this is taking so long.

His eyes soften as he takes my hand from my lap. I have to school my features to hide the internal cringe.

Tightening his grip, he rests it on his thigh, stroking his thumb over the healing wounds.

A cold sweat breaks out over my brow. I want to run back to the house, pack my suitcase, and never look back.

"I know today has been crappy and it's not really the time, but if I don't say anything now, I may never get the chance."

My heart picks up, sending the blood rushing around my body. My stomach dips. "What is it?"

Please don't say you love me.

Please don't say you love me.

Please don't say you love me.

"I love you."

CHAPTER THREE

Luca Leto

JUMPING FROM THE CAR, I stride toward the back door of my club, hands fisted, my mind racing, how the hell did this happen, and why *her*.

Silence greets me when I pull open the door and enter, a sense of dread lingers in the air, a group of employees huddled together advert their eyes as I pass, the faint hum of weeping follows me down the corridor.

Ricardo, the head of security for this club, walks toward me, hands raised in defensive posture, his clothes rumpled, a cut across the bridge of his nose.

"Mr Leto, I don't know how." He wobbles his head, alarm glowing in his eyes, a visible tremor rattling his body.

He's right to fear me, most men do.

That's why it's so hard to grasp the events that's unfolded here.

"Just fucking move," I bark, shouldering past him. I'll deal with him later.

Marcello my cousin and number two has beat me here and is standing by Serena's room, *our room,* his hands on his hips, head bowed.

We've both seen a lot of death, been the cause of most of it, so to see him rattled it unsettling.

My chest thuds violently, his eyes lifting to meet mine, the pinched features are shouting, *No. Don't come closer. Don't fucking look.* But I have to. I have to see her.

The scent hits me first, the metallic tinge clinging to the air coating my tongue with every inhale, my eyes explore the room and land on her, Serena.

Fuck what did they do to you.

Blood.

So much blood.

Everywhere.

It's on the walls, the ceiling, seeping through the cracks of the tiled floor, congealing beneath her naked form. Thick, wet crimson slashes cover every part of her pale flesh, her body discarded at the foot of the pole she'd danced around a hundred times for me.

It was supposed to be only me, she was my exclusive girl. I don't like sharing and everyone knows she belonged to me.

I'm not the sort of man to claim a woman for more than sexual gratification. I'm a selfish bastard, never offering her more than my cock and a paycheck—and she was greedy for both. It works for us —*worked.*

Who did this to you? The questions barrel through my mind coiling my muscles.

A small pile of fabric, what looks like bra and panties have been discarded on the small booth but there's no money—champagne bottles—glasses all the things you'd expect to find in these rooms when a girl is entertaining.

My eyes flick up to the video monitor, the wire deliberately cut to shut off the live feed.

Dropping on my hutches I stroke a strand of hair from her face, she's beautiful even in death, the slash across her throat is deep, vehement, her killer enjoyed this.

"This is an attack on me," I rumble, running my hands through my hair, getting back to my feet. Someone has a death wish and when I find them it's going to be slow and painful.

"We don't know that." Marcello jerks a shoulder, his brow dipping.

"Look at her," I snap "This is my club, my girl, someone is trying to send a message."

Exhaling he places a hand on my shoulder, "No one is foolish enough, Luca, this is just some sick prick who gets off on hurting women, just a coincidence."

"This can't just be another coincidence." I bite, a pounding sounds in my ears. "Not after my mother." I'll burn this city to the ground if someone is inciting a war, every battle scar I own is from victory and this time will be no different.

"The police said your mother's murder was a mugging gone wrong—"

He's words fall flat when I shoot a scathing glare his way, my finger coming up to his face. "You know better than that," I warn through gritted teeth. NYPD doesn't want a battle in their city. They would say anything to keep that from happening.

"We looked into every lead. She was my aunt, Luca. I lost her too. It was an opportunist. Bad luck—nothing more. And the cunt who did it is fucking dead."

"I know!" I bellow, rage festering in my belly. It's always there.

"Her handbag was taken, Sir, nothing else."

My jaw ticks with the memory of that day.

A low life, drug addict piece of shit was arrested close to the scene the purse still on him, he wasn't getting prison, I took that bastard apart piece by piece, peeled the skin from bone, and hung him from George Washington bridge for all to see what becomes of a man who wrongs a Leto—only after making him first watch his own mother and brother die.

My mother was a Queen. It will haunt me to my grave that she was shot and left to bleed out next to the men hired to protect her.

My fist clenches, and I smash it into the door until the skin over my knuckle splits and blood trickles between my fingers.

Startled squeals ring through the air from the lingering workers waiting to be dismissed—be given answers I don't have.

"What do you want to do?" Marcello asks, running a hand down his face, scratching his chin, his own knuckles showing a cut no doubt from Ricardo's nose.

Serena's wide, vacant eyes peer up at me. "We find out who came into one of my places and touched what belonged to me." I seethe, rolling my shoulders.

"Ricardo," I bark.

He scampers down the corridor, lines crinkling his eyes and mouth. "Why the fuck was she back here?" I snarl, gripping him by the throat and smashing him into the wall. The plaster fissures under the force.

"I don't know. She only danced for you. I don't fucking know."

I pinch the cut on the bridge of his nose, enjoying the crunch of bone. His body writhes, eyes squinting closed, "It's your job to know—to keep these women safe."

"I'm sorry. I'm sorry. Please, Mr. Leto. Let me talk to the other girls. I'll find out, I promise." He squirms.

Releasing him with a shove, I crack my neck and run a hand over my jaw.

"Call the precinct. Ask for Detective Morels. He'll deal with this. In the meantime, get the list of every member who came in last night and all surveillance tapes that weren't destroyed."

This business wasn't some walk-in-off-the-street strip joint. It had the Leto name emblazoned on it. Membership was only for rich perverts to come get their cocks hard and if they paid enough, polished.

We had more celebrities frequent here than Madison Square Garden.

Whoever did this wasn't a stranger to the club or Serena.

When I find him, I'll be adding his carcass to the pile of fools who wronged me and if he is somehow involved in my mother's slaying, I'll be wiping his bloodline from existence.

"Did she have family?" Marcello calls out to a couple of the women.

One shrugs her shoulders, wrapping her arms around herself. "This place, us girls. She has a sister over at that ballet school, Swan something." A frown pulls on her features "She worked here to help pay her sister's fees." She says, her voice breaking.

I didn't know that, hell I didn't know anything about her and yet she died because of me.

"Get me her name," I grab Ricardo by the back of the neck shoving his head through the door to Serena's room.

"Take a good fucking look at her, because if you allow something like this to happen again on your watch what happened to her will be a walk in the park compared to what I'll do to you." I warn.

Summoning Marcello with a jerk of my head, I exit the way I came needing to get the fuck out of here.

*

ONCE BACK IN the car I yank my tie loose and pour a stiff drink from the decanter kept in here, my driver rising the privacy screen when Marcello joins me. "How's business, any disgruntled suppliers, buyers I should be aware of?" I ask, tipping the glass to my lips needing the burn of alcohol.

Snorting, Marcello stretches his legs out in the seat opposite me, "There's always rumblings in our type of business Luca, but no one would dare act on them."

Tell that to Serena. *My mother*.

"You did the right thing, letting the police take this one, there was too many employees there when she was found, it could get messy otherwise." He assures me.

Serena didn't deserve to be disposed of like a problem needing buried. She was a good girl, young, *too fucking young*. I had enough officers on my payroll anyway, just means my men will be looking for her killer and so will they, either way he's mine once he is found.

"You, okay?" Marcello asks when I remain quiet.

He's been by my side since we were toddlers fighting over the same toys. I trust him over all others, he's more a brother than my own, but my heart is hollow, it must be to be who I am, emotions can be construed as weakness. I don't let anyone see I have those flaws—not even my closet allies. He will not be getting any emotional confession from me.

"I know what it's like." He adds, tone deeper, head bowed.

"This isn't the same." I remind him.

His pain was because of a woman he loved, and she took her own life. *Annemarie*. Her name is etched into the skin over his chest, and she wasn't even his wife to mourn.

My father thought she'd be better suited for my younger brother, her prominent family line making them a good match.

Marcello was my cousin from our mother's being sisters, he had to work twice as hard to get half the respect my father showed toward me. Relation or not he wasn't the Leto bloodline and my father made sure he knew it.

"I can't believe how much fucking loss we've had to deal with this year." Marcello grunts, his Adam's apple bobbing. He sighs, snatching the decanter and drinking straight from the neck. "Do you think there is a heaven?" he muses.

If there is we won't ever see it. What I did know is this right here is Hell—and we're the demons running it.

CHAPTER FOUR

Alyssa

CLICHÉ. Is that what I am? Eighteen, broke, on a train, leaving my small life in my small town, heading to the city with a dream I'm not sure is mine. From such a young age, being a ballerina was ingrained into me. It's part of my genetic makeup at this point.

Crap. I am a damn cliché.

Clutching the figurine from the jewelery box mom gave me on my fourth birthday, I inhale the doubt, swallowing it back down to the pit of my stomach where it lives. Digging the tiny feet of the ballerina into the pale white scars left on my forearm grounds me.

The scenery outside the window is no longer farmland and nature, replaced with concrete, steel, and glass. That life is behind me now.

I'm doing this.

I'm not trapped inside that house—that life.

I think back to a few nights ago, out in the field with Clint. Telling him I didn't feel that way about him had almost been harder than suffocating Mom.

In a weird way, Clint made me feel normal, like I was enough just the way I was. He didn't want perfection; he was content with just being in a field looking up at the stars. The sad reality is that made me want to punch him in the face.

My thoughts are such a contradiction, they make me seasick.

The devastation that ignited in his eyes made my guilt pocket open up and swallow a few more stones. He picked at the scab bred from my sickness of always needing to please—give in to what they expect from me, plaster on a serene smile, be the dancing puppet. Behind the mask I wore for them, I was screaming, clawing from within to be free. That's a scar that never seems to heal within me.

I think it stems from the disappointment mom would fail to hide whenever I didn't do good enough. She had high expectations, and if I didn't meet them, she was intolerable to live with, and I'd be blamed for making her that way, forcing Dad to deal with her horrible mood swings.

With Mom, affection was earned by achieving goals on the scales, or on the stage floor, ticking off things on her impossible list of perfection.

When I was eight, she first told me I was fat, pinching at my skin almost to the point of pain and calling it rolls.

The diets started then, and never stopped. My relationship with food became so fucked up, I'd get anxiety entering the cafeteria at school.

I had bouts of not getting my periods over my teen years when mom would go on an erratic purge of all things carbohydrates or calorie heavy, forcing me into a deficit well below normal.

Clint used to bring me snacks. Otherwise, I probably would have starved to death.

She loved me, I know she did, but she never saw me for me—I was an extension of her.

"I love you." Like Mom, Clint's words felt hollow when he

spoke them. His eyes dipped to the neckline of my dress, to the small cleavage on display. He swiped his tongue over his lips.

"I think we always knew this would be where things were heading, us being together."

No. No. No.

"I've waited, and now I just want to be with you. Please, Ally."

No. No. No.

"You haven't even tried. Just let me kiss you."

I hate that I allow myself to be weak to empower other people. I did it with Mom. I did with Clint that night in the field. I allowed him into my body because he begged me to give him a chance. Tried to convince me it would change how I feel.

He was right—just not in the way he hoped.

Instead of making me realize I loved him and we could be more, it made me feel cheap, a prize he won at the town carnival. Nothing changed for me. It only reaffirmed what I already knew: there's no sexual spark between us.

Chemistry can't be faked or manufactured—and love isn't negotiable.

He promised it wouldn't ruin our friendship, but that was a lie. He fucked me because he wanted my body. It wasn't about him loving me. And worst of all: he thought it was my virginity he was claiming—in a field—at my mom's wake.

God, he must love me a whole fucking bunch.

Midway through his thrusting, I nearly told him I'd been fucking my coach's son for nearly two years, but I just wanted the night to be over.

I liked sex, needed the relief from it. Dancing is like foreplay, and the frustration needs an outlet. But I didn't enjoy it with him. The memory of Clint on top of me, grunting, kissing me while I laid there hating myself, makes my skin itch.

Never again.

That night, while I scrubbed his cum from my thighs, I

promised myself I'd start taking care of me—my needs, my wants. No more being someone I'm not to appease the needs of others.

"It's bullshit, you know?" A girl not much older than me with bright pink hair pulls me from my thoughts. She jerks her chin to the flyer sitting on the seat next to me.

"What is?" My brows draw in. I've been on this train for hours and not one person has spoken to me. A creeper stared for a while, but he eventually moved or got off. Not that I want conversation. I'm exhausted.

She reaches for the piece of paper, her gaze roaming over the words as her head jerks from side to side, a sneer on her lips. "They say it's an open audition, but in reality, Swan School of Dance doesn't accept nobodies. They invite people they plan to enrol—the rest is just for show."

My stomach knots. My jaw tenses. Snatching the flyer back, I smile. "Good thing I was invited." It's an easy lie that slips right over my tongue, but my eyes betray me as they fill with anxious tears.

If that's true, I wasted the last of what little money I had coming here. I don't even have enough to stay in a hotel. It's why I couldn't travel the day before the auditions.

Our farm is in debt. It's a sinkhole that hasn't sunk yet. I knew coming was a longshot, but there aren't schools that could offer me a career back home.

Back home...

Oh god. I can't go back there and end up like mom. Bitter, and cruel.

She had been a dancer when she met my dad. They married young and moved back to his hometown to take over his family farm. She gave up her dancing dream when her real dream happened: having me.

Lies. Lies. Lies.

When I was young, I'd allowed those words to bloom within

me, to flourish and nurture me. Eventually, her words turned to angry rants about wasting her youth, her ability, me ruining her body. *"It's never the same after a baby. Don't make my mistakes."*

"You must be good," the girl says in a soothing voice, bringing me back from my thoughts. I am good, but am I good enough? Does it even matter?

"Good luck," she quips, shouldering a duffle bag and heading toward the doors. As the train slows, so does my heartbeat.

This is it.

I'm here.

CHAPTER FIVE

Luca

I FUCKING hate being in the same building as my kid brother. The arrogant, drunk prick grinds my gears, and I don't have the fucking patience today.

"It's those motherfuckers opening up new clubs. They want to give ours a bad reputation. It's not uncommon, Luca." His voice erratic and slurred. It's not even lunchtime.

He swipes at his nose, then pinches it to elevate the tingling as he paces my home office floor.

There are multiple wings in this house and yet he always lurks in my damn office spewing out stories he made up in his head to give him a reason to incite violence and chaos.

I like chaos too, but only when it's warranted and controlled. There's no room for rash decisions.

"You're high and not thinking clearly, Antonio. Like fucking usual. Can you not go one day without snorting that shit?" I growl, my nostrils flaring.

His lips pull back. "Stop worrying about what I'm doing and

start coming up with a plan to make these cunts pay. That we're just accepting this kind of attack is an embarrassment."

My hands twitch with the need to tighten around his neck. "It's been one fucking day—and there's no *we*. *My* club, *my* employee, *my* problem."

"Nah." He shakes his head and walks over to my liquor stand. Popping the lid off a bottle of three-hundred-dollar whiskey, he takes it down like it's water. Pointing at me, the bottle curled in his fist, he says, "Leto is the name on that club—not fucking Luka. This is a fuck you to all of us, and Dad agrees."

Motherfucker. Getting to my feet, I round my desk and prowl toward him. Grabbing the little prick by the lapels of his shirt, I smash his back against the wall.

"Stop telling tales to our sick father to get your dick off on a little carnage. When I find out who did this and why, you'll know. If you're sober and not wired out of your face, I may let you play with their insides." I release him and swipe down his shirt to straighten the creases I made.

Snatching the bottle from his hand, his glassy eyes lower. "Until then, go eat something and take a shower, for Christ's sake. You smell like a bum who sleeps on a park bench."

"Whatever." His face twists into an ugly sneer before he leaves the room, slamming the door behind him, rattling the glass bottles.

Ever since Annemarie slit her wrists in their bathtub, he's been drinking from dawn 'til dusk and taking his rage out on anyone foolish enough to look his way.

I allowed him time to grieve. Now, it's time to sober up and come back to the fold. There's no room for reckless assumptions.

We have enemies waiting for us to slip up and do something stupid so they can pluck at the threads until our kingdom unravels. We have to be smart. I have to be smart.

HOW SERENA ENDED up grinding her ass on a pole in one of my clubs while her sister was at this place, I'll never fucking know.

Swan Academy wasn't unknown to my family. My mom loved the ballet. Because of her, I gave a generous donation in her name when she died.

"It's weird Serena had a connection to this place too. Makes you wonder if we're all destined to be linked in some fucked up way," Marcello grunts, and irritation spreads through me.

I don't believe in destiny. Fate is a made-up excuse people use when they fail at life. *If it is meant to be, it will be.* That shit's for people with no backbone or drive to go after what they want.

My father didn't build an empire on luck and the fates aligning. He got his hands dirty, he did the work, rose from the gutter and made a name for himself.

I've lived up to that name and taken it to the next level, carving my own place.

Organized crime has evolved over the generations. It's had to.

The world is ever-changing, and we have to change with it, get our money into legitimate companies from the ground up. We're like mites: unseen until the walls start crumbling around you.

"Let's enter around the back." Marcello jerks his chin to the front steps, an array of dancers all camped out with what looks like a cameraman filming them.

"Let's make this quick," I gripe. I didn't have to come here myself. I have accountants and lackeys for this shit, but I owed Serena at least this much.

CHAPTER SIX

Alyssa

IT'S SO MUCH BIGGER than I anticipated.

The cab drives up a long, winding driveway and pulls into a gravel parking lot behind the building. I hand him a twenty and wince. It's less than a fifty-cent tip. "Sorry."

Cringing, I exit as quickly as possible to lessen my embarrassment. I take in the white stone building. I saw images online, but they didn't do the place justice.

Almost like a castle on grounds of lush greenery—a complete contradiction to the city buildings. This place looks like an estate you'd find a member of the royal family living in, turrets and all.

Mom was obsessed with the royals even though we had no connection to the United Kingdom. She had all the princess Diana merchandise.

Squeezing the handle of my bag, I round the building and take the front steps two at a time.

Inside is a stark contrast to the outside. Modern furnishings oddly placed in the lobby. Simple, bare white walls give a more art environment vibe. Signs guiding applicants lead me through another set of doors into a large room.

I've been to many a cattle market, and this is no different. Hundreds of girls, just like livestock, litter the floor, all numbered and the best there is to offer.

A woman sits behind a reception-type desk, taking people's information, while what looks like a film crew interviews some of the girls.

I join the line, fidgeting with the zip of my jacket.

I should have worn a color that stands out. Instead, like many of the girls, I opted for black leggings and a leotard, my hair pulled back from my face—unoriginal and mundane.

My mother was a beautiful woman. I inherited her smooth skin, jade green eyes, and dainty features, and my figure was in peak condition.

Even though I've been taking care of mom these last couple years, I still trained for when this day would come.

When I finally reach the front of the line, the lady asks, "Name?" A smile growing when the camera begins filming in our direction.

This must be for their website or YouTube channel. The world is evolving, and all industries have to evolve with it.

Leaning my hands on the desk, I tell her, "Alyssa Phoenix."

A nervous pulse hums in my veins as she flits her fake nails over the keys of her computer, searching.

Click, click, click.

There's a list up on the screen, and even though I know my name won't be there, I deflate like a balloon when she says, "A walk in?" All the air pushes out of my lungs on a sigh, my frame sagging.

"Yes."

How many of us were invited and how many are just like me, living on hope?

I look around. Many of the girls have family with them. The room screams of wealth and entitlement.

The woman behind the desk picks up a form and hands it to me along with a number sticker. "Fill that out and give it to the judges when it's your turn."

The girl's words from the train repeat in my mind.

"They say it's an open audition, but in reality, Swan School of Dance doesn't accept nobodies. They invite people they plan to enrol—the rest is just for show."

THE MUSIC MOVES through my limbs like water, flowing powerfully with every leg raise and toe point. I dip, twirl, and extend with precision and determination.

Their eyes flick up every so often from a row of tables, four of them determining my fate. The information sheet I gave them with my dance history, name, address rests discarded at the edge of the table.

One judge is on their phone, no doubt scrolling their Instagram account with little regard for the fact that they're destroying my soul with their disinterest.

I've trained my whole life to get here, to push my limits and earn a spot that allows me to reach the next level. This isn't the only school or audition I've attended, but it's the most important.

If I don't get in, it's back to the farm life for me, maybe teach younger kids at the town hall and marry Clint.

Kill me.

I push myself harder, organically connecting my movements to the music that feeds me.

Do they not see me bleeding out my soul for them—do they not care?

The woman on the train was right. I don't belong here. I was never going to get in.

Darkness rolls over me like invisible smoke. Failure swarms my body. Anger mixed with sadness brings a burning sting to my eyes.

"That's enough. Thank you for coming." Her words are rehearsed, overused, crippling.

Thud.

My heart slows. I want to sink to my knees and scream—beg. *"Please, don't make me go back there."* But it's useless. The position I thought I could earn has already been sold.

"Next," she calls to the woman with the clipboard waiting at the entry door with a flick of her wrist.

Next.

I'm just one of many. They won't even remember I exist once I leave here.

Will I exist?

This is all I am.

I want to force them to notice, to see how good I am, how hard I've worked.

My body has been broken down and rebuilt into a machine. I've spent my life perfecting every muscle. Starving to hit specific weights. Suffering unbearable pain from stretching tendons. Performing on damaged toes.

Blood, sweat, and so, so many tears.

They glorify the life of a ballerina, but behind the lipstick smile and elegant shows, it's hours of continued training on tired joints, hunger to make weight goals, and pain from injuries.

They were all dancers at one point—probably still identify as that. They know the work, the sweat, the hope, yet they're dismissing us without even paying attention to our talent.

A rebellious, aloof brat buried deep inside me shouts, *"Fuck you all!"* But I never give her freedom. Instead, I snatch up my water bottle and the paper with my details on and exit the room, ignoring the looks from the other dancers with the same dream, the same hope that's about to be destroyed.

My mother's face filters into my mind, and my stomach bottoms out.

Sorry, Mom.

I need air.

I need to get out of this place.

Without stopping to change or take off my ballet shoes, I race down the corridor, heat blooming up my neck, goosebumps sprinkling along my skin as my head begins to fog.

My lungs restrict, squeezing. I can't breathe. I fondle with my bottle to open the lid and go to take a deep swig, oblivious to the door suddenly opening in front of me.

A man steps out, colliding into me. My bottle slams against my lip, digging into my gums. A spurt of iron liquid fills my mouth, the sting grounding me, evaporating my mild breakdown.

The bottle clatters to the floor, spilling at my feet and those belonging to a pair of black shoes standing in front of me, almost toe to toe.

My eyes trace up a tailored, suit-clad body, his stance emanating power. My breath quickens when I have to keep looking up, well past my own height.

A broad chest, muscular shoulders filling out the suit jacket. His pulse flickers in his neck as my eyes devour him.

An audible swallow leaves me desperate for more water when I reach his face.

His bearded, square jaw tenses under my scrutiny. Olive skin, thick lips, and the most spellbinding blue eyes peer down at me with dark intent.

Blood coats my lips, pumping from the cut there. His glare fixes on me, rendering me motionless.

More rich assholes.

Probably one of the other dancer's relatives giving a fat check to get her in.

Why, oh why, did he have to be so beautiful? Life is unfair at times.

These places aren't run on talent—they're run on the biggest donation.

The thought forms an anxious pit in my stomach. It opens up, slowly dragging my dreams inside it. Red hot fire flares within me. No matter how good we are, we'll never stand a chance.

"Excuse you," I snap, raising my chin.

The asshole hasn't even apologized or picked up my water bottle.

He looks like he's going to some extravagant soiree. Even has a stupid square stuffed in his breast pocket.

Another man fills the doorframe behind him—another well-fitted suit and stupid good looks. His gaze studies the interaction, not bothering to pick up the fallen bottle or offer aid to my busted face either.

Just another beautiful, bad-mannered prick. They must breed them here.

Blood trickles down my chin, dripping to the floor at my feet. My lip throbs in rhythm to my erratic heart.

"You're making a mess," the blue-eyed asshole in front of me growls. My jaw almost dislocates in astonishment. No *sorry*. No *are you okay?*

"Pardon me for bleeding," I spit, snapping myself out of his thrall.

"Clean it up," he tells me, his tone low, eyes narrowing. Heat spreads up my spine, exploding over my cheeks. My racing heart makes my breathing labored.

Swiping my information form across my mouth, dabbing the blood there, I bend down to grab my bottle.

When I rise, he snatches my jaw between his thumb and forefinger. I squeak out a surprised whine. My eyes enlarge as he takes the pad of his thumb and smears the new crimson across my bottom lip.

I'm frozen, my limbs filled with concrete as he holds me captive.

No one has ever touched me this way before, with such possession and confidence, not even my dance partners over the years.

The action is intimate, the rumbling sound from the back of his throat sexual, making me flush all over.

With an indecent tilt of his lips, he exhales, "My shoe." Leaning in, his breath minty and warm, disperses over my skin.

Fingers tighten on my jaw painfully. I squirm from the pulse of pain and embarrassing throbbing inside my panties.

Part of me wants him to push me against the wall and fuck all this animosity and irritation out of me.

A perfect stranger. A one-time hate-fuck.

He releases me, and my eyes drop to his feet.

There, on his ridiculous clean leather shoe, is a single drop of blood. Mortification washes off the momentary jolt of pleasure, quickly turning to burning fury.

The last week has been a shitty fucking time. I'm sick of people walking all over me. The accumulating bag of crap life has given me makes me give zeros shits about who this jerk is.

Fuck this place.

Fuck Clint.

Fuck this asshole.

Reaching up onto my tiptoes so I'm a little taller, I say, "You clean it up, asshole." Slapping my bloodied piece of paper against his chest and stealing his pocket square.

I move past him and don't look back despite my body screaming for me to do so.

Holding the piece of material to my pulsing lip, I push out into the open air as the daunting thought of returning home hits me.

I didn't make it.

CHAPTER SEVEN

Luca

I ADJUST MY HARD COCK, watching the girl flee out the doors without turning back.

I wasn't prepared for those green fucking eyes, that innocent face dripping blood, the tiny sliver of fabric pulled tight over her body.

Her hard nipples...the outline of every goddam inch of her. An animalistic attraction caught me off guard, and that pissed me off.

I look down at the piece of paper she slapped against my chest, reading her name.

Alyssa.

Marcello's chuckle bristles the hairs on the back of my neck.

"Something funny?" I fume.

Smirking, he squeezes my shoulders before moving in front of me and walking to where we need to be.

"Yeah, really fucking funny."

"You know I'm carrying a gun, right?" I call after him,

scowling at a male dancer walking past, his eyes enlarging at my words.

"I know you don't shoot people in the back. Why do you think I'm walking in front of you?" Marcello grins, then jerks his chin to a door. "She's in here."

He raps his knuckle on the door, then opens it without waiting for an invitation.

A woman stands from behind a desk, a crinkled smile pulling up her lips.

"Mr. Leto. Wonderful to see you again."

I want to ask her what's so wonderful about seeing me after people I care about die, but I don't. This woman would no doubt have a nervous breakdown and throw her bony ass out the window.

"You know why I'm here?" I ask, planting my ass in a wooden chair opposite her desk.

Marcello wanders around the room, picking up trinkets, looking more intimidating than a debt collector visiting someone who owes us money.

Her pale, wrinkled eyes cut between the two of us, her pulse skipping wildly in her neck.

"Marcello," I bark, making her jump. "Sit the fuck down."

His wide, toothy grin directed her way makes her wet her lips. A hand rests against her weathered chest bone, the top she's wearing low cut, a string of pearls around her neck.

"I'm very sorry to learn of Natasha's sister's passing, Such tragic circumstances." She bobs her head, leaning forward slightly.

"This girl's tuition...I want to cover it," I tell her, and her eyes light up.

"That's a very generous gesture, Mr. Leto." Her hands clasp together. These places are money hungry, and they don't care where, or who, that money comes from.

I steeple my hands, resting my elbows on the arms of the chair. "What's with all the cameras out front?"

Her head swivels toward the window on the far wall. A group of girls prancing around for the camera is visible from this angle, "Oh, it's our open audition day. It's a very popular and rewarding program we offer, but it's extremely competitive with limited availability. It's filmed for our websites, and a local news channel likes to write a story on our process." She beams, enthusiastic.

Pulling the bloodied, crumpled piece of paper from my pocket, I slap it on the desk, feeling Marcello's penetrating gaze on my neck.

"I'll also be making a further donation." I tap my finger on the ink, spelling out the girl from the corridor's name. *Alyssa.*

The woman's lips purse, her eyes twitching over the paper. Pulling out a pen, I add, "Name your price."

After a few seconds of silence, she plasters on a serene smile. "I understand, Mr. Leto. Consider it done." She slides the information sheet toward her, circling the girl's name with her pen.

I don't know why I do it, but it's done, and Marcello will never let me forget it.

CHAPTER EIGHT

Alyssa

I STAND on the train platform, my lip busted and ego wounded.

I didn't stick around to hear I hadn't made it.

Instead, I rushed outside, pulled on some sweats, changed my shoes, and began the walk back here, thinking of all the lies I can tell my father and Clint when I turn up with my tail tucked between my legs.

I'm a failure.

Misery is my only future, yet I board the train all the same.

Disappointment stirs inside me as I head straight for the toilets, locking the door behind me once inside the small cubicle.

Checking my reflection, I wince. Dried blood coats my chin. My bottom lip is swollen and throbbing. Mascara smears under my eyes.

My thoughts go back to the man in the hall. He was such a jerk. A good-looking jerk, but a jerk all the same.

My tongue swipes over the cut, the memory of his thumb

there sending a shiver running through me. Who does that? And why did it turn me on so much?

Maybe I was too sheltered growing up and it's how men in the city were. Or maybe he was just a rich asshole used to treating people like they're not his equal.

I imagine him being the type to spit on a woman's pussy before ramming his fat cock inside her. My nipples peak, the throb in my core aching at the thought.

I hate myself.

Splashing my face with cold water, I suck in a lungful of air and pull my phone out to text my dad when it rings in my hand.

I debate not answering it, thinking it's probably Clint asking how the audition went, but it's a number I don't recognize.

"Hello?" I speak meekly into the receiver, shouldering my bag and exiting the toilet.

"Miss Phoenix?" a woman's voice asks.

"Yes. Who is this?" I frown, moving out of the way for people still boarding.

"I'm from the administration team at Swan Academy."

Thud.

"You have been selected as a candidate for a place within our scholarship program. Are you still on the grounds?"

How?

My tongue feels too thick for my mouth but I force the words out.

"Yes. No. I can be," I stumble, a lump forming in my throat as tears brim my eyes. The emotional wave washing over me almost brings me to my knees.

Barging past the stragglers boarding I push onto the platform, elation bringing the tears falling.

I fucking made it.

"Be there within the hour."

I DON'T UNDERSTAND how I got in, but I'm being shown around the studios and living quarters by my very own tour guide.

Scholars get a room situated in a wing of the school and a small living allowance from our benefactor.

The woman who introduced herself as Megan points to a clock.

"Curfew is eleven o'clock on weekdays, twelve on weekends. Everyone must abide by these times. Even a minute late, and the doors will be locked and you'll be out for the night."

I've never had a curfew in my life. Living in a small town, there wasn't much need for one.

Everyone knew everyone and everything was pretty much closed by sundown. It was a graveyard, only the occupants weren't quite dead yet.

On the outside anyway.

We pass a communal bathroom just as a guy wearing a sliver of a towel comes walking out, raising a cool eyebrow at me.

Megan rolls her eyes. "As you can see, the communal spaces are for all first- and second-year students. Be aware some students' modesty is non-existent." This gains her a smirk from the guy, and a head nod from me.

I'm not a shy person. Nudity doesn't faze me. Leotards are like a second skin in our profession, modesty isn't something we have.

"You're expected to clean up after yourselves, and if you have any issues, your house mother will be available between curfew hours." She carries on walking into a small dining hall.

"You eat, live, and train. You should be here ninety percent of the time. Only the best make it at Swan. After your six-week review, we will be cutting the dead meat."

My insides squirm. What if they accepted me just to serve as an example to the others to step up their game?

"Your schedules will be posted on the message board tomorrow. I suggest you make a copy, take a picture, or whatever you do these days."

She points to a table propped up under the message board. "There's an envelope with your room key inside. You're welcome to move in today, but make sure you're fully moved in by next week when your schedule starts."

A nervous flutter takes flight inside me. "Do you have any questions?" She turns to face me, her ginger, shoulder-length hair swaying with her movements.

I look around, rubbing a hand down my arm. "Am I the only one who made it through?" It's a silly question, but it strikes me as odd that I'm the only one here being given the tour.

Lines crinkle her eyes as she squints at me. "No, you're just the one who made an impression, it would appear." Her tone is soft, regretful even. I store that away and tug my suitcase over to the table to grab my key.

Maybe they were paying attention to my audition. I can't believe this is real and pinch myself to make sure I'm awake.

"Do you need to see the first aider for the cut?" Megan calls after me, raising her brow, pointing to my lip. I'd been so excited, I'd forgotten it was even there.

My hand goes there involuntarily. "No, thank you. It will be fine."

When I get to my room, I bite down on the cut, sighing as the stinging fire spreads over the sensitive flesh, heating me in places it shouldn't.

I enjoy the rush of pain, the heat soaring through my veins, I think back to the man in the corridor, his asshole attitude and devilish good looks, my pussy throbs with the need to come.

Maybe I never had feelings for Clint because he's too soft...a boy. I need a man—a brutal, savage bastard.

CHAPTER NINE

Luca

OF ALL THE businesses I own, I find myself most at home in my office at Vino's.

The atmosphere is calming, and none of my family comes here to drink or dine. It feels personal to me, an escape.

Hannah flags me down as I enter my office, loosening the tie around my neck. "What is it?" I ask, turning on the computer.

"There's a detective here to see you." She winces, knowing full well those assholes aren't supposed to show up here.

"Send him through," I growl, balling my fists.

Detective Morels waltzes in wearing a cheap, ill-fitting suit, his hair curling around his ears in desperate need of a haircut.

He looks out of place here. This office was decorated in muted tones, the furnishings modern, expensive—sophisticated. Morels looked like he'd just crawled out of a bad eighties movie.

"Do I have to remind you of the money you receive from me?" I push a few buttons on the screen and spin it for him to see the transfers made to offshore accounts.

"I tried your house and calling you." He paces the floor, irritating me. I can't stand people who fidget. Sit fucking still. "I need you to tell me if you were involved with this girl at the club."

The nerve of this prick, "Involved how?" I push back into my seat, mapping his movements. He appears agitated, wary.

"Involved, like did you kill her?" He runs a nervous hand through his hair. I want to get up from my chair and cut his tongue from his head.

"I'd like to think you know better than to ask me stupid questions." Standing, I round the table. He holds his hands up, shaking his head as I perch on the edge of my desk glaring at this corrupt piece of shit.

"I just need to know what I'm dealing with. There's no evidence of this being a random slaying. The cameras were disabled. The person who did this knew the club, the exits, where the cameras were. They must have known the girl to get her back there. I've spoken to some of the other girls. They say Serena worked the floor but didn't do private rooms unless it was you." He pulls a cigarette from a packet and looks at me expectantly.

"If you attempt to smoke that thing in here, I'll light you on fire and kick you through the door, letting you die in the alley with the rats," I warn him.

Pushing off the desk I palm the back of his neck and tug his face toward mine. "I didn't fucking kill her. I don't get thrills from butchering women. Find out who does and bring me their name."

Once he leaves, I bring up the footage from the club that night on my computer.

I've analyzed the thing over and over, had every visitor that night looked into, and nothing is coming back with red flags—and that coils my gut.

Someone we know did this—one of ours. There's only the staff from the club, Marcello, Antonio, and maybe a handful of others who know the ins and outs of the club. But who could have done it, and why? It doesn't make sense. And it leaves me on edge.

I can deal with enemies coming at me, but not traitors, not people I trust. I imagine her shocked eyes as someone she knew killed her.

Launching the computer across the room, I grab up my jacket and head to the club.

THE ROOM IS STILL TAPED off. We have the biohazard clean-up crew coming in tonight to make it look like this never happened.

The place is empty when I arrive, all but Ricardo who's in his office going through the new surveillance set up via wireless cameras that upload and save to the cloud so we don't get played if this shit should happen again.

It better not happen again.

All the staff has been paid trauma bonuses. Serena will become a memory—a tragic story the girls tell newbies to scare them. Life goes on.

I grab a bottle of whiskey from behind the bar and head to the back room. Yanking the tape away from the door, I sit on the booth and uncap the bottle.

Everything in here is crusted in blood. It needs to be gutted, not cleaned.

Alyssa's bloodied lip creeps into my thoughts. Her wide eyes drinking me in. Flushed cheeks. Needy breaths. Her fat fucking lips bleeding shouldn't have turned me on, but I'm a cruel bastard.

All I wanted was to see tears leak from her eyes so I could lick them clean.

Her tits are bigger than most ballerinas, heavy as she fought to catch her breath, the nipples poking through the fabric, begging to be teased.

I wanted to wrap her hair in my fist and force her to her knees.

I down the first mouthful of amber liquid, relishing the slight burn. I don't know why I interfered in securing her a place at Swan. Maybe it was those eyes, or that ballsy fierce attitude. Fire lives inside her, and I want to feel the burn, the heat wrapped around my cock.

My phone starts to vibrate against my thigh. Pulling it free, Marcello's name flashes on the screen.

"What?" I bark.

"Your father wants to see you."

I end the call without a response and get to my feet. Closing my eyes, I down another drink from the bottle. "I'll find out who did this to you, Serena—and I'll make them pay."

Leaving the bottle on the table next to the pole, I head home to see what mayhem Antonio has riled up this time.

CHAPTER TEN

Alyssa

MY ROOM IS the size of a box.

There's a bed, a wardrobe, and a desk. On the farthest wall, there's a tiny window the width and height of a box of cereal.

I've been living here for almost a week and still keep having to pinch myself.

This is happening.

Mine.

I keep going over my audition in my head. I've met a couple of the other girls who made it, and they said they were called back for a second and third audition before being offered their place.

They had to have a physical exam on their tendons and the length of their Achilles heel. They had to showcase the seven moves of ballet over and over.

Did I get lucky?

Grabbing the little ballerina figurine from the dresser, I push it into my abdomen, sighing as the nip of pain washes over me.

I can't help the pit of dread in my chest telling me my place here is a misunderstanding and they're going to ask me to leave at any second.

My phone vibrates on the bedside table, distracting me.

It's Clint again.

I decline the call and write out a text to let him and my dad know I got in.

Dad already knew I'd be gone a while if I made it through the audition, so he hasn't even attempted to contact me. I don't think he cares whether I make it or come home. We're two adult people who happen to share DNA.

Nothing more.

My phone rings again two-seconds after I send the text. Clint's name has me fisting the bedsheets. Irritation and a hint of revulsion roll through me, but I answer this time to get it over with.

"Hello?"

"I knew you'd get in," he sings down the line. "I've been thinking about you non-stop. Why haven't you called?"

I wish you wouldn't think about me.

"Thanks. I've been so busy. The auditions lasted days." I know I enable him, his feelings.

Enabler. Enabler. Enabler.

Liar. Liar. Liar.

"What happens now?"

I lay back on the small bed, wincing at the hard mattress digging into my back. "I've been given a room and classes start in a couple days."

"I thought you'd have time to come home first." The disappointment in his tone brings a grin to my face.

"This is home now," I tell him, wishing I could see his face fall at that news. *I'm a horrible person.*

"You know what I mean," he moans, and I can picture the creases on his forehead.

"How's my father?" I change the subject, ignoring his sigh.

"Fine. Same as always. Your mom would be so proud of you, Ally."

She would be more for herself than me. She'd be calling everyone she knew, putting up banners, baking a celebration cake she'd refuse to let me have a slice of.

"Sugar rots you from the inside out."

A knock on my door gives me an excuse to hang up. "I have to go, Clint." I end the call without waiting for a response and jump up from the bed.

When I open the door, Megan is standing there, holding out a piece of paper with an address on it.

"The girls with scholarships usually work part-time to make some extra money. We have set you up with a position that works around your commitments to the school."

Wow, this place just keeps getting better. They go above and beyond.

"Thank you." I take the slip of paper, running my eyes over the ink.

Leto Vino Bar

I DIDN'T SLEEP WELL, and it shows in my movements as I make use of the empty space in the studio.

Classes don't start for a few days, and I'm the only one who has been up at dawn training every day in preparation, pushing my limits until everything hurts.

I feed off the pain like a ravenous dog on a bone. My mom used to say I dance angry. My coaches called it passion. I call it hunger—hunger to escape my life. It's my ticket out.

I want to go into the city and find where I'll be working and get a feel for the place, so I grab my stuff and head to the showers, rolling my eyes at the obvious sexual grunting coming from one of the cubicles.

Debating for a second whether to let them finish and come back, I decide to just hit the shower a couple cubicles down and make it quick.

Turning on the spray, I step beneath it and sigh.

The pressure is incredible. The pitter-patter over my shoulders loosens the tight muscles.

The shower at home was like having someone piss on you from above.

Everything is better far, far away from there.

Whoever's getting off reaches their climax, and I smile to myself thinking of Clint's face if I told him I share a communal shower and people fuck in them.

Rinsing the soap from my body, I grab my towel and step out, greeted by a blonde girl putting on makeup in front of the fogged-up mirror.

"Hey," I jerk my chin, straining the water from my hair.

"Sorry you had to hear that." She grins, swiping a pink color across her lips. "We usually fuck in his room, but his roommate watches and it creeps me out."

"No problem," I shrug. "I promise I didn't look." I add with a sly smirk.

She turns to me, pointing her lipstick. "I like you." She winks, clutching up her toiletry bag. "By the way," she calls from the exit, "you're bleeding."

My gaze turns to the mirror. The tiny scab on my lip must have gotten saturated in the shower, slightly re-opening the wound.

Dark blue eyes filter into my mind. The firm grip that left a light bruise on my jaw wakes my libido, my nipples aching.

Pinching them through the fabric of the towel does nothing to ease the desire.

Entering my room, I chuck the towel to the floor and inhale the cold air kissing my fevered skin. I check my lip in the mirror, smearing the blood just like the asshole did that day.

My breathing accelerates, and I close my eyes, conjuring up his image, imagining his rough fingers touching me as I trace down my torso over the mound of my pussy. Separating my lips, I feel the liquid heat there.

Fuck, I need more.

Pulling open the top drawer, I clutch onto the small, stained pocket square I stole from Blue Eyes and move to the bed.

Laying back, I drop my knees and rub the cloth over every inch of my body. Pushing two fingers into my greedy pussy, I force the heel of my palm down on my clit and writhe against it.

I cover my face with the small piece of cloth until my walls throb around my fingers, a warm rush pulsating through my body, peaking my nipples and curling my toes.

THE NOISE and traffic are a huge culture shock.

Everywhere feels crowded and suffocating. I lived in a town with two thousand residents' total. There seems to be two thousand people for every hundred yards here.

A group of women in stilettos carrying handbags larger than my suitcase scurry past me to avoid the sprinkling of rain falling from above, their squeals playful as they rush inside a clothing boutique.

There's so much choice here, so many different stores offering fancy jewelery, shoes, clothing. I own the same three pairs of jeans Mom bought me from the only store in our town five years ago.

I move to the corner of the sidewalk to check the address

again, frowning when there appears to be a few different places with the Leto name, one directly opposite where I'm standing.

I head inside the restaurant, hoping it's the right place. "We're not hiring," a woman says as I approach the hostess stand, wet hair clinging to my forehead.

I hold up the piece of paper lamely, and her eyebrows raise. "That's two blocks away. They're not hiring either."

If this is how she greets customers, it wouldn't surprise me if her job is up for grabs by next week.

"I was told the position was already secured for me." She looks me up and down, and I regret my basic leggings and sweater.

Why do people always have to belittle others?

"If you say so." She shrugs, a smirk on her lips. Bitch.

"You don't have to be an asshole." I clench my fists until the knuckles pale, my jaw aching from my gritted teeth. Her eyes widen, mouth popping open.

Offering her a serene smile, I head in the direction she pointed moments before, coming to a stop up a couple of streets.

This place is twice as stunning as the first. What looks like solid gold wording blazes across an elegant slate colored building. Large, paneled windows give a sophisticated air.

There's a red roped entry and a line halfway down the block, and it's only lunch time.

I'm incredibly underdressed for this place, but there's nothing in my wardrobe that would make me suitable, so I summon up the courage and head inside.

I make it past the doorman and through two sets of glass doors, offering a half-hearted wave to the greeter who scowls at me. "Can I help you?" he asks with a tight smile. What is with these fuckers? Can they smell the poor on me?

"Yes, I hope so. I'm Alyssa ..." I don't get my last name out before a girl behind the bar flags us down with a wave of her hand.

"Send her in, James," she calls with a nod.

Relief brings a genuine smile to my face. I attentively make my way over to her and am greeted by a wicked smirk.

"Hey, I wasn't expecting you for a couple days, but we appreciate your initiative. I'm Hannah, the floor manager."

She has an accent I can't put my finger on, but it's pleasant. With a tight blonde ponytail and painted red lips, she looks like a runway model or an air hostess, tall, elegant.

"Alyssa." I hold my hand out, and she chuckles as she takes it in hers, giving me a little shake.

"I know who you are," she says, like it's obvious despite me only arriving in the city a week ago. Everything happens at warp speed here. It's discombobulating.

"Let's get you the paperwork you need to fill out and we'll arrange your starting date. Does that sound good?"

Sounds great. I can't help but feel they have me confused with someone else. They're so accommodating, and it's been the same at the academy.

Maybe they have me mixed up with another student, probably someone who had a donation.

My heart flutters wildly in my chest. No, they wouldn't need the scholarship if they were rich enough to put a donation down.

"I've never worked in a place like this," I tell her, looking around at the customers in designer suits and fancy dresses sipping out of expensive cocktail glasses. "I can fake it," I assure her and myself.

"It's okay. We'll train you," she assures me, tucking a stray hair behind her ear before adding, "And supply you with a uniform."

She's not subtle when her eyes drop to my attire, but she's not being a bitch either. It just is what it is. I think I'm going to like her. "Do you serve food?" I notice a couple of tables have plates on them.

"We do, but it's a limited menu. We're mainly a wine bar."

She crooks her fingers for me to follow her through the back to an office where I fill out the information needed.

I jot my down what's needed, it only takes a couple minutes to complete, "Here." Hannah says handing me a fancy bag with a black uniform inside.

I don't ask how she knows my size, I just enthusiastically take what I'm given. "I'll see you in a couple of days for training." She smiles.

I think I'm going to like it here.

As I'm leaving through the glass exit doors, a man enters. I'm struck with familiarity as he gives me a slow, confident smirk.

It's the man from the audition day—the one who stood in the doorway watching his friend be a predatory asshole.

What are the odds of bumping into him again off campus?

The thought suddenly occurs to me that I was rude to the asshole who busted my face, and he could be someone important at the school.

Dammit, if I have to see *him* again, I don't know what I'll do.

The man in front of me slips off his mirrored aviators. His dark eyes are like expanding ink pools as he drinks me in.

Trying to avoid the awkward stand-off, I dodge around him, but he anticipates my movements and mimics them.

"You're the ballerina with an attitude," he says, devouring my face with his lingering gaze. His voice is amused, but it rubs me the wrong way all the same.

I didn't have an attitude. I was responding to how I was being treated. "And you're one of the suits with no manners," I quip, wincing inside.

If he is part of Swan, I could end up sabotaging my place there, but I'm done sitting back and taking other people's bullshit.

New city, new me. Or maybe this is the real me...finally.

His grin is stunning, showcasing straight, white teeth. "I like you. This will be interesting." He chuckles, holding the second set of doors open for me to exit through.

Maybe he isn't mannerless after all.

I attempt to turn around to ask what will be interesting, but the door is already closing behind me.

CHAPTER ELEVEN

MARCHING INTO ANTONIO'S ROOM, I yank the covers from the bed, sending a couple women screeching toward the bathroom, their fake tits jiggling.

I've warned him about using this house as a party spot. His pill-popping, waste-of-space friend, Carlos, lays at the other end of the bed in only socks and shoes, a bottle of vodka curled under his arm like a teddy bear.

I pull my gun and bring the butt down on his crooked nose.

Blood sprays up, decorating the white bedsheets. He whimpers and squeals, rolling out of the bed, his skinny frame dropping to the floor.

I grasp the discarded bottle and stalk the bastard around the bed. "What did I do?" he cries, piss leaking from his flaccid cock.

I hate this prick—and Antonio knows it. He's known him since school, so I've tolerated his presence here and there, but I don't like seeing him in this house with such blatant disrespect.

This isn't a frat house or nightclub.

This was my mother's home.

Where my dying father is being taken care of.

Where I live.

"Luca..." he whines, trying to cover his ugly face. Blood drips down his cheeks like tears.

Swinging the bottle, I bring it down over his head. The contact makes a soft thudding sound. His eyes widen before closing as his limp body slumps against the bedside table.

Night, night, asshole.

"What the fuck?" Antonio groans, wincing when he lifts his head from the pillow.

Slipping my gun into the back of my slacks and dropping the bottle to the carpet, I kick the mattress and pat myself on the back for booting the piece of shit in the face.

"Tell that waste of life to clean up his mess when he wakes up."

"Luca?" Antonia calls out, rubbing a hand over his face. "I'm sorry, okay? I know you don't like me being here."

Gritting my teeth, I inhale a frustrated breath. "I've warned you about bringing whores into this house. Do you know what type of business is conducted here?"

"Yes. I know I fucked up." He sits up, the sheet pooling around his waist.

He's lost weight. The body he used to take pride in is wasting away, abused by drugs and alcohol.

"I hate being at home." It's almost a whisper. "I see her there, in every fucking room, in every piece of furniture. I loved her. I know we didn't start out the right way," he fists the sheet, his eyes glossing over, "but we got there."

I think back to their wedding day, it was an honor for her father to have her marry a Leto—a steppingstone to a higher rung on the blood money ladder.

He didn't care whether she wanted to be married to my

brother or not. Hell, no one but Marcello cared, but even he didn't stop it.

We all watched as she choked out her vows, shaking as he placed a ring on her finger.

"It wasn't your fault, Antonio," I tell him for the hundredth time.

Who fucking knows what goes through someone's head that makes them feel they have no other choice but to kill themself.

It's a mental illness. Most doctors don't understand, how the fuck are we supposed to?

"Do you not think it's weird that she died, then Mom, and now Serena?" He shakes his head, his face twisting into a sneer. "I think someone killed them all. A show of power to—"

"Stop," I order, my tone firm, my eyes slicing through him. "No one would come at us that way. No one has the fucking balls. Why would they go after our women?"

"To make us fucking weak—make us look weak. I don't know, Luca. We have enemies all over the place. What about those fucking sewer rat bikers out in Little Rock? They killed one of your men."

A dark chuckle rumbles from my chest. "Those inbred idiots don't even know who they killed. It was over some woman and has been dealt with. Don't go coming up with wild stories and then believing them, Antonio. You escalate things that have been put to bed, I'll be really pissed off."

"You're always pissed off," he grumbles, throwing the pillow across the room and hurling himself back down on the bed like an obstinate teenager.

Storming over to the bathroom, I boot the door open, splintering the wood. Horrified screams make my cock jump, but the sight of the whores' faces caked in smeared makeup and skin coated in crusty cum does nothing for me.

"You wonder why I'm pissed off all the time?" I grate out.

Grabbing one of the women by the arm, I drag her over to the bed and sling her at him.

"The maid found one these thieves in mother's closet."

Jabbing a finger in his direction, I snap, "Get them out of this house and pack up your shit. I want you gone."

He's wrong about Annemarie and Mom, but Serena...her death is a deliberate message. I just needed to find out who sent it.

CHAPTER TWELVE

Alyssa

"YOU TAKE their order and come back here to collect it," Hannah tells me, pointing to the guy behind the bar hanging up glasses on a rack above his head.

She told me his name already. Steve—no, Simon.

"If they ask what you recommend, always point them toward our most popular bottle." She drags her perfectly manicured finger down the menu, tapping on a bottle worth nine hundred dollars.

My jaw unhinges, making her giggle. It's light and beautiful and draws the eye of the men sitting at nearby tables.

I was a little nervous about starting today, but Hannah has a calming presence that puts me at ease. "I'm around if you need me. Don't be afraid to ask questions." She waves her hand in the air before giving me a pad and pen.

Even the notepads are bound in leather, and the pens have "Parker" etched on the side. Everything about this place is expensive.

I breathe in, hoping I can pull this off. I've birthed a cow and raised livestock, this is a cake walk...right?

"Oh, and, Alyssa," Hannah calls out, "stay away from Mr. Leto if he comes in." Her brow pulls into a frown as she disappears into the back.

"Does he come in often?" I turn to ask the guy behind the counter.

Simon smirks at me, a dimple in his cheek. "Unfortunately, he has an office here."

"Is he as bad as Hannah makes him seem?" I picture a white-haired older man with a stick up his ass.

Simon stops pouring a drink to look over at me, his eyes twinkling with mischief. "You're kidding, right?" He laughs, but it's a nervous one.

I shake my head, confused by his response.

"You know who Mr. Leto is—what he is?" The way he's talking makes it sound like Mr. Leto is some mythical dragon. "Just do as Hannah says and stay out of his way."

I'm only here a few days a week anyway.

Not a problem. It'll be a breeze.

I'VE MANAGED to take four orders and only mess up two of them—which feels like a win.

My shift is almost over, I've made eighty-eight dollars in tips, and life feels good. Until the man in the dark blue suit comes walking through the door like a celebrity flanked by two men in black suits who peel off to stand at either side of the doors.

My hand shakes as I try to hold my pen in place.

His friend told him you come here filters through my mind, and I shut the thought down as soon as it happens. He probably doesn't even remember me.

Our eyes clash, electric blue shocking every cell inside my body. My lips part. My breathing accelerates. Shock registers on his features, his eyes narrowing.

Please don't sit in my section. Please.

"We'll take bottle number twelve." The girl I'm supposed to be serving grins up at me, gaining my attention back.

Her smile is infectious. I can't help but return it, despite the butterflies flapping maniacally in my stomach. It's the cheapest bottle we serve and has a fancy name I can't pronounce.

"Good choice," I tell her, taking the menu and tucking it under my arm. When I look up, the blue-eyed asshole is nowhere in sight.

I give Simon my order and head to the back to use the bathroom, needing to splash my face with cold water.

A gasp flees my lips as a hand squeezes around my arm, "Come with me." A familiar voice growls, dragging me into the hall leading to the back offices as I attempt to free myself to no avail.

"What the fuck are you doing here?" he snaps.

My back hits the wall with a heavy thud, rattling my brain. "I work here, jerk." I exhale, looking down to my arm, his red handprint on the skin.

"No, you don't" his chest rumbles, a woodsy scent overwhelms me as his warm body pushes up against mine. "

Try again?" He tells me, my heart ricochets in my chest.

All of him is against me. It's intrusive, violent, delicious, rendering me useless.

Planting my hands on his muscular chest I pathetically push against him to give me space. "Let me go, now," I demand, weakly.

A grunting sound reverberates from his chest, the asshole is actually growling at me, almost predatory, breathing me in like a wolf would a rabbit

I will myself to stay calm, not show how effected by him I am, but my body doesn't listen.

He pushes forward, and my insides squirm, my hips involuntarily tilting toward his.

"I do work here, asshole. What the hell? You can't just go around manhandling people. And this is for employees only. You can't be back here," I snap, searching the hallway for aid while trying and failing to wiggle free.

"I can be wherever the fuck I want to be," he snarls, flexing his hips, implying he doesn't just mean in this corridor, but inside me too if he pleased.

The entitled arrogant fuck. A wave moves through my body, heating my cheeks and dampening my panties.

"I'm surprised you even remember me." My voice comes out weak and pathetic, needy.

A smirk tugs at the corner of his mouth. "No one has ever spoken to me the way you did and lived to tell about it." His words cause a sweat to break out up my spine.

What does he mean by that? "You look different," he tells me, studying my face. The narrow walls closing in.

"Maybe because I'm not bleeding," I force the words out, swallowing the tension pulsing through my body.

His eyes drop to my lips, his pupils expanding. When he leans in, I hold my breath, not sure if I'm dreaming this or it's really happening.

He tugs my bottom lip between his teeth, and although I know I should knee him in the balls, I whimper instead, terrified and curious all at once.

He bites down, and I shudder, the pain sending a shock through my bloodstream.

"There," he groans, licking his lips. Reaching up with his thumb, he smears the blood blossoming from my wound over my lips. "That's better."

And then he's strutting away, and I'm left panting in his wake, touching a fingertip to my lips watching his departure.

Hannah appears from the back office, her brow raised, arms crossed. "I see you've met Mr. Leto."

Mr. Leto?

Well...*shit.*

CHAPTER THIRTEEN

Luca

BARGING INTO MARCELLO'S OFFICE, and slamming the door, pacing his carpet, the smug asshole grins at me.

"I take it you met our new employee."

"Why the hell would you hire her?" I seethe, my cock still straining my slacks.

Seeing her here completely threw me off guard. There's something about her. I want to rip her fucking clothes off and paint her creamy skin in my cum. She has to go.

"Get rid of her."

"Oh, come on. She's harmless. Just lost her mother to cancer. Her family owns a farm, but it's in fucking debt. She moved to the big city to go it alone."

"Are you writing a book on the needy?" I snap. "I don't give a fuck about any of that. And why the hell do you know all of that shit?" I run a hand through my hair, agitated. Every nerve ending is lit without an outlet.

Marcello leans back on the leather couch he uses instead of an office chair, his laptop set up on a coffee table. "Of course, I was going to look into who the hell she was, Luca. You put half a million down for her."

My eyes narrow on him, pinning him to his seat. "That was Mother's money. She'd want it to go to something she loved. It wasn't for some fucking stranger who means nothing. Don't get it twisted."

I hate that I got her a place, that Marcello was with me that day and saw our interaction. I feel vulnerable, exposed, and I can't have that.

"Fire her, Marcello, or I'll cut off your balls," I warn. Exiting his office, I slam the door against the back wall, hearing the faint thud as something falls.

Entering my office, I flick the lock and lean against the wall. Freeing my cock from my slacks, it's heavy in my palm.

The air from the room chases over my shaft, and I hiss out. Gripping the throbbing head, I fuck my fist, thinking about Alyssa's shocked eyes, parted lips, and accelerated breathing.

If I would have dipped into the waistband of her panties, she would have been soaked. The girl wasn't intimidated by me, and that made her either stupid or brave.

Both.

I want to fuck her pretty, pouty mouth, eat her wet pussy until she's crying for mercy, all while fingering her tight little ass that's no doubt never been touched.

"Shit," I rasp, stroking harder. My balls tighten. Warmth spreads over my thighs and up my spine. Her hard nipples come to mind, pushing me over the edge.

"Fuck..." Ribbons of cum spurt pulsing from my bulging head. It's not enough.

Dammit, I'm going to kill Marcello.

CHAPTER FOURTEEN

Alyssa

"HOW DO YOU KNOW HIM?" Hannah asks, offering me a towel. I'd rushed to the staff bathroom needing to clean the wound.

I watch her through the mirror placed above a large basin.

"He was at my ballet school the day I auditioned." I inhale, trying to regain my equilibrium. He knocked me off kilter.

"Is he affiliated with Swan somehow?" I ask, breathless, clutching the sides of the basin to steady myself.

Crossing her arms, she shakes her head, leaning against the tiled wall, examining me. "Not that I know of, but the Leto's have their name in everything, so who knows."

She places a hand on my arm, her brow dipping low. "They're dangerous men, Alyssa. Be careful, okay?"

Silence sits between us for a second and then she's leaving, the door closes with her exit, and my head races.

What does she mean dangerous? In what way?

My hands jitter the effect of him still coursing through my body.

Closing my eyes, I take a few deep breaths before checking myself in the mirror, *"you're fine, it's all fine."*

The bleeding has stopped, so I splash some cold water on my cheeks straighten my shirt and head back out to finish my shift.

I work the next hour, the constant feeling of being watched making my skin itch.

Every nerve in my body is raw. I just want to go back to my room and try to unpack everything that's happened and make sense of it all.

Clearing my last table of wine glasses, I turn and almost drop them when dark orbs track my movements from a barstool.

Like Mr. Leto, this man is dressed impeccably, but his toothy grin is nothing like the predatory one belonging to his friend.

"It's you," I breathe, squinting my eyes at him.

"It's you." He taps his palm on the stool next to him.

"You're a Leto," I say, the pieces coming together like a light-bulb turning on.

"You're perceptive, but no. We're actually related through our mothers. I'm Marcello Benetti." He offers his hand for me to shake, and I timidly give it a quick tug.

My hand is so much smaller than his, it becomes cocooned in his palm.

"But you are related," I state. Slipping onto the barstool next to him, I fist my hands in my lap, wishing I had the little ballerina doll to jab into my thigh to relieve the anxiety Hannah's warning left me with.

"Cousins, but more like brothers. I lost my father when I was a teenager and spent most of my time at Luca's. He's not always an asshole." He tilts his head, his eyes dipping over my face.

He pauses on my lips where my cut throbs. *Luca? He looks like a Luca—or a Lucifer.*

"It's been a tough few months for him."

Silence, then, "His mother dying...that's something you can relate to."

The bartender, Joelle, places a drink in front of him, and he picks it up, taking a sip.

I scrutinize him, unsure if he's trying to be sincere or let me know he looked into me, knows personal information.

Bringing up someone's dead parent is ballsy and oddly intimate. *We all have that in common, how poetic.*

I don't address it, opting for the question burning a hole through my brain like a red-hot poker instead.

"What's his connection to Swan Academy?" I ask, hoping he'll appreciate my no bullshit approach.

He picks up a handful of some fancy nut mix Hannah puts out on the bar. It's an assortment of nuts and seeds mixed with these stick looking things. It looks like it belongs in a bird-feeder.

"Actually, he has no connection to that place. It was his mother, my aunt. She was an admirer of the ballet. Used to tell us there wasn't sophistication in the world like there used to be, but ballet always enriched and we had to appreciate and support the arts."

I wonder briefly about this woman.

Did she have a long illness also?

Was he happy she was gone?

"So, he's a benefactor?" I ask, and the pit in my stomach opens.

The way he looks at me, dissecting, feeding from my movements, my reactions, makes me feel exposed.

He's rubbing at the raw nerves left behind from my interaction with Mr. Leto...Luca.

He throws another nut to the back of his throat, then licks his tongue over his teeth. "Aunt Marissa left a donation in her will. Luca wanted to hand deliver it. End of."

He side-eyes me, and although I don't know anything about him, I do know he's not telling the full truth.

"What about the job? Does he always employ ballerinas? Is that part of the donation agreement?"

"No." Grinning, he winks, then swipes the pad of his thumb at the corner of his mouth before getting to his feet. "You're the only one—and that was on me."

Thud.

"You?" I exclaim louder than I mean to. Hannah furrows her brow in our direction, and I shrink a little in embarrassment.

"I thought you'd be entertaining."

Leaning in toward me, drowning me in his sheer size, his breath tickles my earlobe as he says, "And I wasn't wrong."

His dark chuckle chases behind him like a shadow as he walks away. My heart pounds, palms sweaty.

Hannah hurries over toward me, her fingers tightening around a cloth. "What was that about?"

She doesn't look like the happy, beaming Hannah I've become accustomed to. There's a strain in her voice, her features weary.

"I'm not entirely sure." I sigh, getting to my feet. "How did you know about me when I came in for the job?" I ask, my eyes locked on her features.

Removing his empty glass and wiping the bar she adverts her gaze, "Marcello told me you'd be coming. Just said to be nice and make you feel welcomed."

She dumps the cloth and fidgets with her polished red nails. "Is there something going on with you two?" Her voice catches on the words.

She likes him.

Giving her arm a squeeze, I say, "No. Thanks for looking out for me. I appreciate you."

I hurry to grab my things and a grateful sigh leaves my lips when I find Simon waiting for me out back. "Ready?" He grins over at me as I slip into the passenger seat.

"Ready." I mimic, pulling my seatbelt on and taking a deep breath. He'd offered to drop me off this week so I make curfew.

Instead of asking me questions about talking with Marcello or being done later than usual, he gives me my space, and unlike most people, I like him.

The radio plays low through the car, rain dusting the windscreen as we drive in silence. Hannah's words play on repeat in my mind

"They're dangerous men." Her warning should strike fear inside me, but giddy excitement bubbles to the surface.

I kind of like danger.

"Are you getting out or...?" Simon's voice jars me from my thoughts, I hadn't realized we pulled up.

"Sorry." I giggle, leaning over to dump a kiss on his cheek. "Thanks for the ride." I call, stepping out into the rain I make a run for it.

Once back in my dorm room I strip out of the wet clothes and into a sleep short set throwing myself under the covers.

Sleep evades me, instead, I lay awake staring up at the ceiling replaying the day's events, lingering on Luca and his intoxicating presence.

CHAPTER FIFTEEN

Luca

HANGING my suit jacket on the back of a chair, I roll up the sleeves of my shirt and head to the liquor cabinet, feeling the burn of my father's gaze on my back.

I worked from my home office today, not wanting to bump into the little ballerina at Vino's.

Marcello found tormenting me all too amusing, and because he's my mother's only nephew, I allow him certain freedoms and liberties, but my temper has been frayed lately.

The cool exterior I used to wear so effortlessly has become increasingly harder to portray.

Rage, grief, and irritation lives in my veins, a constant humming vibrating beneath the surface.

We all harbor a darker self-most are too afraid to ever tap into. Mine is seeping through the cracks, covering me in this thunderous cloud of craving blood and retribution for things that were already settled.

Animosity drips from me, and I can't shake it. My mother's death plagues me, and now Serena's...

There's no room for a girl like Alyssa in my world. I can't afford to have any connection with another woman after what happened with Serena.

It's not safe.

But there's something different about her. She's managed to slither under my skin without any effort.

She's nothing to me, no one—a random fleeting encounter of two people. We've spent a handful of minutes in each other's orbit, yet she's left an imprint on me, burrowed in like a seed wanting to grow.

I pour an extra finger of whiskey, and my shoulders loosen as I knock it back.

Seeds can only grow if you nurture them. I'm not going to feed this thing. I'll starve it until it withers.

If Marcello is going to insist on keeping her working at Vinos, I'll make it unbearable for her—force her out.

"HAVE you run out of whisky, son?" my father's strained voice calls out to me from his high-back chair.

The crackling fire makes the room stifling. His paper-thin skin sags on his weary bones, his cheeks hollow. The man is a shell of the powerful force he once was.

"You always have the better bottles." I raise a brow, looking over at him.

"Bring me one of those, will you?" He poses it as a question, but it's not.

Grabbing the bottle and an extra glass, I nod toward Edward, dismissing the man who's been at my father's side for the last two decades.

For people of our status, protection and loyal men are paramount—and that doesn't end when we close our door at night.

This place is teeming with staff and men who work for us. We made a lot of those men wealthy, and in return, they'd kill or die for us.

Edward's large frame casts a shadow creeping across the wall as he leaves, softly closing the door behind him.

He's a beast of a man, tall, with a nasty scar that slashes through his right eye. He looks like a storybook villain.

"I like it in here." My father offers a rare smile. "Your mother liked the view out that window." He lifts a finger, breathing heavy from the exertion, pointing to the floor-to-ceiling window that looks out over the gardens.

Illness for a man like my father is a worse sentence than death. He refuses to leave the house, and no visitors are permitted to his wing of the house.

When he finally does leave this place, it will be in a box. His reputation is brutality and power. He'd rather take a bullet than let his rivals see him weak.

"It reminds me of her too," I say, chinking my glass gently with his. She used to listen to classical music while watching the many young gardeners, but I keep that information to myself.

"Your brother..." he begins, but his words are taken over as he coughs and splutters. He drops his glass to the floor, the liquid seeping over the rug.

I remain quiet until he gets himself under control, then without acknowledging the dropped glass, slip my glass into his hand. "Your brother is getting out of control. If you don't rein him in, he will lose himself."

"I'll deal with him," I state.

Antonio being a pain in all our asses is nothing new.

"You need to marry, Luca. You're my legacy." He pauses, his hand going to his chest as it rattles with his labored breathing.

Hovering between life and death has made him almost frantic about adding to our family name.

He wants grandsons, but that's not the only reason.

He built our kingdom on corruption and blood money—drugs, trafficking, cybercrime—putting our eggs into more baskets over time.

I began building legitimate businesses, collecting on favors, investments, and fear. I helped grow our empire to heights he never imagined, opening legitimate businesses in mother's name.

If the feds ever get one of us, those business can't be touched. They're squeaky fucking clean.

"You don't have to love her, Luca. Just marry and breed Leto sons." He nods his head like it's a reasonable request.

"Did you love mother?" I find myself needing to know. It's a question I once wouldn't have dared asked him, but now...

"She was a special woman—strong, loyal. She gave me sons. Love wasn't important." He tips his glass to his lips as I swig from the bottle. "But I did, in my own way. I still do."

His honesty brings me relief I didn't realize I needed.

I wanted mother to be loved, to have known he loved her.

Marriage for men like us is usually a business transaction—an agreement that benefits both partners. I always avoided it until now.

Maybe it's time to re-think that.

CHAPTER SIXTEEN

Alyssa

IF YOUR BODY isn't sore, you're not working hard enough.

I repeat the mantra in my head as I move across the floor with grace and accuracy despite the blisters on my toes.

I've only been training a couple weeks and have already worn through three pairs of pointes. Breaking in a new pair is hellish.

"Lift up as you descend—point, point, point. I won't tolerate lazy movements," our choreographer, Michael, snaps.

It's a lot harder here than I anticipated.

I'm exhausted every second of the day.

"Feel the rhythm of the music—become it." He waves his hand around like a conductor. "Chin up, extend the knee. Janet!" he bites out. "I've seen cleaner pirouettes from a fourth grader. You're sloppy. Again—again."

The student's name is actually Jewel. I'm not sure if getting her name wrong was meant to further humiliate her or he just forgot her real name. Either way, it brings a smirk to my lips.

She didn't need a scholarship and made sure we all knew it. I despise the stuck-up bitch and will her to fall on her stupid pretty face as she begins cleaner pirouettes.

She's so thin, her movements look fragile. A starving little mouse surrounded by hungry cats waiting to take a bite.

I push through the throbbing sting, allowing the lingering memories of Mr. Leto to distract me.

I imagine him looming like a dark, delicious shadow over me, commanding my body. Pathetic, but I can't help it. My body responds to his in a way I've never experienced before.

My dreams have been overrun with fantasizes of him fucking me against the hallway wall—filthy, rough, deep. I'm sick—and I don't want to get better.

"Enough. Go shower," Michael tuts, waving a dismissive hand our way.

Sagging, I bend over unlacing my shoes flexing the toes as my stomach gurgles, I'm famished and have a shift in half an hour.

I STAND under the hot spray of the shower, letting the droplets massage the aching muscles in every part of my body.

"I think he has some kind of crush on me." Jewel Conway's voice rings out, her tone high and screechy.

Jewel. Even her name makes her seem untouchable, delicate, precious.

Stepping from the shower, I wrap a towel around my body, hating the harsh fabric against my skin. "He's gay actually," I say, squeezing the water from my hair as I walk to the mirror beside her.

Jessica's narrowed gaze burns a scar into the side of my face. She's Jewel's friend, more like a shadow than a person.

Jewel looks me up and down, her nose curled like I'm letting off a bad smell. "How would you know that?"

"I saw him with his boyfriend." I roll my eyes. I haven't seen him with anyone, nor do I know his sexual orientation, but I feel insulted on his behalf.

The truth is, Jewel's movements are hesitant because she'd been gouging at her feet with scissors to remove hard skin or bunions before training began.

That's what I really saw—the blood seeping through the fabric of her pointe. He probably saw it too.

"I did hear you like to watch people together, creep," she snipes, and I grin back at her through the mirror.

So pretty.

So pathetic.

She's everything I'm not.

Blonde. Blue eyes. Porcelain skin. Petite. Rich. And she immediately took a disliking to me. She's worried I'm her competition—and she's right to worry.

"Ignore her, Jewel. She's just jealous he's noticed you and not her," Jessica sneers.

Noticed her for being sloppy?

"Don't you have a thrift store to be rummaging in?" Jewel jibes, raising a brow.

She thinks her taunts are insults. With a gentle nudge as I pass her, her lipstick swipes across her cheek. I can be juvenile too.

"See you later, Janet," I call over my shoulder.

"ALYSSA, drinks are ready for table eight," Joelle calls from the bar to get my attention.

Table eight is Milly's, but I don't see her anywhere.

She only works one shift a week that syncs with mine, but the others have talked about how lazy and stingy she is with the sharing of tips—and that immediately made me dislike her.

I run the drinks to her table and place them down, grateful the customers take their chosen drinks without me having to ask who ordered what.

"Let me know if there's anything else you need," I offer with a smile, then make my way back to the bar to get a fresh order pad.

Tonight had been crazy long. In fact, it's been a long week, and once again, the same as every night this week, Mr. Leto hasn't made an appearance.

I check the clock and sigh. Nearly home time.

"Are you ready to order food?" I ask in my most polite tone, holding in the yawn desperate to break free. This is my last table.

"Can we have a few more minutes?" One of the women ask not looking up at me as she scans the menu.

"Of course." I smile, despite wanting to yell at them.

They've been sitting here for twenty minutes, and fifteen of that was them deciding what they want to drink. We close in an hour, and it will take half of that for the chef to cook their order.

"You look wiped." Simon runs his gaze eyes up and down my body, his brow raised.

A group of women who spent most of the night in a private booth reserved for special occasions giggle and stumble as they leave for the night.

One breaks away from the group and slides a folded-up bill and a napkin with a number written on it across the bar toward Simon.

Smirking, he pockets the napkin in front of her, making her blush.

I take a moment to really look at him.

His dark hair is neatly styled to one side. Amber eyes are rimmed with thick, dark lashes that would make any female jealous. Prominent cheekbones and a slight crook at the bridge of his nose make him handsome in an unconventional way.

"It's been a long week," I groan, looking over at another of

Milly's tables. It hasn't been cleared of the dirty plates despite her customers being finished. "Where's Milly?" I ask.

"She's in the bathroom for the hundredth time tonight. I think her boyfriend dumped her again." Joelle sticks a finger in her mouth in a gagging motion, overhearing our conversation.

"If Hannah comes out here and sees the tables this way, she'll fire Milly—and that would mean more work for the rest of us in covering her shifts next week," she adds, pushing the receipt booklet for their table over to me.

Great.

I go and place it on their table and begin clearing the plates. "Thank you so much for dining with us," I beam.

One of the men slips a twenty into the pocket of my apron, his hand brushing over my lower stomach as he does.

Gritting my teeth, I clear the rest of their plates just as Milly makes her appearance. Narrowing her eyes at me, she follows me through to the back kitchen.

"Are you trying to steal my tips?" she asks, her lips twisted in a snarl.

"What?" I whirl around, astonished she has the balls to accuse me of that. I've been picking up her slack all night.

"I can clear my own tables, Vanessa," she sneers, folding her arms and jutting out her curvy hip.

"It's Alyssa, and the customers were leaving. You still hadn't cleared their tables or even offered a dessert menu."

"I was getting to it," she growls before turning on her heel and storming toward the front of the house.

I follow, scooping the shitty twenty-dollar tip from my apron and scrunching it in my fist.

"Milly," I call just as she steps through the door to the dining floor. I ping the crumpled note off her forehead. "Your tip."

Her screech is over the top and loud—too freaking loud.

Shit.

"Alyssa, in my office," Hannah warns from behind me, startling me. I hadn't heard her office door open.

If I get fired over this, Milly will be getting more than a piece of paper thrown in her damn face on my departure.

Closing the door, I cringe, scratching at a non-existent itch on my arm. "Sorry about that—"

"I need you to stay late," she cuts me off with a shake of her head and crinkle of her nose, looking down at her phone in her hand.

Okay. Not what I was expecting. "I have a curfew," I remind her.

"I'm not asking." She looks up at me over her glasses. I hadn't noticed she wore them for reading before now.

"Can I ask what it is you want me to do?"

"Mr. Leto is coming in to eat."

Thud.

"Why can't he eat during normal hours?" I find the words slipping from my lips before realizing I said them.

A live hum pulses within me at the thought of getting to see him. He hasn't been in all week, and now I'll see him in a real setting—not a fleeting moment in a hallway.

"He owns the place. He can do what he likes." She sounds worn out.

"Everything okay with you?" I ask, moving closer. Taking off her glasses, she rubs the bridge of her nose before sighing and slipping her glasses back into place.

"I'm fine. Send Milly in for me please." I take that as my cue to leave.

"You good?" Simon asks when I get out front.

"Yeah. I might have to sleep in your car if I don't make curfew, though." I cringe.

He chuckles, popping the lid from a bottle of Coke and offering it to me. "*Sugar!*"

I shake my head no, my mom's sour screech churning my stomach. I guess her poison is still inside me.

"Millyyy," I drag her name out, smiling sweetly, "you're wanted in Hannah's office."

Her face pales, and a sick satisfaction fills my chest, enjoying her fear.

AFTER ALL THE customers leave for the evening, Hannah places a bottle of Pappy Van Winkle Old Reserve bourbon on a tray with two glasses. "Leave the bottle—don't pour for him," she states, then excuses herself.

Fifteen minutes later, the front doors open, and in walks the man himself.

Luca.

His tie hangs loose around his neck, no suit jacket just a crisp white shirt, the sleeves rolled up, showcasing his strong forearms.

Two men in black suits flank him, each taking a stance at either side of the doors. They look around, surveying the place.

He doesn't acknowledge anyone as he makes his way to a table on the higher level reserved for VIP guests.

His strides are powerful. He walks with purpose, charging the atmosphere around him. It's breathtaking to see someone command their space and the people around them without even speaking.

Not a minute later, Marcello joins him, dressed down in fitted jeans and a sweater with a shirt beneath it. Tension hardens his features. His jaw is stiff. His furrowed brow makes my stomach tense.

I fidget nervously, feeling dishevelled and worn out. Loose strands fall from my ponytail. I pull my hairband, attempting to neaten it, and the elastic snaps in my fingers, my curtain of hair falling free down my back.

Shit.

Hannah is strict with how we present ourselves—and loose hair isn't tolerated.

Simon clears his throat, gaining my attention. He jerks his chin to the tray. My pulse skyrockets as I take it and walk across the empty floor.

It's so quiet in here, my footfalls echo through the space. With every step closer, my heart races faster, booming in my ears.

They're in a heated conversation and don't stop even as I approach the table.

Being up close with time to catch my breath, I drink Luca in, observing a small scar beneath his eye I want to lick. His features are so beautiful, perfect.

"Your brother is out of control," Marcello snaps, drawing my eyes to him.

"I'll tell you what I told my father: I'll handle him," Luca retorts. I place the bottle down and set a glass in front of each of them.

"What else did your father say?"

I take my time, lingering in their company. They smell so freaking good.

Expensive, woodsy.

"He wants me to marry," Luca states, deadly serious. I almost drop the menus when his gaze slashes in my direction, traveling over my blouse, lingering on the sliver of flesh on display from the extra button I popped opened when I learned he was coming in.

"Then do it, if only to appease him." Marcello rolls his head over his shoulders, tugging at the collar of his sweater.

My belly aches at the thought of Luca marrying someone. It's ridiculous, irrational, and fills me with dread.

Mrs Leto.

"I'm not going to marry some stranger and risk being stuck to a woman I despise for the rest of my life." He twists his watch on his wrist, and I lap up the sight of his strong forearm, the veins straining with his movement, making my pussy ache.

I imagine his forearms working hard while he finger-fucks me, and my mouth floods with saliva.

"We won't be eating." Luca waves away the menu, his tone cold, drenching in me ice.

"He just wants to ensure succession and stability of assets with what happened. Maybe it doesn't have to be a stranger." Marcello's tone softens.

With no excuse to stick around, I leave them to their conversation. "They're not eating," I shrug when I reach Simon.

His brow shoots up, and his bottom lip juts out. "Maybe we'll get you home for curfew, after all."

I chance a glimpse over my shoulder and see them pouring the bottle. "Or they'll want to finish the bottle," I groan, secretly hoping that's the case.

I tuck a strand of hair behind my ear, noting Simon watching me.

"You okay?" I ask, my brow dipping.

"Yeah, sorry. I haven't seen you with your hair down. It's really pretty." A red flush blooms up his neck, and he diverts his gaze, shaking his head. It's cute and makes me chuckle.

"I'll let Darras know he can leave," Simon splutters. "Maybe you can try calling your dorm to see if they'll make an exception?" he adds, and I worry my lip, checking the time.

That's not a bad idea. Julia, our house mother, was actually down to earth and lenient with the older students.

I wait for Simon to make it back out front in case Luca or Marcello needed anything else before grabbing my phone from the staff room.

Ignoring the texts and missed calls from Clint, I dial Julia.

No answer.

Dammit.

A gasp flees my lips when I'm suddenly thrust forward from behind. Luca's scent encompasses me as he pushes against me, forcing me into the cold plaster of the wall.

"What the hell?" I pant.

Tugging on my hair, he gathers the locks into his fist and wraps it around his hand, causing a stinging pain at the nape of my neck. "You shouldn't have this down while working."

Thud.

I'll wear it down all the time if this is the punishment.

My breathing is erratic. His hold and dominance should leave me terrified, but it doesn't. I push my ass back and up, desperate to feel his cock between my cheeks. His hiss from my movements causes a groan to crawl up my throat.

"Why is it down?"

"My hair tie snapped." I quiver, my hands splayed against the wall, the pulse in my neck flickering wildly.

He grunts and growls, breathing me in, animalistic, a ravenous beast straight from most people's nightmares.

Not mine.

"Get the fuck out of here before my willpower snaps," he snarls against my earlobe before releasing me.

I gulp for air and turn to see him retreating away from me.

A whimper escapes. My nipples ache. My pussy throbs for relief. With my cheeks flushed, I swallow. My mouth suddenly dry, I go back through to the bar for water just in time to see Luca exiting with his men, while Marcello stands by the bar.

His eyes clash with mine, ablaze. I bite my lip and take the few feet to reach him.

"Hey, bella," Marcello croons, making my insides liquefy.

Between Marcello and Luca, every woman in their vicinity becomes drenched. It's unfair to be so good looking.

"Marcello." I smile, my nerves still raw with excitement and lust. His gaze lingers taking in my dishevelled appearance.

"Do you have a boyfriend?" His question catches me off guard, I blink erratically, leaning over the bar to grab the water bottle I keep there.

Chuckling, he tilts his glass in the direction of my phone. Clint's name flashes across it as he calls me for the tenth time today.

Damn you Clint.

"No," I scoff, ignoring the call, and turning my phone over to hide the screen. "Dancing takes all my focus." I greedily gulp down the bottle of water and place a hand to my heart, willing it to stop racing.

Pushing out his bottom lip and dipping his head nodding he pulls out a stack of cash clipped together by a silver money grip that probably cost more than most people's car.

Separating a few hundred bills, he drops them on the counter. "A sweetener for staying late." He winks, and my body turns to goo.

Pointing to Simon, his tone turns firm. "Make sure she gets home safely."

"Yes, sir." Simon bobs his head as Marcello turns back to me taking my hand and dropping his lips to the back of it.

"Good night, bella."

"Good night,' I smile shyly, heat setting fire to my cheeks as he makes his exit.

Once we're alone, Simon tugs on my hair, drawing my attention from the exit doors. "Did you get through to your dorm mother?"

Blowing out a frustrated breath, I shake my head, "no."

"You can crash at my place tonight if you need somewhere to go." He lifts his shoulders, unsure of his offer.

It could be messy if there was any attraction or feelings there, but there aren't—at least not on my part.

"Come on, Alyssa. If I leave you on the streets, Marcello will kill me," he says, wiping down the bar and throwing my water bottle in the trash before coming around the bar to join me.

I find myself nodding my head in agreement.

I skim through the cash Marcello left, separating half and handing it to him. "I can't take that." He shakes his head pushing my hand back toward me.

"You stayed late too." I nudge him forcing the money into his palm. "Take it."

He's hesitant, then smiles, "Thanks." He shoves it into his pocket and grabs his coat.

Popping my head into Hannah's office, I find her pacing the floor, "We're leaving if you don't need us for anything else?"

Shaking her head, she comes to the door gripping the wood, "No I will lock up. Drive safe."

Not waiting for a reply, she closes the door forcing my head out.

Simon comes walking up the corridor both our coats in his arms, "All good?"

"Yeah, Hannah's going to lock up."

Holding my coat out for me I slip it on and check I have everything.

It's cold when we push out into the parking lot, a fresh breeze rustling through the tree branches, the moon full, illuminating the sky.

We're not alone, out here the men who accompanied Luca tonight are standing by the car lot exit, a large fancy town car is parked a few rows from Simon's, the lights on but no-one in the driver's seat.

My eyes are glued to it, a nervous jump in my pulse. Is that Luca's car?

"Are you coming?" Simon, chuckles following my eyeline.

"Yeah," I shake my head smiling over at him.

When we drive past the parked car, I bite my lip wondering if he's inside.

Did he not leave?

CHAPTER SEVENTEEN

Luca

COMING HERE TONIGHT WAS A MISTAKE. Seeing her with her hair loose and buttons undone, showing a creamy channel of flesh leading to her perky tits, only made me want to throw her down on the table and take my fill from between her legs.

She wasn't supposed to be there. Her shift had ended, but there she was, thick lips and hungry eyes.

She brings out a weakness in me. Allowing my cock to overrule my head is something I've never allowed before. But now, it's not a choice I'm making.

There's something compelling about this damn woman. I need to fuck her from my system.

Leaving Vino's, my driver and trusted PA, Thomas, is waiting with my town car. He nods in my direction as I approach, my security team covering the entrance and exit to the parking lot.

There are three cars in the parking lot—Hannah's, mine, and a small BMW I'm pretty sure belongs to the bartender. My little ballerina must not have a car.

How does she get home?

"Did you get what I asked for" I ask Thomas, dragging my tie from around my neck.

"Yes, sir." He jerks his chin to the car.

"Take a walk," I order, slipping into the back of the car, need vibrating in my veins.

A static anticipation hangs heavy in the air between me and the woman sat inside on the bench seat opposite me.

"Sir," she dips her head in acknowledgment.

She's a little older than Alyssa and not as pretty but she's styled how I requested.

Observing her black fitted bodysuit—one just like what Alyssa was wearing the day we met, my cock grows.

"Do you know what I want?" I ask her.

"Yes," her eyes darken as she reaches for a purse on the seat beside her.

Slipping her hand in, she pulls out a small razor blade. A heated blush crawls up her neck, her throat bobbing as she swallows.

Labored breathing fills the air between us.

"Do it." I instruct.

Jerking her hand over her lip, wincing on contact, she cuts a small slit through the flesh. "Like this?" she asks, her pupils dilating. A red tear blossoms on her fair skin, making my dick strain against my zipper.

"Yes, it's perfect."

Pulling my cock from my slacks, I grip the base and stroke my fist up. My shaft throbs, pulsing in my palm when her eyes widen.

It hasn't stopped aching since I pushed up against Alyssa's back. She smelled of need and summer, her little frame shuddering beneath me.

Any normal girl would run from the big bad wolf—she stalked the beast, taunted and teased him. My little Red wants to be eaten.

"What do you want me to do now?" The woman asks, shifting in her seat.

"Don't move, I want to look at you."

My phone rings from beside me, Marcos's name flashing onto the screen. Holding my finger up to the woman, I answer the call, "What is it?"

"Sorry to disturb you, sir, but your brother's friend Carlos is insisting he speak with you." That little runt hasn't learned his lesson. Brave to come back to the house after the beating he took.

I un-fist my cock and push the hand through my hair, agitated.

"Keep him there," I order, ending the call and looking back over at the girl in front of me.

"The hair," I growl. Her lips part, small fingers reach up to her hair.

"I was told you wanted a tight ponytail." She quirks a neat brow, the blood dripping from her chin to her chest.

"Let it down," I command, my voice gruff.

Movement in my peripheral view, draws my eye to the back exit door of Vino's opening. Two figures stepping out, laughter chiming through the air like music.

Alyssa.

Her gaze follows the path to mine, only I know she can't see me through the blackout, bulletproof glass.

She not alone, the bartender says something to her making her smile before she gets into his BMW. My fists clench as a growl climbs up my throat.

I should want this—let her be with a nobody like him. It's safer that way.

Small hands rub up my thighs, the imitation of Alyssa getting bold. "Want me to taste you?" she purrs, but my cock is already losing its erection. It wants the real thing.

"No. You can leave," I tell her, pushing her away from me. I stuff my cock back in my slacks. "Thomas will take you home."

"Did I do something wrong?" she asks, her hand swiping across the blood.

"No. I did," I grumble.

I MOVE THROUGH THE HOUSE, a thunderstorm riding my back making the staff scatter like ants.

My office door is open Marcos's frame looms against the back wall hands fisted in front of him, the fires crackling and sat in one of my armchairs like a house pet is Carlos.

"Can I get you something, a saucer of milk perhaps?" I mock, rolling down my sleeves.

He startles at my voice, *was this prick napping?*

The dimmed light illuminates purple bruising under his eyes, a scabby wound across his nose looks angry.

"I need to speak to you." He straightens his spine not giving eye contact.

"Leave us," I order to Marcos, taking a seat behind my desk. "What could you possibly want to speak to me about?" I ask, templing my hands on the wood.

His fingers shake as he brings them up to rub at his brow, looking sheepish, "Antonio...he—"

Motherfucker.

"He what?" I shout, banging my fist on the table, a pen rolls off the desk to the carpet.

"Fire," he blurts, his eyes widening. "He's setting those night-clubs on fire."

What the hell? I shoot from my chair, almost toppling it over. "Where is he?" I stab out each word.

"Downtown," he sighs, rubbing his hands down his thighs. "He's drunk. I thought I'd better come get you."

Of course, he's drunk, when isn't he. Damn that bastard.

"Marcos," I bark. The door opens, his heavy built frame enters walking toward me, filling the space in front of my desk.

"Sir?"

"Take this rat," I jerk a finger to Carlos. "And a few men and go collect my brother."

He nods his head, grabbing Carlos by the back of his shirt, "I'll walk." Carlos cries out, almost lifting off the floor when Marcos yanks him up, Marcos's strength easily over powering him shoves him toward the door, he almost trips on his own feet.

"Move." Marcos warns him.

"I'm going, I'm going, why is everyone so angry all the time." I hear his cocky retort and fight the urge to paint the walls with his insides.

I swipe my phone from the desk and call Marcello, while going to the drink cabinet. The ambiance of this room is warm, relaxed, but I'm anything but.

He answers on the second ring. "I'm busy, cousin. Can this wait?"

I don't wait for anyone.

"No."

THIS DAY IS NEVER ENDING and keeps getting worse.

The tension is thick, Marcello's violent appetite coming to the surface as he paces my office floor, wearing out the carpet, his hands clenched behind his back.

My brother sits in the chair Carlo favored earlier tonight wearing the same suit jacket he's been wearing all week, stains splashed up the sleeves. His dark hair is greasy and parted in the middle.

He's an embarrassment. "Are you going to say something or just scold me with your disapproving glare?" he slurs out.

Moving across the room like a feral beast, Marcello scoops him up by the lapels of his jacket. "Do you know how much damage you caused tonight? You're reckless and a disgrace to your name."

He drops him back into his chair, rubbing his hands down his sweater, wiping the remnants of Antonio's scum off.

"You're a mess, little brother. And you created unnecessary issues with those fires tonight."

"I didn't set them myself. Could have been vandals." He throws his shoulders up like this is all a joke.

"No, you're not man enough to do the dirty work yourself. You ordered our men to do it for you." Marcello swipes a hand over his mouth.

"Luca wasn't going to do anything." He flings his arms out in my direction.

"Because Serena's murder has nothing to do with the Blaydon brothers building sex clubs in the city!" I bellow, gripping the arms of my chair to stop myself from wringing his neck.

"So, we pay for the damage or tell them to fuck off," he muses, thinking because it's his mistake it will be overlooked.

My fingers twitch. Marcello balls his fist and plows it into Antonio's jaw. The impact twists his face as he slams back in his chair, hitting the floor.

"Enough!" I stand, rounding the desk.

Antonio is on his feet in an instant, the punch sobering him up. "You will pay for the damages." I tilt my head, studying him. He glares at Marcello, his breathing heavy.

"I will deal with the brothers. In the meantime, you're going to get clean so you can start thinking straight again." I warn him.

Spitting blood at Marcello's feet, Antonio jabs a finger into his chest. "Don't ever fucking hit me again."

Shoving him away Marcello retorts, "Don't make me hit you again."

A heavy silence looms like a thunder cloud, before Antonio wipes his forearm across his bloody mouth storming from the room with one last look at Marcello over his shoulder.

Once he's gone, I grab a bottle and a glass before taking my seat behind my desk again. "What now?" Marcello asks, flexing his fingers.

"Get me a meeting with the Blaydon brothers."

"Are you sure you want to take the blame for the fires? We could go with the vandals route."

Drumming my fingers on the desk, I shake my head. "Let's get in front of this. We don't need small problems becoming bigger ones." I tell him, my attention turning to my computer screen.

With a firm nod of his head, he swipes his hand through his hair and makes a move toward the door. "Send Thomas in, will you?" I call after him.

Tapping my fingers over my keyboard, I bring up the staff list for Vinos and tap on the file for the person I haven't been able to get off my mind since seeing them tonight.

A minute later Thomas enters the room, his suit coming to stand at the opposite side of my desk, "Sir?" He asks.

I save the file to a memory stick and hand it to him. "Find out everything there is to know about this person."

Slipping the memory stick into his slacks pocket he bows his head, "Yes, sir."

Sitting back in my chair, I grab for the glass of whiskey, telling myself it's intrigue and not jealously pushing my actions as I glare at the picture ID on the screen—the one I'd copied for Thomas.

Simon Greene.

CHAPTER EIGHTEEN

Alyssa

A LIGHT SHEEN of mist coats my skin from the routine we've
been repeating for the last three hours, "Lift," Michael snaps out,
with a sharp tongue full of scrutiny, "Enough." He holds a hand
up dismissing us with a grunt.

Jewel walks beside me to the shower rooms, her eyes flitting
toward me. "What is it?" I sigh, stopping just outside the door, too
tired to deal with her drama or bitchy attitude.

"I noticed Michael paired you with Nathanial today."

Nathanial is a great dancer, tall and strong. I trust him to lift
me and feel at ease with him. "And?"

She thins her lips, folding her tiny arms over her flat chest.
"I've been working with him."

"Jewel, I'm just doing as I'm told—not trying to steal your
boyfriend. If you have an issue, take it up with Michael."

Nathanial and I had chemistry on the floor, I'm not going to
give that up because of her fragile ego.

"Like you could steal my boyfriend." She huffs, narrowing her eyes.

If I wasn't running late for work, I would drag him into the shower with me and let him help me release some of this tension just to spite Jewel. But I made a pact with myself.

I'm not going to put myself in an awkward predicament that can cause drama with my peers or jeopardize my position here.

"Are we done?" I ask exasperated, I have to cover an extra shift at Vinos I don't have time to play who can be the biggest bitch.

"You'll be done if you keep getting in my way." She snides.

It's one step too far for my own ego to accept, my earlier promise not to cause drama flying out the window. I grab her forearm before she can strut away happy with herself, jerking her against my chest.

"Oh my god, let me go." She gasps.

Tightening my hold, I lower my voice so I can't be heard by passing dancers, "Don't fucking threaten me, you spoilt, little bitch, or I'll snap your leg and use it as a toothpick." I bite out, releasing her with gentle shove.

Her eyes are as wide as saucers, mouth agape, her hand wrapping around her arm.

"Now we're done." I add, waltzing into the shower room.

"YOU'RE LATE." Hannah tuts, wobbling her head like a hula girl on a dashboard in jest as she plays with a bottle of water and forks a mouthful of salad leaves into her mouth at the staff room dining table.

"It's six on the dot," I rush out, dumping my things in a locker, tying my apron in place and taking the bread roll Simon offers me, devouring it like a starved animal.

I burn so many calories dancing, I'm slowly trying to unlearn all the bad habits Mom instilled in me.

"The king is at his table." Simon nudges my shoulder, exiting the room. He looks a little different tonight, a new hair cut maybe?

My stomach dips, thinking about what he just said, a fluttering of butterflies taking flight. Hannah offers me a worried half smile.

"How's things at school?" she asks to make conversation, watching me add extra plasters to my feet before pushing my feet into my work shoes.

"Exhausting, and painful." I chuckle wiggling my foot in her direction.

She swipes up her salad and takes it to the trash dropping it in half full. Walking to where I'm looking in the mirror tightening my ponytail.

Her hand rests on my back, "You should take better care of your wellbeing."

The door swings closed behind her not giving me a chance to digest and reply to her.

I check my face in the mirror, pinching my cheeks to give myself a bit of color before heading out to the shop floor.

Soft music and the purr of voices hums through the room as I scan the occupants. My heart skittering in my chest when my eyes land on Mr. Leto in the raised private area.

"He's only here because you're working," Joelle whispers in my ear from behind jolting my body. I hadn't even noticed her.

"He never takes his eyes off you." Her lips tug up into a mischievous smirk.

"Liar," I scold, feeling naked.

I'm covering Milly's shift. He would have had no idea I'd be here.

She busies herself making up an order, "I'd wish he'd notice me, but three years—and nothing." She winks.

I drop my head to sneak a peek over at him. My breath catches when I feel his penetrating gaze burning a hole through me.

Seeing him at the table dressed in a designer suit with perfectly styled hair...he looks like he fell from the pages of a magazine. It's intoxicating to be in his trajectory.

Joelle pushes a tray in front of me, mouthing, "The king," before biting down on her lip and cutting her gaze to Luca's direction. "He likes the bottle placed down and left." She jerks her head firmly.

My throat dries, and my nipples tighten under my formfitting shirt. I'd gone braless while in a hurry to get dressed and now regretted that mistake.

His very aura makes my heart hammer in my chest. His tense jaw sends a wave of nerves dancing in my blood stream—excitable nerves, exhilaration.

"Sorry for the delay," I lie, placing the bottle of bourbon on his table and the glass with two ice cubes on a napkin before him.

Turning to leave, he barks out, "Pour."

The husky, rich tone of his voice incites a nervous giddiness within me.

I should be intimidated.

He's much older than me, I'd bet his thirties easily, and an air of fear surrounds him, like an invisible fire, keeping most people from even daring to look his way.

Not me, though.

I like the burn.

He has a dominance in his movement. His speech has a way of making you feel inferior to him. And in my fucked up, broken way, I like that too.

His thick lips cause heat to pulse in the lower part of my stomach. My eyes trace down his throat, watching his Adam's apple bob as he swallows.

The suit he's wearing is dark gray tonight and fits to perfection. Strong muscles show through the fabric, summoning the memory of the way the hard planes of his body felt pushed against me.

He's reading a newspaper like it's ten years ago despite having two smart phones placed on the table before him. I'm not sure why anyone would need two cell phones.

I pour two fingers worth of the tawny liquid, acutely aware the bottle costs more than my salary, willing my hand not to tremble and spill. "Did you want to eat?" I ask, licking my bottom lip to moisten the sudden dryness.

"Steak."

His eyes move to mine before dropping to my lips, sending my pulse roaring.

"Rare. I like to see blood on my food." He closes the paper discarding it on the table.

My lips part, a small puff of air pushing free. His eyes bore into me, loosening every part of my body. He releases me with a jerk of his chin, and I almost lose my footing when I back away to relay his order to our chef.

"You're blushing," Joelle gushes, nudging my side. "Did he say something to you?"

Glancing a quick look over my shoulder. I feel the room close in around me when I find his eyes still fixated on me, stripping me bare. I feel my pulse everywhere.

"No, just the usual." I jerk a shoulder trying not to show how affected I am by him.

"That man," she sighs, fanning herself.

"What man?" Simon asks, pulling open the fridge behind Joelle and taking out a tonic water. I advert my gaze, jotting down a scribble on my pad.

Smirking, Joelle croons, "That one." Flitting her eyes in Mr. Leto's direction.

Rolling his eyes, Simon scoffs, "You know the devil had a pretty face too, right?"

The devil, is that who he is?

Joelle's glorious laugh brings a smile to my lips, "Don't worry, Si, we think you're cute too." She turns to me winking.

"Gee thanks." He snorts, going back to his customer.

My gaze finds its way back to *him*.

Mr. Leto.

That man.

That devil.

I SENSE the moment Marcello enters. The way the atmosphere shifts and all eyes track his every move.

Dressed beautifully in a light suit, mirrored shades hiding his eyes, his towering height descends on the bar.

My pulse jumps in my neck when he smirks in my direction, skimming past me with a hand on my back while murmuring, "Bring me a glass, Preziosa."

Every inch of my body is aware of the powerful men in my vicinity.

Taking a glass to the table, I place it down in front of Marcello, highly aware of Mr. Leto's gaze on me.

He's paying me more interest today than he has before, and it makes me a little on edge.

"Are you hungry?" I ask Marcello, meaning to ask if he's staying for food. My brain isn't working around them today.

The corner of his lips twitch as he devours me. "Ravenous," he quips, his eyes dropping to my chest blatantly. My breath hitches, then accelerates.

"He will have the same as me," Mr. Leto barks, drawing my attention to him. His eyes have darkened, narrowing on me.

"Yes, sir," I say in a mocking tone. I turn to leave, hearing Marcello say, "She's quite something." My heart blooms.

"She's a child," Leto scoffs, dousing me in humiliation.

Embarrassment heats my cheeks as anger tears through my body. Was I a child when he was rubbing his cock into my back?

I linger near a table close by, pretending to wipe it down.

"Her body says otherwise."

"The body is pointless if the mind can't handle the things you do to it."

My heartbeat skyrockets. What the hell does that mean?

I take off to place the order for Marcello's steak before running to the restroom to splash my face with some cold water, needing to get a hold of myself.

"You're fine, he's an asshole we knew this." I tell myself patting dry my face.

BUSYING myself with other tables I try not to think about what Mr. Leto said but it's like a virus in my brain infecting every thought, I can't focus.

Joelle calls me over for Mr. Leto and Marcello's order. I think about sneezing in Luca's before delivering it but rein in the petty bitch inside me.

Taking an even breath, I still my nerves and rapid heart rate walking to where they're sitting, and placing their food down in front of them.

"Anything else I can get for you?" I ask, looking directly at Marcello, forcing a cool smile deliberately dismissing Mr. Leto.

"We're good," he grunts anyway, his tone a clear warning for me to leave them alone.

"Actually, my glass needs refilled." Marcello smirks a wicked look, dazzling his eyes.

Picking up the bottle, I pour a small amount in the glass and hover it near Luca's glass.

He twitches his head slightly, giving me permission.

Moving the bottle over his lap, I spill a drop on his crotch, making him startle.

"Oops, so sorry. Must be my childlike hands." I grin, placing the bottle down and walking away.

CHAPTER NINETEEN

Luca

MY CROTCH IS DAMP. Marcello's roar of a laughter draws all eyes to our section. I'm going to kill that ballerina.

Getting to my feet, I march through the bar. Gripping her under the arm, to the shock of the barmaid, I drag her to my office, she doesn't fight it, complying like a good little princess, all the while knowing she's anything but.

I slam the door behind us.

"Do you have a death wish?" I scorn, angry and turned on all in the same damn breath.

Her face is breathtaking. No makeup, naked, and still the best-looking girl in any room.

Her chest heaves, her nipples poking through her shirt. Is she not wearing a bra?

"Look at this mess. I have a meeting after I leave here," I fume, gesturing to the wet patch she made.

She lifts her shoulder. "I can blow on it for you." Her brow quirks, those fat lips offering a knowing smirk.

I want to strip her naked and fuck the life from her over my desk, make her scream so everyone can hear her come undone beneath me.

"You do realize I'm your boss, right? Your disobedience won't be tolerated," I growl.

A light giggle of disbelief filters through the air daggering me in the chest, "Tell my boss grinding himself on employees is sexual harassment, so don't tell me what will and won't be tolerated."

My legs close the space between us before I realize I've even moved.

Once again, I pin her against a wall, pushing my body against hers. "Are you making threats, little ballerina?" I breathe down on her, and she matches me glare for glare.

She's exceptional. I want to keep her, but I can't. Someone killed Serena because of her link to me. I need to stay away. But then she licks her bottom lip, and my cock pushes against the zipper of my slacks, desperate to be slapped against her ass.

Her breathing accelerates, making her shirt gape, offering a view of the swell of her tits.

"Like making wet patches, do you?" I taunt. "I bet your panties are soaked."

Her lashes flutter, "Not that people can see. Yours looks like you can't hold your bladder," she mocks. "Is it an age thing?"

"You're angry about my comment," I smirk, pushing further into her. "Yet acted very childlike with your response," I inform her.

"What do you want from me?" She squints her eyes, and I want to say *everything*.

"I think it's you who wants something." I raise a brow, dropping my eyes to her nipples pushing against the white fabric of her blouse.

"Then give it to me," she dares, and damn her, I drop a knee and suck her nipple through the fabric of her shirt, flicking my tongue over the small bud, coating her shirt in saliva.

Her hands grab at my hair, a whimper coming from her lips.

I pull away, standing, leering at the wet spot allowing me a clear view of her sexy rosebud nipple.

"Now we're even," I state. "Get out."

WHEN I MAKE it back through to the bar, Alyssa has changed her shirt and is busying herself serving customers. I track her movements for a few seconds, then go back to the table.

Marcello has finished eating, and my food is stone cold.

"She's very entertaining," Marcello taunts, pleased with his hire. Prick.

I sit back in my seat as a girl enters, her fiery red hair like a beacon.

She's flustered, blaring my name to Simon, "Where is Luca Leto?"

My guards flank her, grabbing her arms. A silence falls over the room. I jerk my head for them to bring her to me.

Alyssa focuses on me, her brow crinkling with worry. She moves to the bar, talking to Simon, never taking her eyes from mine.

Marcello moves his chair around to get a better view of the girl. She's young, red, frizzy hair bouncing off her head like cotton candy. It looks ridiculous.

"You," she says my name like it's tar on her tongue.

"And you are?" I ask, jerking my head for my guards to release her arms. I think I can protect myself from this child.

"Natasha, Serena's sister."

Interesting.

I look her over with new eyes, trying to find pieces of her sister within her features, but she's nothing like her.

"I don't want your money," she sneers. "You killed my sister."

"Lower your voice," I command, standing, buttoning my jacket, my appetite gone.

"I didn't kill her, but I will find out who did and make them pay for what they did to her," I assure her. Running my gaze through the bar, the customers go back to their drinks but I know they're all straining to hear what's being said.

Scrunching up her nose, she twists her lips, shaking her head. "I know who killed her." She looks at me like I'm an idiot.

"Her ex, Eddie, hated that she was with you—that you wouldn't allow her a life outside of the nights you'd let her suck your cock," she bellows.

My jaw tenses, her crass, loud mouth causing another scene.

"Out back," I grind out to Marcello, marching through the bar, feeling the burn of eyes on me from every angle.

Entering my office, I sit behind my desk giving a barrier between us so I don't snap her neck if she insults me again.

She's brought in, tugging herself free from Marcello's grip.

"Quite a potty mouth on you," I offer a seat with a gesture of the hand to the one next to her. She shakes her head, the ginger fluff bouncing with her movement.

"Tell me about Eddie," I encourage.

"Like what?" she glares over at me. If looks could kill I'd be a pile of ash right now.

When I don't speak, she rolls her eyes. "He's a drug addict piece of shit who used to slap her around." Pursing her lips she adds, "She was a glutton for punishment. She'd always go back to him—until you." She crosses her arms, defiant.

What is it with these ballerinas?

"What is Eddie's last name?"

"Johnson. He's a dangerous man," she warns me, softening.

I want to laugh. If only she knew how dangerous the man she's been mouthing off to is, she'd bite that tongue of hers.

"Take the tuition. If not for you, then for Serena. She would want you to take the money," I tell her.

Her stubborn chin juts forward. "Fine. But it doesn't mean you're forgiven."

I don't need forgiveness, just retribution.

"Understood." I give her a nod, letting her have closure.

She smacks her lips and leaves a little less fiery than she arrived.

"See she finds her way out," I instruct to Marcello. "And find this Eddie, bring him to me."

"It will be my pleasure." His eyes light up.

Eddie Johnson is about to meet his maker.

CHAPTER TWENTY

Alyssa

WHEN THE GIRL passes me guided by Marcello, I want to grab onto her and demand to know what's going on, but she's rushed through to the exit and would probably tell me to fuck off anyway.

"Who is she talking about?" I turn to Simon. All the warmth has left my body. "I know that girl." She's unmissable, I've passed her in the halls at Swan.

"Don't ask questions, Alyssa. It will only lead to bad answers," he warns before turning back to his customers. I feel rattled, and for the first time, a little afraid of the man I've been daydreaming about and who he really is.

Moments later, Marcello deposits her on the sidewalk waiting for her to walk away before returning.

"Marcello?" I call as he makes his way back toward us.

Holding his hand up to us, he says, "All sorted. Just a misunderstanding. Take a house bottle to every table and apologize for the interruption." Not leaving room for questions he disappears again.

It's another hour working on Jell-O legs before my break comes around. I find Hannah in her office, looking queasy.

"Did you hear about what happened?" I ask, making my way over to her desk, taking the seat opposite her.

"Are we friends?" I flinch at her sudden question, a warmth stirs in my stomach, it takes me off guard. We don't really know each other, but I've felt a connection to her throughout my short time here.

"I'd like to think so," I tell her honestly. I could use friends.

Worrying her lip, she tracks a path to the door making sure it's closed.

"I wasn't being cautious when I told you the Leto men are dangerous." She frowns, swigging from an open bottle of water.

"What do you mean?" I ask, sitting forward.

"The girl who came in is the sister of a worker at one of Mr. Leto's other businesses."

"Okay?" My stomach knots in anticipation of what she's going to say next.

"Her name was Serena. She was a server at a private club. She was Mr. Leto's girl—exclusively." My insides want to be on the outside. Jealousy and envy spawn inside me.

"Everyone knew she belonged to him. Especially her. She liked it, flaunted it," Hannah sneers.

"Did he love her?" I ask, the possessiveness spreading inside me like a disease.

"God no." She pulls a face like it's a ridiculous question. "Mr. Leto isn't built to love a woman, Alyssa. This is what I warned you about."

Thud.

Not everyone needs or wants love.

Screwing the cap on her bottle she folds her hands into her lap, "Serena would never be more than his good time girl, and I think it broke something inside her. A sadness surrounded her, you know?" she swallows, I think she knows more about that than I.

"She could never truly be his. You don't make women like her into wives." She scoffs. "No one knows for sure what happened, why she went to a back room with someone other than him, but they found her in their private room, murdered." She watches my face, waiting for the fear or shock to show, but I just want more information.

"So, who did it?"

She clasps her hands onto the arms of her chair, lifting her shoulders. "They don't know. But this freak really did a number on her—carved her up until she wasn't recognizable."

Again, she stares at me waiting for me to gasp, or run-in fear.

I won't.

"The cuts were so deep, it had to be someone really fucking nasty, brutal, strong." Taking a breath, she adds, "And it came only months after Mr. Leto's mom's death."

So much death surrounding us both.

"How did she die?" The way she said it implies her death wasn't a normal death either.

"A mugging, of all things. Supposedly." Her brows pinch. Worry tugs at her lips.

"His mother was murdered as well?" I breathe aloud, wanting to soak in all the information she has to offer.

"I know. It's suspect."

Is it?

"Do you think he could have done it?" I ask, bewildered by this new information.

Tension builds suffocating the room.

"Honestly? I don't know," she's whispering now, concern watering her eyes. "But it scares me. I've seen the way he watches you."

Which way is that?

Like I'm his next victim...

I reach over and squeeze her arm. "Don't worry about me, but thank you."

Swiping at her eye she sniffles chuckling, "For what?"

Smiling I say, "For being honest and genuine." I check my watch. Break's over.

I CAN FEEL his eyes on me as I move around the lower floor.

Always freaking watching, stirring my insides.

He's returned to his table, having lost his suit jacket and tie. He's now in a white shirt, the sleeves pushed up his arms.

I often wonder what he'd look like without clothes on, and what I've learned about him hasn't quelled that thirst.

Shaking my head to rid the thoughts from distracting me more, I move to the new customers and take their order.

The man, thin with leathery, crinkled skin, looks much older than the girl he's with. The atmosphere between them makes my stomach churn.

There's no spirit in her dull, bruised eyes. His large, bony hand clenches her smaller, pale one, making the tips of her fingers turn white.

"My usual bottle," he tells me flippantly without even raising his eyes to mine.

Another rich, entitled asshole.

"I'm sorry, sir, but I'm new here. I'm not sure what that would be."

His jaw flexes with annoyance. "Then ask someone," he snarls.

The girl he's with makes a whimpering sound, her shoulders dropping from how hard he's squeezing his hand on hers.

Bastard.

I want to ask if she's okay, but I fear it will only anger him further and his aggression will be taken out on her.

"I'll be back with your order," I say through gritted teeth, plastering on a fake smile.

When I get to the bar, Simon raises his brows at me, shaking his head. "What's got you worried this time?"

"Just another asshole who thinks he owns the world," I grumble.

"Do you know that man?" I ask, nodding my head to the man in question. Simon's lips curl, answering without words. He disappears out to the wine room and returns with a one of the rare bottles.

"He's a rich prick. Likes his wine mature but his women not so much." He shudders.

I look back over at their table, my instincts telling me to go rescue the poor girl. "She doesn't even look like a woman," I input, playing with a strand of my hair from my ponytail.

"Alyssa," he says my name in warning, gaining my attention back to him. "Trust me. Those girls know what he is. She's not here against her will."

Taking the tray, he scoots across the bar toward me with the wine, I blow out a breath and head back to the table.

Holding out the bottle, I get an arrogant head jerk in response, confirming it's the right wine.

I pour for him, then move the bottle to the girl's glass. The asshole shoots his hand out, covering her glass, but it's too late for me to stop the wine from pouring out of the bottle and over his hand.

A gasp leaves both me and the girl.

Shit.

"You idiot," the man roars, his chest vibrating. I can't move, my legs solidified to the spot, my heart raging.

He begins shaking his hand, sending wine splashes all up my shirt. The blemishes sink in, painting a permanent stain.

"I'm sorry," I say, despite wanting to hit him over the head with the bottle. His beady, narrowed eyes finally raise up to mine.

"You useless little bitch." He cracks, the bitter, evil beast in him raising to the surface and spilling free all over me.

My stomach bottoms out with the pure intent of his hateful glare. Instincts have me scanning the table to use something as a weapon if I need to.

All eyes peer our way, putting me in the spotlight. "Clean the mess and get me your manager." His tone is loud and spiteful.

Words fail me.

I've never been spoken to so rudely by a stranger before. Hell, by anyone—not including Luca.

The atmosphere in the room shifts, and a dominating figure suddenly appears behind the man.

My eyes sheen with tears of anger and humiliation. I travel the length of Luca's form and lose my breath seeing the murderous look in his shocking blue eyes.

He moves, unwavering with precision, and slams the man's head down on the table surface.

My mouth drops, gaping in disbelief. A horrid crunching sound makes the girl scream.

Covering her mouth, she scoots back in her chair as the flurry of movement from nearby tables clearing echoes around us. The man is out cold, slumped against the table, blood oozing from his nose, forming a pool by his glass.

The weight of his limp body slowly drags sideways and slides off the chair, landing in a heap at the girl's feet.

Luca jerks his chin to the two men in black suits situated at the doors. "Take the trash out," he tells them before he turns to me. "No one makes a scene in my establishment but me. Go home. Take the rest of the night off."

Thud.

I want to throw my arms around him, thank him for coming to my aid. For having my back. Adrenaline soars through my veins making me jittery. There's a charge in the air, vibrant and intoxicating.

Twice in one day, someone has made a scene, and both times, I've learned there's violence and darkness inside Luca...maybe darker than my own.

CHAPTER TWENTY-ONE

I LOST IT. The beast I work so hard to subdue, to keep locked inside its cage, ripped the doors off and brought all eyes on me.

Why did it have to be her serving that entitled prick?

His behavior wouldn't be accepted in any of my businesses regardless, but I wouldn't have lost my tempter the way I had if it hadn't been *her* he was speaking to.

The possession I felt in that moment rippled through my bloodstream, roaring in my ears.

Mine.

She belongs to me.

This is what I needed to avoid.

Goddamn Marcello.

The tables all around have cleared, the scene causing a tsunami effect. "Clean up and re-set," I bark to the staff members all staring at me.

Pushing through the door to the back, I overhear raised voices from the staff room and know it's my ballerina.

Going to the door, I listen, gritting my teeth when I hear Simon's voice. "You can't get involved with him, Alyssa. You saw what he is—what he did."

A smashing sounds, something being slammed down.

"And he was the only one who actually did something! I sure as shit didn't see you coming over to interfere and tell that perverted, disgusting asshole he couldn't talk to me that way." She's angry, her voice breaking.

"I was getting a replacement bottle," he tries to justify. In reality, he's a weak boy—she needs a man.

"He didn't deserve another bottle," she hollers. "You should have told him to leave."

Feet shuffle about.

"That's not my place, I don't have authority for that."

"You mean backbone," she sneers.

I step back as the door swings open. Her eyes clash with mine, the green glistening bright through a sheen of tears.

Her cheeks are flushed. Those fat lips of hers are pouty and in need of kissing. I need her out of my goddamn system—I need her out of here.

"I know you didn't do it for me, but thank you all the same," she tells me, her brow dipping low.

I want to grab her and tell her it was for her, push her into that room and force Simon to watch me claim her. Instead, I summon the bastard in me and jerk my chin.

"You need to be more careful when pouring drinks, it seems. Consider this a warning. One more discrepancy—and you find a new place to work."

Her bottom lip quivers for a second before she schools her features.

I'm an asshole, but it's necessary, if Simon is warning her to stay clear of me, he must have noticed the attention I pay her, and that's not good for her.

Straightening her shoulders, she nods. "I understand, Mr. Leto."

ROUND AND ROUND, Alyssa's image plays in my damn mind. It's a compulsion. I can't concentrate.

Never in my thirty-two years of life has a woman had such an effect on me. All I want to do is claim her. Not allowing myself the indulgence of fucking her is making me stir crazy.

Once Serena's killer has been dealt with, I'll be able to relax and take what I want. After a week of making her sore, she'll be out of my system.

A knock on my office door draws me from my thoughts. "Sir," Thomas says as he enters, placing a memory stick in front of me.

"There was nothing unusual or worrisome about Simon Greene." He adds a folder to my desk. "The reports pulled when he was first employed were thorough, and not much has changed. I put everything there is to know in the folder, he's bland."

Picking up the stick, I place it in my jacket pocket and swap the folder for a photo taken from the security camera of the man whose face I broke today.

"I need everything you can get on this man. I have to know if he's a problem that needs to permanently go away." I lean back in my chair, my intense stare telling him everything he needs to know.

"I understand, sir." Nodding, he slips the photo into an envelope and leaves just as Marcello enters.

"What the hell happened?" Marcello asks, jerking a thumb over his shoulder, referring to the empty bar.

Narrowing my gaze, I grate out, "Alyssa happened." I get to my feet and take the few steps to where he's standing, meeting him toe to toe. "She has to go."

"We have to go," he counters. "I got us the meeting with the Blaydon brothers. They know it was Antonio who set the fires." He slaps his hand down on my shoulder. "Are you sure we don't go the fuck you route?"

Releasing an exasperated breath, I shake my head. "No. Let's try to calm the waters without getting our hands dirty. We have enough light shining on us right now."

SITTING opposite these men in one of their clubs is slumming it.

How they got their hands on real estate within blocks of my club is questionable.

The red leather and poor lighting makes the place look like a cheap diner with stripper poles.

It's a shame Antonio didn't burn this one down.

The brothers are similar is stature and appearance. Short and stocky. Hair that's been bought and badly plugged. Over-tanned skin with bright veneers.

They both busy themselves with a tray of cigars. I shouldn't be here giving them my time, but I don't want more unresolved issues catching me off guard—especially with my own club opening back up Saturday for the first time since Serena's death.

"I'll cut straight to the point," I tell them with a tight smile, attempting to keep my voice calm to disguise my annoyance for even being here.

I should have let Marcello deal with this without me.

"The fires were a misunderstanding. I'm here to extend an olive branch."

The men look between themselves before both sets of brown eyes land on me, the eldest of the two speaking first.

"You will cover the damage, time lost, salaries, etcetera. As for your brother..." he smirks, puffing on a cigar, the smoke billowing between us, "He will come and apologize face to face."

There's a dangerous edge to his tone. I fight the urge not to crack the bottle of bottom shelf liquor they put out and slit both their throats with it.

I don't think they realize he's gambling with their lives.

I was willing to admit fault and pay for the damages, but on my terms. I won't be disrespected and talked down to by these nobodies.

Marcello is tense beside me, his hands fisted on his knees.

"I think you misunderstand our positions," I tell them in a mocking tone. "I'm not here as your bitch. I was willing to pay for damages, but don't mistake my gesture of goodwill for weakness." I stand, straightening the lapels of my jacket. My feet sticking to their disgusting floor. "And don't ever give me orders."

I lift my chin to Marcello. "We're done here."

"We'll be seeing you, Mr. Leto," the youngest chuckles to my retreating form.

"You better hope not," I call over my shoulder.

Once back in my town car, Thomas hands me an antibacterial wipe before closing my door. That place could give you an STD just by entering.

Marcello punches the leather seat beside him. "Who do those motherfuckers think they are? This is all Antonio's doing," he fumes. "What do you want to do?"

Looking back to the club my rage tells me to go in there and gut them both but I'm not Antonio, I need to act using my head.

"Nothing."

My phone vibrates against my thigh, and I dig it out of my pocket. "We tell them to fuck off after all," I add before answering the call.

"Detective?"

"Someone called in a complaint to the precinct against you today," his gruff voice drones.

There are snakes everywhere as of late. "Is that so?"

"A Mr. Angelo? He's in the hospital with a broken nose and jaw, said you attacked him at Vino's." A grin tilts my lips as I watch Marcello furiously type out a message, no doubt to Antonio.

Maybe this temper thing runs in the family.

"If his jaw is broken, how did he make the call?" I inquire, running my hand through my hair.

I'd hoped the asshole would come after me via the money route. Men like him usually sue, but if it's the police he wants to involve, that's bad news for him.

"It was his wife, a Bridget Angelo. The precinct will be sending someone over to their house tomorrow morning. He should be released tonight. I'll forward the address," He informs me.

That man won't be alive by morning to say anything to the police.

"Any update on Serena's killer?" I ask while I have him on the line.

"Nothing yet." He blows down the receiver, no doubt sucking on a cigarette.

"Did you know of her ex-boyfriend, Eddie?" My gaze shifts to the window. Why didn't I know about this boyfriend?

"We questioned him and just released him today, actually. I'm following up on his alibi now."

My ears prick, hairs raising on my arm. I want this man. If it was him who killed her, I didn't want the NYPD getting him. He's mine. "Where did you pick him up?"

Silence.

"Tell me," I instruct, my tone lethal.

"He's a permanent resident of a dive bar downtown."

"What bar?" I reply with a cold retort.

A sigh, then, "Wild Rover."

The line goes dead, and my adrenaline spikes. "Change of plans. Turn the car around," I call out to Thomas.

"Are we going back to Blaydon's?" Marcello questions, opening his jacket to palm his gun.

"No." I jerk my chin to his ankle where he keeps his blade. "I know where Eddie is." I loosen my tie. "Have the boys prepare the factory and call in the dentist."

CHAPTER TWENTY-TWO

Alyssa

I WISH he would either fire me or fuck me. Just put me out of my misery. This back and forth is becoming exhausting.

He wasn't something I planned for when I came here. Dance was supposed to be my only focus—put every part of me into perfecting my form, learn all I can, and use it to give myself a better life.

I'm messing all that up because of a man who has infected me. I feel him burning me up from inside, the static humming in my veins. It's driving me crazy.

He's a fever taking over my insides. I need to stamp him out, flush him from my system.

The way he dismissed me with a warning coaxed the darkness inside me to rise up. Tomorrow, I'll give him what he gives me: a cold indifference.

I find Jewel in the kitchen when I make it back to our dorm.

Leaving without Simon meant I had to walk on already tired legs. I just want some food and sleep.

"Hey," she says, immediately putting me on alert.

"Hey?" I frown, watching her from my periphery.

Laura lingers by her side like a wart on Jewel's ass.

"So, you're working at Vino's?" Jewel says, dunking a teabag in a cup of boiling water.

She calls it skinny tea. It's supposed to be some magic drink that helps you lose weight. The girl is one pound away from death. She can't afford to lose more.

"That's right. Why?" I blow out a breath, hoping the news about today's drama hasn't already reached them.

Laura lets out an obnoxious giggle, and I go on high alert. This isn't just a general conversation. An insult or something is coming.

"We were wondering if you could get us a table there?" Jewel twists one side of her mouth in an attempt at a sweet smile.

It's not what I was expecting. "You and Laura?" I pull the premade salad I bought yesterday from the fridge and grab a fork.

"No," Jewel screws up her face, looking over at Laura like it's a ludicrous thing to think she'd have dinner with her friend.

"Nathanial and I." She smiles, her lips thin and cheekbones almost tearing through the skin. "I want him to see you waiting on us—how it should be," she jeers.

Little bitch.

"I'm sorry," I look her up and down, "Vino's only serves clientele of a certain class. Mr. Leto does, however, have a strip club you'd be perfect for." I plaster on my most serene smile and push her cup of tea off the counter, spilling a drink for the third time today.

They both screech as the hot water splashes their feet and legs.

"You bitch!" Jewel yelps. "We know all about Mr. Leto and his strippers. He likes to fuck them and they wind up dead.

Better hope you don't end up on his pole. Or, better yet, you do." She crosses her arms, the edge in her voice harsh and bitter.

Stab her in the eye with your fork.

Before I can react, a female voice drifts in from the foyer. "Jewel, my office. Now." The house mother's timing just saved Jewel an eye.

Red-faced and like a child, Jewel stomps away, leaving Laura standing there on her own. It's odd to watch her wilt in the darkness I cast.

Her shoulders drop, face paling. "Night, Laura," I say in a velvet murmur, holding up my middle finger for only her to see.

CLOSED IN MY ROOM, I abandon the salad and throw myself down on the bed. Jewel's spiteful words spin around in my head.

Was that girl who died his only lover, or did he have a habit of fucking the strippers the way Jewel implied? How would she even know any of that?

Reaching under my pillow, I bring the small figurine to my lower stomach and push her sharp feet into my flesh, gasping to contain the pain of the burn and relief of the cut. I need to bleed out the darkness.

A violent voice fights my mind for control. If Jewel slipped in the shower one day, I doubt anyone would be shocked. They'd say she probably fainted from hunger.

No. No. No.

Grabbing my phone, I wince. Clint has texted and called again today.

Letting out a sigh, I hit call, hoping he doesn't pick up.

My hope is dashed by the third ring.

"Hello?" he chimes down the line, a pitch of surprise in his tone.

"It's me," I say, gaining an answering chuckle.

"I know it's you, silly." I turn onto my side, squeezing the ballerina in my grip. "It's so good to hear your voice," he croons, sounding nervous.

A female voice in the background groans for him to come back, and the ruffling tells me he's moving.

"Who's that?" I ask, both intrigued and agitated.

If he has another girl occupying his bed, why is he constantly blowing my phone up?

"It's no one," he says dismissively.

"Does she know she's no one?" I ask, insulted on her behalf.

Why do men think they can just decide who is worthy of being more than just a fuck?

"She knows she's not the girl you marry." His words are hollow, used often by shallow, entitled assholes. "It's just sex, Ally. You're the girl I'll marry." My insides want to disperse over my bedroom floor.

Isn't that what Hannah said about Serena? *She's not the girl a man like Mr. Leto would marry.*

Getting into a sitting position, I clutch the phone in my shaky hand. "That's so funny, because the guy I'm fucking said the exact same thing about me."

Once the words leave my lips, a sense of giddy joy washes through my system like a drug.

"What the hell did you say?" he asks, his tone full of contempt.

"Also, Clint, you're a shitty fuck, so expect a no when you do propose." I end the call, throwing my phone onto the mattress, and let out a weird squeal before walking over to the mirror.

The small swell of blood blossoming on my lower stomach makes me smile. Smearing my finger through it, I bring it to my lips and swipe across them. A tap on my door makes me jump.

"Who is it?" If it's Jewel, I may drag her into the room and force feed her until she loses her *hangry* attitude.

"Nathanial, I can come back?" his baritone voice rings out.

"No," I pull my shirt back into place and stuff the ballerina figurine into my dresser drawer.

"Hey?" I say as I open the door, more as a question than a greeting. His eyes shift to the bed where my phone vibrates incessantly.

"I never see you home at this hour and wondered if you'd like to get some extra training in?" He's sweet and seems genuine, and I need to release some of this energy.

"Do you need to get that?" he asks, stuffing his hands into the pockets of his jeans.

"No. It's no one important." I shrug. "Training sounds great. Let's do that."

CHAPTER TWENTY-THREE

Luca

EDDIE IS PREDICTABLE, it would appear.

Thomas gives me a nod in confirmation as a picture message pops up on my burner phone.

"What now?" Marcello asks.

"Now, we wait." I fist my hand. Patience is a must in these situations. We need to take Eddie without being seen.

I usually wouldn't be the one to handle the grunt work, but I can't let him out of our sight now we have him.

We park in the shadows. Thomas checked the building for outside cameras and there aren't any.

"I'll need you to drive. I have another job Thomas needs to take care of," I inform Marcello.

He quirks a brow. "You going to elaborate or...?"

"You'll know soon enough." I tell him.

Getting out of the car, I make the call for another car to come collect Thomas and tap the window, gesturing for him to join me.

"Sir?" Thomas asks, waiting for instruction.

"The job I gave you today—the man in the photo at Vino's?"

"Yes," he confirms.

"It's turned cold. Both occupants. Accidental," I tell him, giving him the address Detective Morels sent over.

"I understand, sir. I'll make arrangements for tonight."

He moves across the street to wait for his car while I await Eddie. The air is cold, causing condensation to billow from my lips, making me less invisible than i'd like but it's dark and anyone who does exit the bar is too drunk to notice their own feet let alone us.

It only takes ten minutes for Thomas's ride to arrive, and just as he slips inside and drives away, Eddie exits the bar.

I bring up the picture to be sure, then stuff my phone back in my pocket.

There's no mistaking it's him. He sways as he stumbles around the building and drops his jeans, pissing up the wall. I knock on the window to alert Marcello, and he jumps into the driver's seat.

Walking over to Eddie's naked ass, I survey the area, ensuring no one's around. The car tires kick up gravel as Marcello brings it across the lot, gaining Eddie's attention. Looking over his shoulder, he frowns.

"You finished?" I ask, slipping on my leather gloves.

Dropping his eyes to his cock, he jerks it, then tucks it back in his jeans. "What the fuck—?"

I hold a finger to my lips, then palm the side of his face and ram his skull into the brick wall.

It takes two hits to knock him out. Marcello pops the trunk and jumps out to help me dump the bastard in there. "What the fucks that stench?" Marcello screws up his face, grabbing Eddie's arms, straining from the dead weight.

"He's covered in piss." He whisper—yells.

He may have landed in his own piss

"Just lift the fucker." I grunt, heaving his body over the lip of the trunk.

I'll have to burn this suit.

"Feels like old times." Marcello grins over at me as we slam the lid closed.

Wiping my hands down my jacket, I smirk. "This is how criminals are made," I remind him.

Getting into the passenger seat beside him I add, "We all have to get our hands a little dirty every now and then."

WE PULL up to the warehouse, greeted by my men who take Eddie from the trunk and tie him to a chair in the middle of the space reserved for these types of meetings.

Slipping out of my jacket, I place it on a hook on the far wall, then take my time undoing the cuffs of my shirt and rolling up the sleeves—a deliberate action to give Eddie time to adjust to his new predicament.

"I know who you are," he stutters, eyes flickering open, wincing in pain. The side of his face already swelling.

"That's good, we can skip the introductions then," I mutter, scraping a chair along the concrete floor. Placing it a few feet away from him, I sit, resting my elbow on my knees. "Tell me what you did to Serena." I cut straight to the chase.

"Nothing," He shakes his head vehemently.

"You see..." I wag a finger, shaking my head, "I don't believe you." I look up at Marcello who is standing a few feet away. His legs slightly parted, arms crossed, he gazes down at Eddie with dark intent. "What do you think, Marcello?"

"I think he's a lying murderer." His skin stretches into a snarl.

"I swear, I didn't fucking touch her."

I give the subtle nod to one of my men we call The Dentist.

Wheeling a trolley over, he unwraps a leather binding, revealing a set of tools inside.

"When was the last time you saw her?" I ask, and Eddie jerks a shoulder.

"I don't fucking know. We broke up."

"Take a tooth. Let's see if it will help him remember," I command.

"No. What? Wait." He bucks, trying to free himself from his bindings, but this place was built for torture. He isn't going anywhere.

Another one of my men grabs his head from behind, forcing his jaw down to open his mouth.

The dentist doesn't hesitate despite the screams. The sound is like biting into a strawberry when he plucks the tooth from gum.

It's extraordinary how much the mouth bleeds when injured.

Gurgling on the blood, Eddie spits down himself and thrashes, cussing me out.

"When was the last time you saw Serena?" I ask again, my tone bored.

"Fuck you, you fucking cunt motherfucker." He spits in my direction, blood and saliva spattering the space between us.

"Take another," I command.

The tooth clinks when it's dropped on the metal trolly. Molars are surprisingly large.

"She hated you." He dribbles, his eyes rapidly blinking, sniffling, I'm not sure if he's trying to convince me or himself.

Checking my watch, I blow out a bored breath. Serena loved me. She wanted more than I was willing to give, but was content with our arrangement.

"We were going to get married, have kids." His breaths come in heavy pants, and he slumps over.

Snorting, I fold my arms and lean back into the chair. "From what I hear, you were into beating her." I give a silent demand to the dentist, and he fists his hand. The punch comes from his right, twisting Eddie's head to the side.

The chair is cemented into the ground and doesn't move. "That doesn't sound like a good foundation for marriage and kids." Another punch.

"Why did you kill her?"

"You killed her," he wheezes, his eyes unfocused.

"Her sister seems to think you did it," Marcello interjects, grabbing him by the jaw, putting pressure on the gums. Eddie howls in pain, fighting to pull his head free.

When Marcello finally releases him, he says, "Natasha is a stuck-up little bitch." His lips flex, taking in a breath. "If she weren't an ugly cunt, I'd fuck the snob out of her."

"Where were you the night she was murdered?" I growl.

"I can't remember," he attempts to roar, but chokes and splutters.

"Hang him up. Let him think for a while," I tell them. Getting to my feet, I collect my jacket. "I'll be back tomorrow. You stay and keep an eye on things," I tell Marcello.

*

ANTONIO IS WAITING for me when I get back to the house.

He's wearing clean clothes, and there's clarity in his eyes as he greets me in the foyer with a tilt of his chin.

"I had Miranda make you a plate," he says. "She made your favorite pasta."

Miranda has been serving in his house since before we were born. She's old as shit, but the woman can cook and is part of the foundation of the house.

"What's that smell?" He leans in wincing when he gets a whiff of me.

Piss.

"Should I be worried about you being civil?" I raise a brow and begin stripping off the clothes from tonight as I take the stairs to my room.

"I've been off the rails," Antonio calls up to me, rubbing a hand through his hair. "I'm just angry all the fucking time, but I'm trying to work on it."

I watch him over the handrail, nodding my head. "I'm glad to hear it."

I've heard the words before, and they don't usually last.

I enter my room, the fire already burning how I like it. Dumping the suit on the flames, I head to the shower, washing the night off my skin.

Antonio is waiting for me when I make it downstairs.

"You smell better." He notes, looking over my lounge pants and white tee, following me to the kitchen where I pull the pasta Miranda made out of the fridge.

"I can have her warm it up." He gestures to the door leading to the housekeepers' living quarters.

If he was hungry, he would wake Miranda at any hour to cook for him. He's spoiled, it would take him a couple of minutes in the microwave.

"I like it cold. Come sit." I tell him, pulling out a stool and sitting at the breakfast bench. "I don't think I've sat here since we were kids." I chuckle, stabbing the fork into the pasta and placing a hearty serving into my mouth.

"Marcello said you had the meeting with the Brothers Grimm." He smirks, folding his arms to hide the shake in his hand. The withdrawals are kicking in.

"Yes, it was enlightening," I grumble.

"They're thugs, Luca. They started out selling street drugs and moved up the ranks, gaining position through manipulation and blackmail." His jaw clenches.

"They must have someone influential or rich backing them." I swipe up another forkful. No way those lame fucks got their hands on more clubs through being business savvy.

"They're corrupt and degenerates." His nostrils flare. "I hear they had leverage against someone with money, but not power, so they cashed in. They're scum who blackmail using sex tapes of people's daughters. They need to be taken down a peg or two."

He did that. Setting their clubs on fire put him right down on their level, playing their games.

"We're above that kind of petty bullshit, Antonio. They're so far beneath us, it's not worth me even entertaining their company."

"So, what are you going to do?"

I swallow the last bite and wipe my mouth with a napkin. "I'm going to do nothing. They can pay for their own damage." Uncapping a bottle of water, I take a mouthful.

"They have me at the club while the fires were being set," he growls, his corded neck straining.

"Then, if they're the men you say they are, they have leverage and will come to blackmail us," I say calmly.

"And then what?" He throws his hands up.

My father's frail frame emerges from the shadows, walking with the aid of a stick like Death creeping in with his scythe. "And then you do what you always do with an infestation: you exterminate," he rattles, placing a hand on Antonio's shoulder. "It's the only way with men like that. Trust me," he adds. "Now, go wake Miranda. I'm hungry."

CHAPTER TWENTY-FOUR

Alyssa

NATHANAIL and I hit the lifts to perfection, all our practicing paying off. Michael claps for the first time since we've been here, and pride blooms in my chest.

"This is the level I expect from all of you," he beams. "We have the benefit Sunday, and then next week, we begin training for our first performance of the summer. If you think I've been hard on you so far, it's nothing compared to what I'll expect from you in the coming weeks." He points around the room, his hand movements animated. "Now, rest, rest, rest."

The showers are always swamped after classes let out, so I forgo and head for the kitchen, needing sustenance.

Julia calls me into her office when she sees me in the dining area.

My stomach twists from her concerned expression. "What is it?" I ask, my skin itching. I want to scratch myself until I draw blood.

"There's a boy who keeps calling here for you. He's very persistent." She clasps her hands, her brow dipping low.

Thud.

Clint.

"Is there anything you want to talk about? Is this boy bothering you?"

"No!" I shake my head, laughing away her worry with a wave of my hand. "He's just a friend from back home. I've been so busy, I haven't had time to take his call. He's probably just worried. I'll call him." I back out of her office.

I'm going to kill that little stalker shit.

Rummaging through my bag for my phone, I call his number, getting no answer. I find a quiet corner of the room and wait for his voicemail.

"You better stop calling my dorm, Clint, or I swear to god, I'll never speak to you again. I need space—give me that," I snap, ending the call.

My appetite gone, I head to the showers, thankful there's no one in here when I arrive. Dumping my bag, I begin peeling off my clothes when a snivelling sound echoes through the room.

"Hello?" I call out, waiting. No reply but more whimpers.

Pulling my clothes back into place I seek out the sound, checking each stall stopping at the last one in the far corner. Wishing I hadn't bothered when I see Jewel huddled on the tile floor, cradling her foot.

"What happened?" I ask against my better judgement.

"Nothing, leave me alone." She sniffs, tears staining her cheek.

Bending down, I pry her hand away from her foot. The toenail on her big toe is loose. "It's best to take it off and let the new nail come through," I advise her.

This won't be the first time she's lost a nail. "I'll bandage it up for you. You'll be fine."

"Why?" She wipes her cheeks screwing up her face like she's tasted something bad.

Pulling her to her feet, I help her hobble to a bench along the back wall. "Because I'm not an asshole." I tell her dropping her onto the bench seat before going to the cupboard for the first aid kit kept in all communal areas.

I pull out what I need and join her on the bench.

"Ready?" I ask, pulling her foot onto my lap.

"Ok," She bops her head, swallowing and looking away.

Pinching the loose nail with tweezers, I lift the nail away, wincing when she gasps and a tear leaks to her cheek.

"It's over." I cringe, depositing the nail on a piece of tissue, dabbing the blood with a sterile wipe.

"Nathanial says it's because I'm malnourished." Her mouth curls. "He doesn't understand the pressure I'm under." She hisses.

I begin wrapping her toe, daring a glance up at her. "I thought if anyone could understand, it would be a fellow dancer."

Snorting, she swipes at her runny nose. "His parents aren't like mine. My mother..." she bristles. "She expects so much."

"Was she a dancer too?"

"How'd you guess?" She shakes her head, inhaling a deep breath.

Sticking some tape on the bandage to keep it in place, a sigh leaves my lips. "My mother was the same way. It's taken forever to get her voice out of my head. If I'm being honest, it's still there. I'm not sure being a dancer would have been my choice," I say aloud, feeling a weight lift.

"*Was* the same way?" her head tilts, studying me.

"What?" I ask, lost in a moment of thought.

"You said she *was* the same way—past tense."

The cold chill of her memory wraps around my neck like a noose. "She died before I came here."

I finish with her toe and gently place her foot down. "Toxic is toxic, Jewel. It doesn't matter who the person is."

Silence lingers and then she murmurs. "Are you going to take Nathanial from me?" her voice is broken, vulnerability wrapping around her question.

She's just as damaged as the rest of us.

Placing the left-over medical material back in the box I get to my feet. "He's not interested in me like that. How could he be when he has you?" I rest a hand on her shoulder and gently squeeze.

"This doesn't make us friends," she calls out to me as I head toward the shower.

No, it makes us human.

***

A LIGHT SWEAT covers Joelle's brow as she marches up and down the bar making orders, my signaling to her going unnoticed.

The noise is loud tonight, every table is full making me flustered to be dealing with so many customers.

Simon makes his way down the bar to me, holding his hand out. Begrudgingly I hand him my next order for a table of six, all women celebrating a friend's birthday, I fan my face to attempt to cool my heated flesh.

I've been awake for sixteen hours and keep daydreaming about my bed. Simon pushes a drink I didn't order across the bar to me. "Drink this. Trust me, it will help you make it through the rest of the night."

I narrow my eyes. "What is it?"

"A peace offering. And energy." He winks.

I know he wouldn't give me anything illegal, and I hate bad energy so I greedily gulp down the liquid, enjoying the bubbles popping over my tongue. "Thanks." I pretend to tilt my hat and startle when a warm breath whispers in my ear.

"I thought little girls knew not to accept drinks from men at bars?" Mr. Leto scowls, narrowing his eyes on Simon, who scurries away to clean some glasses.

Coward.

"Not that I see any men," he adds louder, so Simon has no choice but to hear the insult.

Being so close to him clouds my mind, his allure trying to erase all the asshole shit he's done to me, but I steel my back and take a step away from him, turning to face him.

"Actually, it's all girls, not just the little ones." I glance around the room, then drop my gaze, looking him up and down, ignoring my whore vagina begging me to sit on the bulge in his pants. "And you're right, I don't see any men either. Excuse me."

I feel the heat of his scolding gaze on the back of my neck as I busy myself, my pulse pounding in my ears.

I shouldn't antagonize him, but I can't help myself. He's the type of man who makes me want daddy issues, and I promised myself I wasn't going to give him the satisfaction of my attention tonight.

He makes it easy for me when he leaves the building.

Going back to the bar I take my order from Simon, the women at my table all dressed with a certain sophistication, purses I've only seen in magazines placed next to them like they're a beloved pet.

"Who was that man speaking to you at the bar?" One of the women ask, while the other's giggle taking their drinks.

"That ladies, wasn't a man. It was the devil dressed as one." I whisper, in warning.

With that I leave them to enjoy their night, busying myself with clearing a couple of my tables grateful to find large tips left for me.

By the time I finish wiping the tables over my shift comes to an end. I didn't see Mr. Leto not making a reappearance.

It's pitiful that I miss his presence.

"Alyssa?" Hannah summons me with a gesture of her hand for me to follow her to her office as I'm packing up my things to leave for the night. My shift was only three hours, but it felt longer.

"What's up?" I ask, closing her door behind me, a tired thumping beginning in my head.

Walking to her desk, I take the offering of a cracker from her watching as she inhales one herself.

"Water?" She offers gesturing to a couple of bottles on her desk. Uncapping one she sips from the lip.

"Are you ok?" I ask, she's awfully pale tonight.

Waving a hand in dismissal she wipes her mouth, "Just a little queasy."

I take a seat holding my bag on my lap and nibbling the cracker she gave me.

"How would you feel about making some extra money Saturday?"

I was going to go shopping Saturday for a dress for the Swan benefit on Sunday. It's mandatory that I go, and I have nothing to wear.

When I don't answer she perks up leaning forward on her desk. "You'd be doing me a favor, Alyssa. I know it's a lot to ask, but a couple of the girls from Club S are refusing to come in and I've been asked to cover, but I'm not feeling good."

Club S?

"Isn't that the sex club?" I ask, incredulous.

Releasing a tired breath, she scratches her eyebrow. "You won't be working the floor or back rooms, just serving drinks."

That's no big deal.

And the extra money would be nice.

But it's a sex club and wasn't it where that woman was murdered?

"Maybe you'll be feeling better by then or Joelle can cover?"

"You'll make three times in one night what you make in a month here." She places a cherry on top.

That's a lot of dresses.

"What will I have to wear?"

She laughs, leaning back in her chair holding a hand to her stomach. "I promise nothing revealing. You'll only be covering the early shift. It's the first night re-opening and may not even be busy. I'll take you over and show you around."

That sounds easy enough. "Okay. I suppose...if it's a favor for you."

"One time, I promise," she agrees.

CHAPTER TWENTY-FIVE

Luca

ALYSSA'S ATTITUDE only made my cock hard. She wants to taunt me about being a real man. Soon, she's going to learn just what type of man I am.

Once Eddie confesses, there will be nothing holding me back from taking everything I want from her. I have to be sure he's the one responsible and eliminate him as a threat.

Pulling up to the warehouse, I exit the car and find Marcello sleeping on a cot in one of the rooms.

I should have relieved him this morning, but I wanted to give Eddie time to re-think his options, and I needed to be seen in public should any police come asking questions when Eddie turns up floating in the Hudson.

"Afternoon, Eddie." I walk over to where he's hanging, his hands in chains wrapped around a meat hook, his toes barely scraping the concrete floor.

His body is shuddering, dried blood crusted around his lips, a dusting of sweat coating his skin. Hanging there like that will be agony, the stretched tendons in his arms almost tearing from the sockets, his skin on fire. The bruising has come out blackening his face.

"I took the liberty of removing his fingernails, but he's still not talking," the dentist informs me.

Piss and blood coat the concrete beneath his feet, the stench revolting.

Marcello steps announce him joining us, yawning and scrubbing his hand down his face. "Do you want me to break a few bones?" he grins.

A text pings on my phone.

Detective Morels.

Eddie's alibi checks out.

Goddammit.

Irritation rolls through me, I wanted it to be him, for this to be over. Leaning down, I pull Marcello's knife from the strap on his ankle, "A confession won't be necessary now." I growl, stalking Eddie. I plunge the steel blade into his chest.

"Or we could just do that," Marcello pipes up. "What's going on?"

"Eddie was clean. Get rid of him," I order. Taking the blade to the sink, I clean it to remove my prints and hand it back to Marcello.

Fury roars in my chest. I thought this was going to be over, but now we're back to square one.

WHEN I ARRIVE BACK at the house, Detective Morels is sitting in my driveway, his car idling.

Getting out of my car my shoes crunch across the gravel, the wind hinting of a storm brewing howling against the windows of the house.

Opening the passenger side door, I slip into his vehicle. It stinks of cigarette smoke and fast food.

"Did you get my text?" he queries.

My eyes flit down my body conscious that there may be some blood splatter there but I'm clean.

"How solid was his alibi?"

Exhaling a deep breath, he leans an elbow on the window ledge. "Rock solid. It couldn't have been him." He opens the glove box and pulls out an envelope. "There's something else. I pulled the tapes from the surveillance cameras out of evidence."

Opening the seal, I tip the photos out, looking them over. Pictures of the animal who murdered my mother take up the image. "What's this?"

"The alleyway these were pulled from was three blocks over from where your mother was killed."

A static noise buzzes in my head. My heart pounds in my ears, my veins pushing the blood through my body too fast. "What are you saying?"

"I was re-examining the tapes, to see if we could have missed anything useful to this new case, a connection." He picks at the stitching on his seat.

"The police handling the evidence mislabelled the tapes, the cameras." He slams a palm down on his steering wheel, "It was a mistake, they had him down as in the wrong alleyway. It couldn't have been him who killed your mother."

How incompetent is the NYPD? Reckless, idle assholes.

"He was still a piece of shit, but..."

"Are you saying my mother's killer is still out there? That they have been this whole time?" My chest tightens as the world unravels around me.

I killed a man and his family because the police can't do their fucking jobs.

"I'm sorry. I believe these are targeted attacks. The scenes are clean. Someone knew where these women would be."

"Why? Why come at me this way?" It doesn't make sense. Nothing makes sense.

"Someone with a grudge, is there anyone who comes to mind? An employee you let go maybe?"

"No," I grit my teeth, irritated by his implication that someone under my own nose, my own employee, could have done this. Why not just kill me?

No, it has to be someone else.

"Don't tell anyone else about my mother. My father needs closure. Him thinking it was an opportunist killing in a messed-up way is something he can deal with, but the thought that she was sought out...it would kill him."

He looks over at me, his appearance more ragged every time I see him. "If I bury it, then we won't have anyone looking into it."

Like they can be trusted to find answers anyway. They got a man killed because they're morons.

"I will," I snarl. "This isn't a debate, just get it done."

Exiting the car, I call Marcello, telling him to meet me here.

THE GLASS HITS my office wall, raining down a shower of crystal shards to the carpet. Sinking into a chair, Marcello drops his head into his hands, his actions mimicking how I feel inside.

I can't rid myself of the thoughts of my mother being ambushed and murdered. What must have gone through her head?

"I want you to look into what Antonio's been doing. Go back to Annemarie's death," I inform him, his head snaps in my direction.

"You think the Blaydon brothers aren't the first mess he's

gotten himself into?" he asks in astonishment. "If this is something he's caused..." he adds, his face turning red.

I hold a hand up to placate him. I can't have him wringing Antonio's neck—not without cause.

If he is the one who's made enemies, it will be my hands doing the wringing. "I don't know anything. I just want to be sure," I tell him. "Keep this on the downlow."

"This will devastate my mother." He rubs at his eyes, inhaling a deep breath.

"She can't know. Only you and I know—and it stays that way until we have answers."

He jerks his head in agreement.

"And, Marcello..." I frown, pouring another glass of whiskey, "I want the ballerina gone. Fire her."

I hate that she has to go, but if something happened to her...

"I'll do it."

<h1 style="text-align:center">CHAPTER TWENTY-SIX</h1>

Alyssa

"SCARY, RIGHT?" Nathanial takes the seat next to me on the couch in the communal room, jolting my body with his movements. "One minute, you're living your life, go to bed, and then you don't wake up."

My heart jitters in my chest as I look over the image he's showing me on his iPad.

Two people dead.

Carbon monoxide poisoning.

"Apparently, he was a benefactor here." He jerks his shoulder, resting his arm behind me on the back of the couch.

It's the man from Vino's, the one Luca put in his place.

Dead.

Thud.

He's a benefactor here? How crazy would it be if he was mine? "What happens to the people his money pays for?" I frown.

Swiping across his screen to a new article he wags his eyebrow at me. "They don't have to stroke his ego at the benefit Sunday. It's a blessing, trust me."

I would have hated if he showed up here and I had to be nice to him. I'm glad he's dead.

Pulling an energy bar from his pocket, he unwraps it and points it in my direction offering me a bite. I shake my head, holding up my mug of soup.

"What are you doing tonight?" he asks, changing the subject.

I check my watch and get to my feet. "Actually, I have to pick up a dress and then I have a shift to cover tonight."

"You work too much. All work and no play..."

"Means I get to eat," I finish for him. Kicking his foot, I gesture to Jewel making herself tea in the kitchen with a tilt of my head. "You should take Jewel out. Aren't you still dating?"

He studies me for a silent beat before looking over his shoulder in Jewel's direction. "We were never official."

"Does she know that? It's not fair to string her along." I tell him grabbing my bag.

Jewel's a bitch, but ever since learning she has a mother who rides her back, I feel a kinship toward her.

"I'll talk to her," he assures me.

"Good."

Walking to the kitchen I rinse my mug offering Jewel a small smile which she ignores. Maybe the kinship goes one way. I'm trying to build a bridge and if she wants to burn it down, then that's on her, she can choke on the smoke.

*

CLUB S IS nothing like I expected. It's luxury. Black leather and silver velvet booths line the walls. Mirrored tables sit in front, bottles of champagne in the centre.

A runway platform extends out through the centre of the

main floor. Crystal chandeliers hang like jellyfish from the ceiling, giving the room a soft glow.

It's beautiful, and Hannah looks at home here, her elegant frame glides through the club talking me through what's what. We get to the bar and a familiar guy is arranging bottles.

"Simon?" I say stupidly.

Hannah turns to me pointing her finger at him, "I forgot to tell you Simon will be helping out behind the bar tonight." She says, rubbing her temples. "This is MJ, Katy, and Brittney. They'll be serving drinks with you tonight."

I offer an awkward wave to the blonde beauties in snug leather pants and corset tops that push up their breasts to form two perfect mounds with a valley between them, it's like replicas of Hannah, maybe management had a type.

Or Mr. Leto does...

"Katy will show you where the uniforms are. You can wear a black tee if you prefer." Hannah breaks through my internal ramblings.

A warm heat blossoms over my cheeks. I'm not a prude or a child. "The leather is fine." I ignore the raised brow from Simon and follow Katy into a hallway with numerous doors branching off.

She stops at one labeled "Girls," and pushes inside.

My mouth pops open at the dressing room. A wall of mirrors and vanity tables, shelves of shoes stacked from the ceiling to the floor, clothes racks overflowing with outfits, a shower room...

"Help yourself to what you need. Just be quick before the dancers arrive. It's a bitchfest in here when they're all together."

She signals around the room. "You're not allowed to take anything with you when you leave. Your uniform goes here to be steam cleaned after use." She points to a chute in the wall.

"If you need help tightening the corset, give me a shout." She winks before leaving me alone in the space.

I go to the rack of clothing and find the server outfits. Picking my size, I strip my clothes and slip into the leather it's harder than putting on leotards, sticking to the skin.

Closing the corset around my waist, I tug on the bindings getting a tight pull, my boobs pushing up, matching the other girls.

Walking to one of the full-length mirrors I stroke a hand down my body, I don't look like myself, but maybe tonight, I don't have to be me.

Swiping on a little lipstick, I pull my hair into a high ponytail and opt to wear my own leather boots. They're comfortable and won't risk blistering my feet.

I can do this.

Plastering on a smile I head back out to the bar.

"IT'S weird seeing you dressed like that." Simon dips his head, a rose tinge heating his neck as he leans over the bar checking me out.

"Bad weird?" I ask, looking down my body. The leather is like a second skin, leaving nothing to the imagination.

"Just different weird. You pull it off. I think that's what makes it weird." He chuckles.

"I'm not going to be working the pole, Simon," I tease.

"Hey, that's how the favors start out," he jests, and I throw a coaster at him from the bar. He ducks, and it hits another bartender on the back of the head.

"Sorry." I cringe, biting my lip to stop from laughing.

A dark-haired man walks out onto the club floor, and all talk ceases, a shift in the atmosphere brings my eyes to him.

"It's our first night opening since we lost Serena," he booms. "I know most of you are eager to get back to work and others apprehensive. But let's give them high energy and show them what they've been missing." Cheers ring out, and the lights dim.

Show time.

ONE HOUR into my shift and the place is packed. The ambiance is seductive, with a relaxed energy, despite how busy the servers and I have been.

I walk over to one of the private booths taking away their empty glasses ignoring the hand that slides money into my back pocket.

I've had more hands slipping cash down my pants tonight than some of the dancers. "Thanks," I wink down at the guy. I'm getting the hang of how to work the men out of their cash.

Swinging my hips as I leave, noting them watching my ass a grin lifts my lips. I can see why the girls work here, it's easy money.

Getting back to the bar Simon points to a table close to where the pole dancers are working their bodies like gymnasts.

Their agility and fluid movements are so impressive, where do they learn to do this, is there schools for pole dancing?

"That table wants a booth when one opens up." Simon informs me, looking ruffled.

"You, ok?" I ask, seeing his eyes keep flitting around my body. *Is he watching the dancers?*

"Heads up," he warns, motioning to something behind me. I chance a look and feel a warm glow heat my skin.

Mr. Leto is walking the floor. He shakes hands with a couple VIP guests before heading in our direction.

His eyes find mine, and my heart flutters violently in my chest when his features darken. The anger transforming his face steals my breath.

Hooking me under the arm, he marches me through the staff door, I attempt to pull myself free but he just tightens his hold.

"Oh my god, you can't keep grabbing me like this and dragging me away like a caveman." I snap. As he pulls me down the long hall into an office.

Finally releasing me with a gentle shove, making me almost stumble. I right myself and wail on him. "Excuse you!" I shove at his chest, and it doesn't move him one inch.

"Stop manhandling me like I'm a child, do you know how many of your bruises I will be wearing tomorrow because you're an asshole?"

The atmosphere is heavy, his breathing like a snarling beast.

I attempt to pass him to get out of the room, but he grabs me from behind as soon as my palm touches the handle.

His hand wraps around the front of my throat, placing pressure on my windpipe. He jerks my head against his chest and tilts my chin up, using my ponytail as leverage.

Every damn inch of him closes in on my body, his heat scorching all the sacred places inside me.

"What do you want from me?" I choke out. His hand tightens, cutting off my airway.

His hard cock pushes against my spine, and I think I might pass out.

I reach for his arm, clawing for freedom, but he only growls, deep and animalistic into my ear. My pussy responds, throbbing, soaking my lips.

"Stop wiggling around like you don't want to be right here with my cock so close to your needy cunt, little ballerina," he snaps. I can't help my body fighting; I'm craving freedom and captivity all at the same time.

"Why are you wearing this?" He bears down on me, his hand slipping from my hair, creeping around my torso, and skimming the waistband of my pants.

Air floods into my lungs as his other hand loosens from around my throat and the heat flees my back. He paces the floor, moving farther away as I turn around.

Yanking at his tie, he fists his hands, turning to face me. "What the hell are you doing in this place?" he demands.

"Helping out a friend. Why does it bother you so much to see me here?" I exhale, still a little breathless.

"You don't belong here," he snarls.

Blowing out a breath, I run my hands down my body. "I think I pull it off, and the tips would suggest the same."

"Don't play games, little girl," he warns, his jaw clenching.

I should be terrified, but he's so fucking beautiful my insides squirm to be closer to him.

My body coming alive responding to him like he's a conductor and I'm a slave to his music.

"Why? Games can be fun." I wet my lips, every inch of me on fire.

I'm provoking the beast. I know it's dangerous, but I'm willing to play for survival...I'm just not sure whose.

CHAPTER TWENTY-SEVEN

Luca

HER FACE WAS the last thing I expected to see at the club tonight. It's like the universe is testing me.

Being around her is like stumbling in the dark. She does something to me, takes control of my body and makes me want to be a different person.

I'm not a different person, though.

And someone out there wants to take things I care about.

Until their blood coats my hands, she can't be near me.

I can't keep myself from gravitating toward her whenever she's in my vicinity—and that's dangerous for her.

She glares at me, a mix of hate and lust in her green eyes. The leather outfit is skin-tight, showing me everything there is to unwrap and discover beneath.

She stands out amongst the other women. She doesn't belong, and every man knows it. She's royalty—something special to treasure.

"Why do you look at me the way you do?" I ask, having to fight the fiend inside from taking a big bite out of her.

"What way is that?" She licks her bottom lip, and my pulse jumps.

"Like you're hungry," I growl, wanting to feed her my fat cock deep past those plump lips and down the back of her throat.

"I'm not hungry, Luca," she purrs, her hand gripping her throat over the marks I left there, her brow crashing down. "I'm starving," she all but whines.

"Famished—desperate for you to fill me up." Her chest rises and falls, her breath coming out in needy little pants.

"With what?" I stalk her, slow, predatory.

"With you! Everything that is you," she exhales.

"You're how villains are made, little ballerina," I growl. "Tempting fate, wanting to play with the wicked."

The corner of her lips twitch. She tugs at the string on the corset she's wearing, and the front comes apart, exposing her pert tits and hard, rosy nipples.

My cock strains against my slacks, begging me to take my fill.

"I am the wicked," she tells me, allowing the material to fall to the floor.

The heat of her skin warms my own, her body so close I can taste her scent over my tongue.

Tension cords every muscle within me, if we give in to this, I'm not sure we'll recover.

Heady desire pulses through my veins, warming my chest and thickening my cock.

I place a hand on her chest, feeling the wild beat of her heart. Skimming my palm over her nipple causes her to suck in a breath. I want to bite and tease them.

Just a little fucking taste.

I grab her under the arms, and her legs wrap around my waist as we crash against the office door.

Her bare tits press against my shirt, eyes dance with anticipation. Her mouth parts slightly, glistening with a swipe of her tongue.

I crash my lips against hers, consuming her. She tastes sweet and deadly. The soft thickness of her lips caress mine. Our tongues spar for dominance. Hands pull at my hair, desperate for a deeper connection.

I drag my teeth across her lip and bite down until she cries out. Her body shudders against mine, and I thrust my hard length into the apex of her thighs, seeking the heat of her cunt.

I bring my lips down her jaw, kissing, licking, biting.

The intense need to devour her makes my touch rough. Fisting her hair, and yanking her head back, causes a hiss of pain, but she fucking loves it.

Her hips move, grinding on me. My cock throbs with the need to fuck her until she's breathless. She's sin and savior wrapped up in a delicious forbidden package.

I want her colored in my mark, soaked in my cum, whimpering beneath the firm hand of my spank.

Palming her tits, I squeeze, pinching the nipples between the pads of my forefinger and thumbs while scraping my teeth along the collar of her neck.

Our heavy breathing fills the room. The need is so strong, it's intoxicating. I want to redden her ass with my palm until her release coats her thighs.

Nimble fingers fumble for the zipper of my slacks, but if I let her touch my cock, I'll be buried up to the hilt within a heartbeat.

We can't do this.

Pulling my lips away, I shake my head and push her down my body until she's on her feet. She sways slightly, then rights herself.

A cold chill snakes up my spine, expanding through the room, coating her in my cruelty. This was a mistake.

Shit. What the hell was I thinking?

Her pouty, bruised lips open and close, but nothing comes out. Her tits are red from my roughness, and it speaks to the alpha male inside me.

Claim her.

Fuck her.

Make her mine.

Schooling my features, I grab her top and toss it at her, forcing the next words from my lips. "Get your shit together. You're fired."

CHAPTER TWENTY-EIGHT

Alyssa

NO, he can't.

Cold air replaces the heat as he moves away from me, leaving me whimpering like a needy little girl.

Did he not enjoy my touch, our kiss, my body?

"You can't fire me," I choke out, rubbing at my tender throat.

"I can do what the fuck I want, little ballerina. You're not right for my establishments and I'm sick of your disobedience."

My mouth dislocates. He can't be serious.

"I've been doing great at Vino's, why are you such a bastard?" I vomit the words, a bad taste forming in my mouth. I can't lose this damn job.

His eyes narrow, glaring at me. "Because I have to be. Now, get the hell out," he barks, jerking his chin toward the door.

Hannah made me come here tonight. Had she known this would be the reaction it would cause?

I wasn't wrong for his establishment. I could be what the men here expected: a little entertainment and a pretty face.

"If I'm not what you want in that way, then fine, but don't take my job."

I will the floor to open up and swallow me whole. I've never felt so rejected in my entire life. Tears threaten, a lump forming in the back of my throat.

A smirk kicks up the corner of his mouth. "It has nothing to do with my dick. It's your job performance. Now, get your boyfriend Simon to take you home. I won't tell you again."

My heart skitters in my chest, darkness expanding out. "You're an evil bastard, you know that, right?"

"Yes," he roars. Picking up a chair from near the desk, he tosses it across the room like it weighs nothing.

It crashes into the wall, and I still my spine, not giving him the reaction he wants.

"It's you," he points in my direction, his tone sharp and demeaning, "who doesn't know that."

Scoffing, I wrap the leather corset around my torso. "You're wrong. I do know, and I wanted you anyway." I sling open the door and slam it behind me as I leave.

I move through the hall into the girls changing room. Tossing the corset, I search the shelf I left my clothes on and make quick work of getting changed.

Once I have my clothes on, I go back out to the club floor to find Simon. His brow creases as his concerned gaze scans my face and drops to my neck. "Are you okay?"

"Apparently I'm not good enough for Club S." I swipe at my neck, hoping he doesn't see marks there.

His hand rubs my shoulder. Dipping his knees so he's eye level with me, he smiles, warm and affectionate.

"It's probably for the best, Alyssa. You're a dancer. If someone saw you working here, it could affect your status at Swan."

I hadn't thought about that. Could they really discriminate

over where I worked? And does Leto know this? Did he fire me for my own protection?

No, he's just an asshole.

"He fired me from Vino's too." My voice is rough, broken.

I sense him as soon as he appears from the door to my right, his gaze tracking me. "I have to go." I reach up and give Simon a hug. "Don't be a stranger, yeah?"

"Alyssa?" He sighs, but I'm already moving through the club, underdressed and out of place amongst the elite members.

A SLIGHT BREEZE picks up my hair, blowing it across my face as I push out onto the street, blinding me for a few seconds.

I wish it would make me invisible to the rest of the world.

Noise from a car honking alerts me to a headache forming, a marching band drumming through my head.

A light feather of rain drops to my cheek in warning of an imminent downpour.

Cars screech to a halt a few yards away from the club entrance, drawing attention.

My heart skips when a flurry of men begin jumping out, sending my stomach to my feet.

They're carrying guns.

Not like we have on the farm, but the ones you see in action movies.

My head whirls. My bag drops to the ground.

Noise, loud and piercing, all around me.

Glass shattering.

Deafening screams.

Fear has its own distinct sound. The pitch of terror clawing its way up the oesophagus before pushing past the lips, alerting everyone around to the horror happening.

That sound will forever be stained on my memory.

Pop. Pop. Pop.

Bullets fire, making a small thud as they connect with the soft tissue of a security guard standing just in front of me.

The man topples to the sidewalk, and people on the street attempt to flee.

The air leaves my lungs in a whoosh.

I push back through the door and run down the steps toward the man whose eyes are filled with dread.

Luca? My cold obsession.

I've never seen that look from him before, it douses my soul in horror, my heart ceasing to beat.

"Run," I scream, my voice sounding distorted to my own ears just as the doors behind me open.

Luca reaches me and picks me up. Rushing through the second set of doors, he shouts, "Code red!"

The security guy guarding the second door punches a code into a panel on the wall. A clanking sounds, then a steel shutter falls from the ceiling, almost decapitating one of the gunmen as he opens the door, but not in time to stop the metal shutter from sealing the door with us inside.

The soft pinging of bullets can be heard by us standing close, but the music is so loud, everyone else is oblivious to the carnage that awaits them outside.

"Check all exits," he orders his men, not releasing me. "The code sends an alert straight to the police. It's going to be okay," he assures me.

A sob shatters my chest. I came close to being shot and killed tonight, yet it's being back in his arms that brings on the sorrow and fear.

Now that I know how it feels being his focus, being kissed by him, I don't think any other man will ever come close to inciting what he does within me.

"It's okay, Alyssa," he tells me, his grip tightening as he moves us through the club and into the office he broke my heart in moments before.

"Who were those men?" I ask when he deposits me on a small leather couch.

"Dead men walking," he states firmly. "Are you okay? Did you get injured?" His hands roam over my body, his eyes searching.

"I'm okay," I tell him, rubbing up my arms, suddenly feeling chilled. "What was that shutter?" I ask, never having seen something like that before.

"It's a security precaution—something I never thought we'd need. A lot of clubs have them installed now."

I think of the times on the news when nightclubs became targets for terrorists and hate crime. Acid stirs in my stomach.

"I need you to wait here. I'll be back, okay? Don't leave this room," he orders me, his word such a contradiction to the ones minutes before.

Is this why he said he doesn't want me around, because bad things happen around him?

I think of the girl whose ghost must be haunting this place. Is he afraid I'll end up like her?

The gravity of the situation hasn't sunken in, but takes its toll on my body.

I lay down on the couch, my eyes closing. I need to sleep.

CHAPTER TWENTY-NINE

Luca

LOCKING the office door with Alyssa inside settles the racing of my heart.

I can't believe how close she came to being killed.

I underestimated the threat level of the Blaydon brothers.

This was a revenge attack—and it's going to cost them everything. I will wipe their bloodline from this world, decimate everything they've built and turn it to rubble.

"Bring up the cameras at the front entrance," I bark to the security guy as I enter Ricardo's office.

Flitting his fingers over keys he points to one of the large monitors. There's no one outside now, droplets of rain move past the camera, the wailing of sirens sound. There are a few bodies lying on the sidewalk. How did they think they'd get away with this? The tendons in my neck strain, I need to fucking kill these bastards.

"Mr. Luca," Ricardo says, holding up a phone receiver, his face pale, "it's for you."

Taking the phone, I hear Marcello's voice sigh with relief. "I've been calling your cell. What the hell is going on? Jared said shots were fired at the club?"

"Not on this line," I warn, ending the call.

"What do you want us to do?" Ricardo asks, stepping from foot to foot.

Blue and red lights dance across the video monitors. Officers fill the streets. This is bad for business. "Open the shutters."

FIVE PEOPLE DEAD. Three civilians, one of my security men who took the bullets that could have hit Alyssa, and one of their men who took a bullet from it ricocheting off the shutter door.

Idiot.

This is not how the re-opening was supposed to go, a lingering strain coats the air.

"They're just thugs for hire. We already have three of them in custody. The other car has been found abandoned," Detective Morels informs me, breaking away from other officers.

The club has been cleared out. The media is swarming the place. It's a shit show. And I want blood. They've declared war and have no idea the mistake they've made.

This isn't warfare, it will be annihilation.

"I want them," I tell him, fury burning through my veins.

"They won't be released. Once processed, they'll be trans-ferred to a holding prison until they get a court date." He rubs his jawline with one hand, the other placed on his hip.

He knows what's coming.

"I want to know where and when. This was one of my clubs—me," I growl, fisting my hands, my eyes closing briefly.

There's nowhere on this earth where these men are safe from my wrath. Prisons give me easier access. I'll make sure they share a cell with the vilest creature in there. By the time they're done, they'll wish for a bullet.

"Do you know who's behind this?" he asks, awarding himself a scathing glare.

"Someone well out of their league," I grumble, splitting away from him when I see Marcello coming down the hall from the back entrance, a visible pulse in his neck.

"What the hell happened?"

"Those brothers," I growl, planting my hands on his shoulders, squeezing to alleviate the coiling of my muscles.

I want blood.

I want to throttle the life from those bastards until their pulse stops, only for me to bring them back to life and start all over again.

"Bring it all down," I tell him though gritted teeth. "I want everyone on this. Deplete their accounts. Send a Leto message to everyone who ever supplied for them. Make their men suffer—but save those bastards for me."

His eyes gleam with pleasure. "On it."

"And, Marcello," I call before he makes it to the exit. "Don't involve Antonio. He's done enough."

CHAPTER THIRTY

Alyssa

THE DOOR OPENING causes me to jolt up from the couch. I'd fallen asleep, the adrenaline fleeing my body as fast as it came.

Luca stands there, staring at me, another man at his back. "Take her home," he tells this man, making my stomach lurch.

Do I not need to speak to the police or stay with him just to be sure it's safe?

The man with him is wearing a cheap tweed jacket and week-old scruff covers his chin. Stress lines wrinkle his face when he asks, "Who is she?"

Am I invisible?

"She's no one of importance," Luca tells him, turning his gaze from me. The cruel words wound me like a physical attack.

My breath shudders from my lungs. An overwhelming cloud of sorrow sits heavy over my heart.

I could have died tonight, doing Hannah and what I thought would be *him*, a favor. Simon reminded me that being here could put a stain on my position at Swan, and this is what I am to him?

No one of importance.

Getting to my feet, I will my legs to carry me and not buckle beneath me.

"I'm Detective Morels," the man informs me, opening the door. I don't give Luca the satisfaction of my gaze.

I'm taken through the same back entrance I came through earlier tonight. This is the exit I should have left through. If I had, though, those men would have made it inside. I quake at the thought of how many would have perished.

When we get outside, I give the detective Simon's address. The dorm curfew has passed.

"How do you know Mr. Leto?" he asks once we're inside his car. I squirm a little. Fast food bags and wrappers litter the floor and it reeks of smoke and sweat.

"I don't know him," I say honestly, looking out the window as we pass reporters camped out in front of the club.

"Just got unlucky, huh?" he muses.

"It would seem so, yes."

He lights a cigarette, the toxic plume of smoke filling the small space.

Inconsiderate asshole.

"What about those marks on your neck?" My hand instinctively reaches up to stroke the skin there.

"It's a sex club, Detective. Some of us like it rough."

The lie empowers me.

I like the bruises Luca's hands and mouth left on my flesh—a reminder of how badly he wanted to mark me, taste me.

We fall into an uncomfortable silence. I don't even wait for the car to come to a full stop outside of Simon's apartment before I open the door and jump out.

"Thanks," I mumble, slamming the car door closed and running up the steps, rapping my knuckles on the door.

My heart lodges in my throat when he doesn't answer.

What if he's not here? I'd slept a couple of hours on that couch but maybe he was held up giving a statement back at the club.

My heart skitters when I hear movement.

When the locks click and the door opens, tears spring to my eyes and I launch myself at him, needing comfort.

He catches me, his arm tightening around me, squeezing. "Oh my god, Alyssa. I've been so worried about you," he breathes. "I've been calling you."

Pulling free, I wipe my hands down my face and pat my pocket. My phone must have fallen out in the mayhem.

Ushering me inside, he pours me a glass of water and brings it over to the couch where I sit down before, I fall.

"I wasn't sure if you made it out of there." His brow creases. He's wearing loungewear, his hair rumpled.

"Did I wake you?"

His brows raise and he swipes a hand through his hair.

"No, I couldn't sleep. I have to go down and make a statement tomorrow." He jerks a shoulder.

"I don't know anything, and even if I did, I know not to say anything." He drops to his knees in front of me, searching my eyes.

"What do you mean?" I ask, meekly.

There's silence, and it stirs acid in my stomach before he captures my clasped hands in his. "I don't know what your connection is with that man, but for your own sake, please stay far away from him."

It's not like I've been given the choice. Where is this even coming from?

Pulling my hands from his, I smile weakly. "Is it okay if I crash here tonight?"

An awkwardness hangs between us when he gets to his feet.

"Sure. Let me get some blankets."

I don't like it, that both him and Hannah have warned me

away from Luca. If they knew how insignificant I am to him, they wouldn't have to.

I don't wait for him to return before I huddle into a ball and silently cry myself back to sleep.

LIGHT CREEPING in from a gap in Simon's drapes stirs me.

I can hear a shower running. I need a shower—and food.

Pushing a blanket I don't remember being placed on me off, I stretch my limbs and pad to the kitchen, grateful Simon has a kettle and an addiction to coffee.

I potter around, finding the mugs, retrieving the creamer from his fridge, and begin searching for the sugar.

"Top cupboard," Simon speaks up from behind me, startling me.

Placing a hand to my chest, I chuckle. "You scared me."

"Sorry." He holds up a hand. I didn't hear the shower turn off over the gurgling of the coffee maker. "No cream in mine," he tells me, rubbing a towel over his head.

Another is wrapped around his waist. I avert my eyes from his naked torso. This feels too personal, too cozy.

I don't like it.

"I have to go down to make a statement, but you're welcome to hang here, shower, watch some TV until I get back," he offers.

I finish making the coffee, hand him a mug, and move past him to the living room.

"Tonight is the benefit. It's an annual affair held at the school for all the beneficiaries." I smile tightly when he takes a seat next to me.

"I need to get back and make sure I have everything ready."

"Are you sure you're okay?" He reaches over, placing a hand on mine.

"Yeah, I'm sorry I dumped myself on you last night." I lift the mug, and his hand has no choice but to move.

Have I given him the wrong impression by showing up here?

"We're friends, Alyssa. You're always welcome to come here if you need to." Him being practically naked is awkward. I'm not sure where to look, or if it's intentional.

"Yeah, you've been a good friend to me. I'm grateful," I say, smiling over the top of my mug but not keeping eye contact.

I'm not sure how to read his interest in me. I hope he's content with friendship but fear he may eventually ask for more, and I don't feel that way about him.

He's sweet and a good man, but I don't feel an attraction to him.

"I should get dressed," he announces, finally moving down the small hallway to his room.

I rush back to the kitchen cleaning my mug and finger brush my hair, folding the blankets and getting myself together.

By the time he comes back, I've finished and ready to leave.

"I can drop you if you want?" he offers. An uncomfortable tension hangs stagnant in air between us.

I just want to wash my skin and figure out what I'm going to do now.

"That would be great. Thank you."

IT'S A SILENT DRIVE. I'm not sure where are friendship will go now that I'm not working at Vino's anymore.

"What will you say to the police about last night?" I ask, trying to make conversation.

I sense his eyes shift to me, then back to the road. "Nothing, I value my life."

My gaze cuts to his side profile. "You talk about Luca like he's the boogieman." Why does he have such disdain for the man?

"Luca?" he says, a hint of shock in his voice. "Mr. Leto is worse than the boogieman, Alyssa. He doesn't need shadows and myths to incite fear. He comes at you in the daylight. Do you know what happened to Mr. Angelo, the man who made a scene at Vino's with you?"

Thud.

"That was a gas leak or something." As soon as the words leave my lips, I want to snatch them back. I sound naïve. *Have I been naïve?*

We pull up to the edge of the car lot at Swan. Simon grips his steering wheel, bowing his head.

"Luca Leto is king, and his rules are law. If someone wrongs him—hell, even looks at him in a way he finds disrespectful—they find themselves dead in a gas leak or floating in a river. The man who killed his mother was found with his entire family skinned and hanging from a bridge."

My heart pounds so wild and loud in my chest, I can feel it in my neck, wrists, and ears.

It should rise fear within me, but all I can think is that man killed his mother—he should have been punished.

Should I be punished for killing mine?

Tension pinches his features. "Mr Leto, *Luca,* built an empire of legit businesses, but it all stemmed from the blood and carnage his father paved for him. Their hands are filthy, fucking rotting in corruption, blackmail, murder, trafficking, and every other illegal activity men like him were born into. He's based here, but like a weed, his roots have reach. His businesses are far and wide, sprouting out in all directions."

He's becoming so angry, veins bulge in his forearms from clutching the wheel so tight.

"You sound like you hate him, hate what he is, so why do you work for him? And how do you know so much?" It feels like a personal attack, an insult.

If he believes all that, hates him the way it comes across, then why take his money every week in a paycheck? Why serve in one of his businesses?

He releases an exasperated breath. "I wasn't planning on being there as long as I have, I suppose. I don't know."

"He doesn't seem like what you portray," I whisper, looking out the window so I don't have to see the disappointment on his face.

He wants me to hate him too, and I do in an angry way, but it's superficial anger and will dissipate.

"Because he hasn't shown you his true colors yet. Take being fired as a blessing, Alyssa. Stay well clear of that man."

Pushing open the car door, I smile, but it holds no joy. "I will. Thanks for the ride."

*

I NOD my head in acknowledgment as a few dancers' wave as I pass them.

Nathanial is standing with his arm slung over Jewel's shoulder on the couch when I move through the communal area on autopilot.

"Walk of shame?" Laura snorts, then shuts up when I give her a contemptuous glower. I'm in no mood for childlike, bullying bullshit today.

"You okay, Alyssa?" Nathanial calls out, and Jewel's lips thin.

"I'm fine. Thanks." If I have to say I'm fine one more time, I'm going to lose it.

Grabbing my shower bag and little ballerina figurine, I head to wash the night from my skin.

The spray of the water hides the tears I allow to fall as I dig the small feet into the skin of my hip.

It's strange the emotion swirling inside me. Something akin to sorrow. I feel like I may float away, grief shredding my insides, I'm grieving the loss of Luca knowing I may not see him again.

It's crippling, my chest tightens, the muscles clenching my stomach threatening to spew my insides over the shower floor.

My shoulders drop my breath spluttering as I attempt to gain control.

It can't be over, can it?

Turning the shower off, I step out and go to the mirror, examining the bruises blossoming around my neck and teeth puncture wounds on my shoulder.

It's so pretty. It's the only accessories I enjoy wearing.

Tears well in my puffy eyes, the red veins prominent against the white. Agony clenching my insides, is this the last time I'll adorn his mark?

THERE'S a sense of wealth in the room. Diamonds drip from the women, their husbands constantly surveying the room in their designer suits with golden check books.

I love the dress I bought off a sale rack, but it's going to take some getting used to.

The silk green fabric brings out the jade in my eyes and shows off the condition my body is in from years of training. The back of the dress hangs low, showcasing my full back.

A nervous energy sizzles in my bloodstream. The events of last night still live inside me, making themselves known. I'm once again out of my comfort zone and don't like the eyes following me around the room—like I'm on display for their indulgence.

My stomach dips when I notice a familiar face.

Marcello stands across the room, gazing at me.

Why is he here?

His gray suit molds to his physique, giving a peek at all the treats that lay beneath.

Luca is like the sun. The closer you get, the more at risk of burn. Marcello is the moon. The closer you get, the more amongst the stars you feel. *I like the burn.*

I realize I've been staring too long at him when his lips kick up into a knowing smirk. He walks toward me, all eyes following his path, curious or just admiring the view of his rear end.

"Well, look at you," he beams, flicking his tongue out to wet his lips as he takes his time caressing his gaze over my body. I feel exposed.

"I didn't realize ballet was something you enjoyed," I say, thankful my voice doesn't betray me with just how affected I am at his appearance here.

In a way, it makes me feel closer to Luca. *Why does he have such a hold on me?*

Reaching out, he swipes a lock of hair from my bare shoulder, sending a wave of shame pulsing through my veins.

It's nothing, a drag of his knuckles, but it's not Luca's touch.

Embarrassment tinges my cheeks. I'm pathetic, allowing someone who rejected me to still have an influence on my body.

Maybe I should date a little, get rid of some of this pent-up sexual tension. Then Luca won't feel so special, so alluring.

"I didn't either," Marcello murmurs, his attention making the tension between us grow.

His Adam's apple bobs in his throat as he swallows.

"I wanted to check in on you after what happened last night. Hannah told me you were there covering her shift."

Digging my nails into the palm of my hand, I inhale a calming breath, trying not to allow the memories of last night bring tears with them.

"You didn't have to come all this way to this to ask me that." I blush, resting my hands on one of the tall tables set out through the room.

"That's not the only reason I'm here, but it is the most important one."

He holds up his hand to signal for one of the waiters to bring him another drink.

"I want you to take some time off. A couple weeks maybe." He leans against the table, his arm muscles stretching the fabric of his suit.

"Luca fired me." I exhale, searching his face to see if he knew. His brows pull in.

"Really?" He rubs a hand across the back of his neck, grimacing. "A lot happened last night. It was an intense situation. Let's just say you take a break and then see how things go from there."

My chin drops to my chest. Is he pitying me, or is it because firing me may look bad with what happened at the club?

She's no one. The phantom words sting just as heavy as they did when they fell from his lips. My body jolts when Marcello places a hand against my bare back.

"Just think about it, bella." His tone is soft, playful, and then he's gone, disappearing into the throngs of people.

TWO GLASSES OF CHAMPAGNE, and I already feel the warm glow of alcohol giving me a little confidence to walk the room. Jewel is standing with an older couple.

The woman has the same eyes as Jewel and a dancer's posture.

Lifting a hand to give a small wave isn't reciprocated. Instead, Jewel lifts her chin and adverts her eye. My gesture gains the eyes of her father, however.

He whispers something in her ear, never taking his eyes from my dress.

His interest is like tar coating my skin, sticky and unpleasant.

I sense other eyes on me as I move through the room, a man watching me with blazon curiosity.

I move to the bar and order a club soda. My heart races inside my chest. The need to get out of here makes my legs vibrate when I sense his approach.

"So, who are you?" The male voice vibrates so close to my ear, his body brushing against mine. I take a step to the side to rid myself from his overzealous advance.

He's handsome but intoxicated and entitled, uglying any pretty he may have had.

I don't want to come across as rude and get reported, so I force a tight smile.

"Alyssa," I hold my hand out toward him.

"I saw Marcello talking with you. Is he the reason you're not in the other room?" He gestures to a door separating the function rooms, ignoring my hand.

I have seen some of my peers being led in there tonight, but there are security guards to prevent anyone from just wandering inside.

I didn't know what that room was for, thinking maybe it was there for family members to hangout—for students like Jewel who didn't need to swan around the investors, showing them the product they're pumping their money into.

The same feeling of shame from earlier returns under his attention.

"I work for Marcello at a wine bar. He was just saying hello, that's all." I don't know why I feel the need to clarify that, but this guy is making me feel unsettled. "How do you know him?" I ask, curious.

Mischief dances in his eyes. "He's..." a pause, "my brother." I must look as shocked as I feel, because he chuckles, placing his finger under my jaw to close my mouth. "Well, he could be anyway," he adds.

"Alyssa," Madam Georgina beams, walking toward me, her gown swaying behind her like a tail.

I'm not sure how she knows my name. I've only ever seen her in passing. She's the director of the school and a former, renowned ballerina. "I've been looking for you," she informs me, seemingly nervous.

Her words cause me to pause. "Please, come with me."

Abandoning my drink, I take a step toward her.

"I'll be seeing you, Alyssa," the man pipes up with a curious tilt of his head.

"I didn't get your name," I say. He places his drink on a tray a waiter is holding as he passes, and then he too disappears into the crowd.

"Alyssa?" Madam Georgina snaps, clicking her fingers at me like I'm a pet. She hooks her arm with mine and begins guiding me through the crowd of people toward the exit.

"Where are we going?" I ask, but she just gives me a once over, pursing her lips at my attire.

She pulls me into the foyer where a couple dancers linger, no doubt as uncomfortable as I am.

Why didn't I come out here to hide? My stomach dips when she continues to guide me into a hallway.

It's eerily quiet and most of the lights are dimmed.

"What's going on?" The knot in my stomach tightens.

We come to a stop outside an office door and she turns to face me. "It's not good news, I'm afraid. Your beneficiary has pulled your funding."

Thud.

I stare at her, trying to read for signs that she's joking, but I'm not sure this woman knows how to joke. "How can they do that?"

"It's very rare, and usually, if we were farther into the year, we may have found room in the budget to cover the costs, but that's not possible at this time."

Is it hot in here? Sweat breaks out over my brow, my heart pounding.

It's over.

Back to the farm I go.

Back to face Clint.

Back to mother's ghost haunting me.

No. No. No.

"How can they just pull the funding?" I'm on the verge of tears, my voice cracking.

She rubs a pitying hand down my forearm. "It happens. Circumstances change." Moving in closer, she says in a hushed whisper, "There are other beneficiaries here tonight. One actually asked me about you and wants an audience with you."

An audience? What does that mean?

"If you have the means to cover your costs..." She holds her hands up, already knowing I don't.

I wouldn't need a scholarship if I had the means.

This seems so unfair—and not the treatment you'd expect from a place like Swan.

"Just meet with Mr. Howard. Things may work themselves out." She bobs her head.

Mr. Howard?

She opens the door to an office and ushers me inside, but she doesn't follow.

The hairs raise on the back of my neck when a clicking sounds signals the door locking.

I sense I'm not alone, the shadows creeping out to greet me. A lamp on a large wooden desk is the only offering of light.

My hands clutch nervously in front of me. "I've been watching you tonight," a voice croons as the silhouette of a man steps into view.

I look back to the door, biting my lip.

"I have a key." He pats his breast pocket. "Don't worry."

I recognise him from earlier, standing with Jewel. "You're Jewel's parent?" I croak, feeling uncomfortable being locked in a room with this man.

Does Jewel know he asked for this meeting? Is the beneficiary pulling my funding a ploy to set up this unkosher meet-up?

I feel dirty and cheap. My ideals of this place become smeared in ash. This can't be legal or approved by all members of the board, surely.

"I'm not here to talk about Jewel. Let's talk about you. I hear you're in need of a beneficiary?" He moves closer, his eyes undressing me.

My skin crawls, a thousand beetles skittering around under the flesh. "I may be open to funding someone with promise," he leers, slipping his jacket down his arms. "I'd have to see what it is I'm paying for, of course."

Thud.

"A demonstration?" I straighten my spine, the festering darkness that lives inside me being summoned to the surface.

"Yes," he licks his lips, "a demonstration."

"You want me to dance for you?" I give him the benefit of the doubt, but it's clear what he wants from me—what's expected.

It's a disgrace that I've been served up to this old man. His daughter is my peer.

I came tonight with a price tag and didn't even know it. How many other girls are paying for their place here tonight?

Snorting a callous laugh, he narrows his eyes on me. "Don't be naïve, child. I want to see your fucking body. Take off the dress."

My breathing hitches. A buzzing sounds in my head.

"I'm not property. My body isn't for sale," I push out, the vulgar pig's entitlement making me want to cut his balls off and drop them in his wife's cocktail glass like a pair of olives.

With this animal as her father, it's no wonder Jewel has issues.

He moves in on me, and I take a step back, knowing I have nowhere to run.

My ass hits the desk. Miss Georgina locked me inside this room with a predator.

"Everyone is for sale, we just need to find your price."

His hand reaches out, cupping my breast. I smack it away, gasping in shock at his audacity. "Don't fucking touch me," I warn.

His beady stare turns into a scowl. "A feisty one, are we?"

When he takes a second pass, his hand rougher, launching at me, tugging at my dress, tearing the thin strap, it catches me off guard.

He's stronger than he looks and overpowers me for a couple seconds before I gain advantage.

Shoving him, I turn my body, putting a sliver of space between us. "Don't touch me," I holler, the disbelief that this is happening causing my breathing to become labored.

"Stop playing hard to get. It's unbecoming," he snipes.

My head clouds. His movement is like slow motion. Once again, his hands reach toward me.

I counter his move, grabbing his wrist and slamming his hand down on the desk. Swiping up a letter opener from the pencil holder, I jam it through his hand with all the force of anger and disgust I possess.

It pierces through his skin, cartilage, and muscle, until the shiny silver blade stands upright inside him. I back away, my eyes wide and lungs taxed.

His shriek is delayed, his body taking its time registering the gravity of what just occurred.

"Get this out of me," he squeals like the pig he is.

Breathe, I will myself, a rush of adrenaline empowering me.

"I bet you didn't think it would be you getting penetrated

tonight," I mock, shoving my hand into his breast pocket, retrieving a key.

Blood drips from the table, his hand impaled there. His face pales, shock rendering him speechless.

When I open the door, the corridor is empty.

My broken dress strap causes the fabric to gape, exposing me. I pull it together, my feet faltering when I see Jewel standing by the entryway.

I need to walk past her to get to the exit.

I debate trying to find another direction when her gaze lands on me, assessing what she's seeing. Her chest begins to rapidly rise and fall, her eyes glossing over with tears.

She knows—she knows what he is and what just played out. I don't want to pass her and have everyone see me looking dishevelled. I'm no one's victim.

Slipping her glittering shawl from her shoulders, she holds it out to me. A moment passes between us before I take her offering. It's an understanding that she's not responsible or part of her father's predatory actions.

"Thank you." I wrap the material around my shoulders, hiding the destroyed dress and red marks discoloring the skin on my arms. "Have you seen Georgina?" I ask her.

She sniffles, folding her small arms under her breasts. "She went to the bathroom." She tilts her head in the direction of the lady's room.

Perfect.

There's a girl at the mirror fixing her lipstick and one washing her hands when I get in there.

One stall door is closed.

Turning to the girls, I muster up my cruellest tone. "Out," I snap at them, narrowing my eyes and baring teeth, my veins still full of adrenaline and fury.

They hurry to exit, and I flick the bolt at the top of the door so no one else can enter.

The stall door opens tentatively, and Georgina holds her hands up in front of her chest in a defensive manner. "I'm sorry, Alyssa," she attempts to placate.

"What the hell was that?" I growl, images of me tearing her hair out dancing through my mind.

"The man who paid for your enrolment...he wanted you gone. I thought if I showed you the darker side of this business..."

"No." I point my finger in her face. "Don't say that like it's not a choice you make. You allow men like that to pray on dancers who trust you, who come here to progress and learn, not sell themselves to the highest bidder."

She thins her lips, jutting out her jaw in defiance. "The world is built on rich men paying for the privilege of women's company. Don't be naïve, Alyssa. There is no greater prize than a swan."

"You disgust me," I tell her, my muscles coiling under my skin. "I want my place secured here. No one gets to see or take my body as payment."

"It's not possible. I was told to get you out of here, send you home. I thought you'd never look back after..." She diverts her eyes, crossing her arms.

I step into her eyeline, forcing her to look at me, feel the shame of what she did. "After you locked me in a room with a pervert?" I finish for her.

"He's harmless. He just likes to think he has some power here."

Her words cause an abrupt unhumorous laugh to erupt from my chest. "Have you listened to yourself?" I open the shawl, letting her see what her harmless power-hungry animal was capable of. "Maybe we should lock you in a room with him?"

She scans the marks left on my arms, the bruises from Luca I've hidden with concealer.

"I'm sorry. I didn't think he would actually touch you." She sounds sincere, but I'm past listening to her excuses.

"Why would my benefactor want me gone? What does it matter to them if I move home or stick around?" I push her for information, and her shoulders bristle.

"I don't know the answers to the questions you have," she informs me, exhaling a tired breath.

"Then tell me where to get the answers," I demand.

A flash of fear shadows her face. "I can't." She shakes her head adamantly.

"If you don't, I'll tell anyone who will listen just what Madam Georgina is willing to sell in order to gain funding," I threaten.

"Alyssa," she warns, her tone returning to that of authority.

"I have nothing to lose," I remind her, knowing what she's going to say before the words leave her mouth.

Bastard.

CHAPTER THIRTY-ONE

Luca

FOCUSING on any task is difficult knowing I've sent Marcello to Swan to have Alyssa's funding pulled.

She can't be here any longer. Returning to her little farm life where she's safe is what's best.

When this is all over, if I still can't shake this draw to her, I'll go there and take my fill.

I turn her phone over in my hand. I decided not to give it back after I found it stuffed down the couch at the club where she'd fallen asleep.

It's best she doesn't have the contacts she's made here tempting her to stick around.

There are a ton of missed calls and texts from a Clint I'm trying not to look at.

It's beneath me to be jealous, yet the green acid burns in my chest when his fucking name flashes up for the hundredth time.

My finger hovers over the answer button just as Hannah

appears at the entrance of my office, preventing me from answering.

"How long do you want us to remain closed?" she asks, holding an iPad, taking notes.

I closed all our New York businesses to err on the side of caution after what happened at the club. The wheels are already in motion for dealing with the Blaydon brothers.

By the time I'm done with them, they're going to wish they'd never met me.

"A week."

"Okay. I've informed all but one of the staff members. I can't reach Alyssa." She looks at me, scratching her chin, a slight tremor in her hand. "I was going to stop by her dorm and see if she's there."

Holding my hand up, I narrow my eyes. "This doesn't seem like a *me* problem, Hannah. Why don't you just spit out what you really want to know?"

"Have you seen her? She covered for me at the club because I was sick..." She places a hand to her chest.

"You've been sick a lot recently." I wouldn't normally notice, but being here more lately—*because of Alyssa*—I had.

"Actually..." she moves from one foot to the other; another fidgeter, "that's something I wanted to talk to you about—"

Her words cut off when a door opens, beckoning her attention. She swivels her head to someone coming up the hall. "It doesn't matter," she rushes out as Marcello and Antonio force her to step back so they can enter my office.

Antonio smirks at her, and she blanches. His eyes follow her departure.

"Is there a reason you're here?" I raise a brow. I liked coming here because it was somewhere Antonio never came.

"Now, now, brothers, what's with the hostility?"

He's been drinking again.

"I found him at Swan." Marcello looks pointedly from him to me. "I thought I'd drop him here with you. I have some business I need to tend to."

Why was Antonio at Swan? Marcello leaves the way he came, and the door softly clicks shut.

"You should have listened to me about the Blaydon scum," Antonio says when it's just the two of us, pacing the perimeter of my office.

"If you hadn't gone around starting fires like a child, I wouldn't need to do anything. Now I have our names slashed across every newspaper and outlet there is. It's bad for business," I state, feeling the muscles in my neck straining against my skin.

He infuriates me.

"You've gotten too used to your suits and fancy buildings, brother. It's still kill or be killed out there in the jungle. No matter how much money you make, how many checks you write for ballet schools, you'll always be a Leto. Our name will always be drenched in blood and targeted for power."

"Why were you at Swan?" I change the subject, knowing he's just trying to get a rise out of me.

I haven't forgotten who I am, where I came from, or where I'm going.

He struts to the chair opposite my desk, throwing his weight into it and cocking an ankle on his knee.

"There was an invitation at the house, some ball." He shrugs, rubbing a piece of lint from his trousers.

"It reminded me of Mother. Thought I'd go and see what you've been spending our money on."

"Her money," I correct him.

"She's dead, Luca."

I'm on my feet in a heartbeat, leaning toward him, my hands on the desk. "Watch your tone when you speak of her." Anger radiates from me.

"You miss her?" he questions. It's a stupid fucking question. She was our mother.

"Do you not?" I ask, retaking my seat.

He reaches for the bottle of whiskey I have on the desk, but I grab the neck before he can and move it out of his reach.

"We both knew two very different mothers, Luca." He sighs, rubbing a hand down his face.

"What do you mean by that?"

He looks me over for a few silent beats before saying, "She had secrets."

Shifting on the leather, I open the liquor and pour myself a glass. "What kind of secrets?"

Everyone has secrets.

It's normal.

Human.

"I heard her and Marcello's mother talking a few months before she was killed."

"Aunt Mary? About what?"

He holds his hand out for the bottle, and this time, I shove it into his palm. "About Uncle Beni."

Marcello's father?

He swigs from the bottle, wincing at the burn, then asks, "Do you know how he died?"

I was a teenager when he died. I was told it happened in his sleep. "Sleep apnoea."

"Nope." He pops the P. "Aunt Mary killed him."

"Ludicrous." I scoff, leaning back in my seat. Aunt Mary is a sweetheart. She couldn't kill anyone.

"It's true, brother. She found out he was having an affair."

All men like him—like our father—had affairs. The wives knew and didn't care so long as they wore the wedding ring.

"With our mother," he finishes, wiping all humor from my face.

He's mistaken. My jaw clenches. His words are dangerous.

"Aunt Mary knew if our father found out, he would punish not just him, but mother—and maybe Marcello too. You know how he is. Sins of the father..."

My heart is pounding, my thoughts trying to make sense of what he's telling me. "She thought it best he went away."

The world feels out of focus. My mother and aunt were close —best friends. There was no animosity between them.

If it was true, surely, they wouldn't just remove the problem and carry on as normal?

"Why were they talking about it after so long?"

"Because of Annemarie."

He guzzles the remainder of the whiskey and gets to his feet, slamming the empty bottle on my desk.

"They were talking about how much was taken from Marcello." He grits his teeth.

"He may have loved Annemarie, but she loved me." He jabs a finger into his own chest.

"Me."

"Antonio," I call out before he can leave. His hand lingers on the door handle, his head bowed to his shoes. "I went to Annemarie before the wedding, offering her an out."

His eyes spark, widening. "And?"

"She didn't want it." He squeezes his eyes closed and drops his head.

"Is there anything you need to tell me?" I ask him, needing to know if he had anything to do with Serena.

Twisting his head a fraction, he says, "I just did."

Alyssa's phone rings once again, offering a distraction from Antonio's departure and the bomb he just dropped on me.

Clint.

I swipe the answer icon and bring the receiver to my ear.

"Ally? Don't hang up please."

"This isn't Alyssa," I growl. He sounds young and desperate.

"Who the hell is this? Where's Alyssa?"

"Who the fuck are you calling her phone non-stop? Take a hint." I end the call, switching the phone off and tossing it in the top drawer of my desk.

I'm heated and worn out all at once.

Dialing Thomas's number, I wait for him to pick up and ask, "Is it done?"

"Yes, sir."

I end the call and crack my neck.

Antonio underestimates my capabilities. He's like our father in a lot of ways—a natural craving for brutality and chaos—but he didn't have the business sense or knowledge to make a real life from it.

If he were next in line, he wouldn't live to see his forties. There is a darkness inside me willing to come out and make itself known, but you have to be smart about it.

Antonio will never understand that.

It's why I'm king and he's a brat grounded for being an idiot.

CHAPTER THIRTY-TWO

Alyssa

"MR. LETO."

The name from her lips rings in my head the entire way to Vino's.

I don't even know if he'll be there, but I need to find him.

I pay the cab driver and exit the car.

Cupping my hands to the window of Vino's, I look inside, eyeing his security team surrounding the doors. A couple of others are sitting at the bar, talking to Hannah.

Hannah.

Slapping my palms against the window, I gain their attention, my heart leaping when the security men place a hand on the weapon holsters strapped to their hips.

Hannah waves them off as she comes to the door. She's here late, but I'm glad. I may never have gotten past these men otherwise.

"Alyssa?" My name is a whimper from her lips. She wraps me in her arms. "I've been so worried about you."

"I need to see Luca."

"Alyssa?" This time, it's a plea.

"Just let me by, Hannah, please." It's my turn to beg.

"Fine." She holds up her hands, then lets them collapse against the side of her upper thighs.

One of the security men follows behind me as I move through the bar like a tornado.

Barging into his office, I spit, "You bastard."

He's on his feet in an instant, his gun pulled, aimed directly at me.

Thud.

"What the fuck?" he bellows, his stride eating up the space between us. "Leave," he snaps at the security guy. Slamming the door closed in his face, he grabs me around the throat.

The shawl Jewel had loaned me flutters to the ground, exposing my torn green dress.

His hold is so strong, my body has no choice but to comply when he forces me back farther into the office before crashing me down on his desk, my back hitting the hardwood with a painful thud.

The oxygen pushes from my lungs, dispersing from my lips in a distressed gasp. The air kisses over my exposed breast, the flimsy satin fabric gathering around my ribcage.

"You don't fucking learn, do you?" He places the gun against my forehead the black of his eyes expanding, swallowing the blue. "What's it going to take for you to get the message?"

His words are a contradiction to his body.

My legs are parted on either side of his thighs, the hard length of his cock pushing against my pussy, making me grateful for the long slit up the side of the dress.

He applies pressure, choking. Water springs to my eyes, my lungs desperate for air.

Black dots fill my vision before he loosens his hold slightly.

"You're playing with fire, little girl. Do you know how easy it would be for me to just make you go away?"

His threats are useless when his cock is telling me how badly he wants me—almost as bad as I want him.

I reach up, wrap my palm around his hand with the gun tight in his grip, and drag it downward.

When I get to my mouth, I open, flicking my tongue out to caress the edge of the barrel. His hiss only encourages me to slide the barrel past my lips, sucking.

The lust clouding his eyes tightens my core, need drenching me. His hand on my throat goes slack. I pull the gun from my mouth as he takes a step backward, his body sagging, allowing me to sit up.

Every nerve-ending inside me is hyperaware of him and the danger hanging between us.

His eyes drop to my exposed flesh, the nipple hard and tight. "If you're going to make threats, at least do it without the safety on," I pant.

The second it's out of my mouth, I know it was a mistake. The veins in his neck bulge. He strikes fast, grabbing a fistful of my hair, yanking my head back, making me cry out.

"You really are testing my patience." He shoves my legs wider apart, tearing at my dress to give him better access, and pushes the gun against my pussy, the only barrier my soaked panties.

"You like fucking with danger?" he provokes, digging the gun into me, stealing my breath. I bite down on my lip, fighting to control my arousal.

"You don't scare me," I grit out, anger and lust fighting for dominance.

"I should," he snarls. Gripping my jaw cruelly, the pads of his fingers bruise the flesh beneath them.

Pushing my panties to the side with the gun, he thrusts the end of the barrel past my lips and inside me.

The shock of the entry jerks my body backwards. "Be as rough as you want, Luca. I fucking love the pain," I tell him, grabbing his wrist and forcing the gun deeper inside me, the steel painful.

"Enough," he roars. Pulling the gun free, he removes the safety and fires a bullet into the wall, startling me. A tiny screech pushes past my lips. Without missing a beat, he stabs the end of the barrel against my inner thigh, the burn snapping the lust into pain and back again.

When he pulls it away, a red rising mark throbs in its wake.

The lust in his eyes nearly floors me. His body almost vibrates trying to control his beast.

He likes pain too.

Inflicting it.

"I have a proposal," I exhale, struggling to catch my breath.

"If I wanted to fuck you, ballerina, I would have," he mocks.

Smirking, I push him away from me and slide down my skirt. Slipping off the table, I cup his cock through his slacks, the bulge heavy and thick. "Your cock has been telling me for weeks you want to fuck me, Mr. Leto. What I'm proposing is a marriage."

Amusement tugs at his lips, releasing in a boisterous laugh. When I don't return it, his eyes narrow. "You're joking, right?"

"No," I tuck my hair behind my ears, trying to retake my composure. "You need a wife."

Dark brows tug down. Amusement creases his lips. "And what is it you need?" He tilts his head, his tongue flicking out to dampen the thick bottom lip. I hate and love how beautiful he is.

Bastard.

"You get me back in Swan, pay my fees and some extra for the inconvenience you've caused me..." I slip the fallen satin over my breast, holding it in place, "the cost of living, my supplies, etcetera."

Tracking my actions, he dissects every inch of me. "That's an awful lot you're asking for."

"It's what you were paying for before, for nothing in return. Why didn't you tell me you were my beneficiary?"

He turns and moves to a cupboard, pulling out a fresh bottle of whisky and two glasses.

Shovelling ice in his glass from a canter, he pops the lid off the bottle and fills them.

He brings one to where I'm standing, an offering.

"What happened to your dress?" he gestures with his finger at the broken strap.

"I'm not here to talk fashion," I snap, throwing the glass he gave me at him. With catlike reflexes, he ducks. The glass splinters against the unit behind him, decorating the office floor in crystal shards.

Within seconds, I'm bent over his desk, my dress pushed up around my waist. My panties tear in his hands as he yanks them from my body.

His palm comes down on my bare ass cheek, and I quiver.

The slap rings out through the room, and an exhilarated giggle chokes from my chest, angering him further.

He pants like a dragon breathing fire. I suck in a breath when the soft wisp of him pulling his belt through his belt loops alerts me to what's coming next.

"Don't fucking move, little ballerina," he warns me. "You've had this coming."

The snap as he folds the leather and pulls it taut has the oxygen held hostage in my lungs. A moan crawls up my throat the moment the air hits my butt less than a second before the sting of the belt ignites my flesh in a delicious burn.

The crack rings out again, the leather kissing my skin with its cruel tongue. I crave another lashing, and he obliges.

My core tightens, warm energy spreading through my body. I feel drunk on lust. "I won't marry you, Alyssa," he tells me, moving away from me, yanking off his tie and rolling the sleeves of his shirt up his strong forearms. "Get out," he orders, pointing to the door.

Bastard.

Righting myself, I blow out a breath, trying to cool my overheated face. "Don't dismiss me. You're rude and belittling," I announce, tentatively sitting my ass on the lip of his desk.

His eyes track me over the rim of his glass. He refills it with ice and amber goodness, taking a sip.

"I think you value yourself more than I." He raises a brow.

"Why can't you hear me out at least?" I argue, desperate for something to drink but after throwing his last offering at him. I doubt he'll be accommodating a second time.

"Because it's ludicrous,' he punches out.

Swiping a curtain of hair from my shoulder, I shrug. "Why? Because of my age?"

He stares at me, drinking me in like a man parched. "Amongst other things."

He looks me up and down in such a way, I can't help but feel the caress of it.

"What other things?"

The air in this room is so thick, you can choke on it.

"It has to be believable, little ballerina. Real."

The nickname he uses for me sends a warmth blooming in my chest. I hate myself for being so easily softened.

This man has been an asshole to me. I should hate him. But amongst the hate is a lust and desperate need to stay here, stay with Swan, *with him*.

"I can role play, make it believable. Eventually, who knows? It may become the real deal." I jut my chin forward, showing confidence.

"How many men have you fucked?" he asks, and I blanch, the question catching me off guard. Clint's face forms in my mind, and I fight the urge to shudder.

"What does that matter?"

"Because it matters." There's light amusement in his tone. He wants me ruffled. "How many boys have you let between those thighs? How often do you seek pleasure?" He chuckles when I glare at him. The sound tightens my stomach. It's stunning.

"Pleasure doesn't have to come from men fucking me," I retort. "I prefer to see to my own needs. Too many disappointments in that area."

Surprise flashes in his eyes. "And yet you want to get married?"

"Not want. It's an arrangement that will suit us both."

"I'll be fucking you if your finger wears my ring—and I'm no little boy. I like it rough. I'll want to coat you in my cum every chance I get. Make you sore for days on end. There's not a hole in your body I won't try to stick my cock in. Chains, cuffs, dildos, whips—I will use them all to bring you to surrender. How do you feel about that?"

The room closes in around me, his form seeming to expand, the ego an entity of his own.

He's trying to get me flustered, make me back out, but all he's done is excite me.

"So, added perks we both can enjoy. Win, win." I swallow, trying not to pass out from the need inside me.

"Show me," he says, stepping closer to me.

My brow pinches. "Show you what?"

"Show me how you pleasure yourself. That's what you said you do, right?" A flush burns my skin. "You want to prove you're mature and able to play your part, prove it."

Bastard.

He tilts his lips into a smug smile, a gleam in those impossible blue eyes. Lifting his drink to his lips, he says, "Well?"

Has he not been in the room for the last hour? I'm not shy.

My arousal is leaving a wet spot on his desk right now.

His belt has my ass imprinted on it for fuck's sake.

I swallow down the disobedient girl inside me and call on the girl who wants to be his whore. I'll gladly let him fuck me until I can't breathe his name anymore, then let him resuscitate me to fuck me all over again.

Standing, I walk to his cabinet and take the bottle of whiskey, downing some of the contents while watching him.

The amber liquid stirs a warm burn down my throat. I grab a handful of ice and drop them in his glass. "You'll need this," I tell him, smirking.

I take my position back on his desk, and he takes the seat opposite, getting an eye level view of my bare pussy as I tug at my dress until it sits just above my thighs.

His eyes widen, jaw tensing. He didn't think I'd do it. Screw him. The alcohol loosens my limbs and my mind, and I give him a show.

CHAPTER THIRTY-THREE

Luca

SHE KICKS off her shoes and slides her bare feet up my calves before resting them on my thighs.

The ice in my glass chinks, slowly dissolving in the liquor.

My thighs spread, opening hers further, causing her pussy lips to part slightly, giving me a view of her glistening pink cunt.

It's pretty, just like expected. It takes everything I have not to lean in and devour her.

I swallow thick, willing my cock not to rip through my slacks and impregnate her.

It empowers her seeing what she does to me.

She's right, she is wicked.

I don't think I've ever met a match more perfect for me.

She came undone under the punishment of my belt, wanted more. The red welts on her skin elicited a drop of precum to soak the tip of my cock.

She leans back on one hand, keeping eye contact. Slipping her free hand down the front of her body, she bundles up the fabric of her dress, hissing when her fingers meet the heated skin of her cunt.

They slide through her folds with ease. She's soaked and in desperate need of fucking.

The sound of her slickness as she pushes two fingers inside her almost buckles me.

Both our breaths catch, and she bites down on her lip, pushing her hips into her hand, moaning.

"I feel so fucking good, Luca. Listen to how wet you make me," she teases. "I'm thinking of your juicy fat cock right now, fucking me, stretching me, making me a bad, bad girl."

Fuck me. She's going to kill me.

"I'm on fire. I want you to mark my body, claim every inch with your teeth, your tongue, your bruises." She bucks her hips. The dress shifts, the material falling away, exposing her tits, her rosy nipples hard and ready for sucking.

Scooping up a piece of ice from my glass, I drag the cold cube across my lips. "You're hot, little dancer. Let's cool you down," I tell her, dripping the cube up her thigh and over her mound.

She uses her fingers to open herself up for me, the scent of her arousal speaking to the animal in me.

Claim her.

Fuck her.

Make her yours.

Slipping the cube down her clit rewards me a groan and hitch of her breath. Crooking my fingers, I push past her folds into her needy hole, thrusting the melting ice inside her.

"Luca," she calls out as I enter her, her needy walls clutching onto me.

"Your fingers are so much thicker than mine. Fuck me with them," she pleads. Her brow crashes as a wave of euphoria washes over her, her cunt pulsing, holding onto me greedily.

I thrust harder, fucking her tight hole. Adding a third finger, I stretch her, the ice water turning warm from her heat.

She's on fire and about to erupt.

Her head swings back, her tits bouncing as she bucks her hips up to meet every thrust.

I pound my fingers harder, the juices making a delicious beckoning sound. I want to feast on her.

This is madness.

When she cries out, her body shuddering, toes curling, I almost come in my slacks.

I pull out of her, a sheen of nectar coating my fingers.

Grabbing the bottle of whiskey I tease her entry with it, getting all her flavor on the rim before backing away, leaving her gasping on my desk.

"You've made a mess," I spit out cruelly. "Clean it up, then have one of my men drive you home." I swig from the bottle, letting my tongue linger on the lip to taste her.

"I don't have a fucking home, Luca. You took it from me!" she screams, righting herself.

"I don't owe you anything!" I roar, launching the bottle across the room and exiting before I do something crazy like take her up on her offer.

I want her too fucking much. It's more than need, it's everything.

I want everything from her.

***

THE DRIVE back to the house gives me too much time for reflection. She laid herself bare for me tonight, and I rejected her—left her with nothing and sent her on her way.

They can't kick her out of the school tonight. They must have to give her time to collect her shit and make arrangements.

Dammit.

She's not my problem.

She has to go.

"We're here, sir," Seth, my driver for the night, informs me. I hadn't noticed us pull up.

The house is buzzing with activity. A couple of my father's nurses wait for my return. "What is it?" I ask immediately, wary of their concerned expressions.

"Your father took a nasty fall in the bathroom tonight. His body is weak, sir. He refused to go to hospital. We have treated him the best we can, but I think he's broken his wrist."

"Can he not be treated here?"

Her face crinkles, worry lines like craters on her forehead. "We can get the equipment, but not until tomorrow. Please try to get him to rest until then," she pleads. "He doesn't listen to me."

He doesn't listen to anyone. He's fading, losing himself.

Hushed grumblings greet me when I enter his room. "How are you feeling?" I ask, taking in the IV he's attached to.

"Parched. Those women I pay to wait on me are savages." He coughs on the last word, his frail body jerking around from the strain of it.

A smile tilts my lips. "They're here to medicate you," I correct.

"Whisky is medicine," he grunts.

Can't argue with that.

"Have you dealt with the problem your brother created yet?"

"It's in motion," I tell him, pushing my hands through my hair. It's been a long night. Hell, it's been a long week.

"Am I going to get to see my son marry before I die?" he croaks, vulnerability like a chink in his armor.

Alyssa twirls through my mind, eating away at me. She would be safer here wearing my ring under my watchful eye.

My heart thuds hard. The thought of her being mine loosens the tightness I've had in my chest since leaving her tonight.

"There is someone, actually."

He perks up, his eyes sparking with interest. "Really?"

Yes, really.

I need to own what I'm feeling. I'm Luca Leto, I take what I want. And trying to push her away is having the opposite effect. We're drawn to each other.

"She's young, but mature. There's something about this girl. She's special," I say honestly, releasing a knot inside me.

"Tell me more."

My whole life, my father was a man feared, a man always busy, always dealing with some crucial conflict.

His love came in the form of praise the more involved in his world I became.

This...talking about a woman, is something that would have never happened before.

His illness has changed parts of him, giving us some sliver of a normal father and son relationship.

Pulling up a chair, I tell him all about the ballerina who's weaved herself inside me.

CHAPTER THIRTY-FOUR

Alyssa

ONCE AGAIN, I find myself at Simon's apartment, humiliation and exhaustion making me emotional. When he answers his door, his eyes widen, "Alyssa?"

"Sorry to dump my drama on you again, Simon." I lift both my shoulders, sighing. "I have nowhere else."

"Come inside," he tells me, placing a hand on my back and looking around the street, no doubt to see how I got here. "You look..." his words halt as he jogs over to an open laptop and closes it.

Had he been watching porn?

Awkward.

"A mess," I finish for him, tightening the shawl around my destroyed dress. "I don't suppose I could borrow a shirt and some sweats to?"

Rubbing the back of his neck, he laughs uncomfortably. "I do, but they will drown you."

"Can't be worse than this," I cringe, gesturing down my body.

"What happened to you?' Worry tugs his lips down.

"Can I tell you over coffee?" I ask, and get rewarded with a smile.

"Sure, make yourself comfortable. I'll get you some clothes."

I plonk down on his couch, looking around the room.

It's barren in here. No home comforts or pictures. If I didn't know it was Simon's apartment, you'd never know someone lived here.

He returns a couple a minutes later holding up a white shirt and gray lounge shorts. "The best I can do, I'm afraid."

"It's great. Thank you." I take his offering and head to his bathroom to change.

Slipping the dress down my body, I collect it up and stuff it in the small bin, never wanting to see the thing again.

I don't chance looking in the mirror. Instead, I turn on the shower and blast cold water over my fevered flesh. Goosebumps dust my skin, the memory of Luca manifesting, caressing.

Damn him.

He played me tonight, getting me to show him I'd be a good match for his appetites, then flung me aside like a trash bag.

Turning off the shower, I grab a towel from a folded pile and pat my sore skin, my ass cheeks on fire. I hope the marks scar but know they won't.

"Coffee's ready," Simon calls out.

Wrapping the towel around my head to keep my wet hair from dampening the shirt, I slip on Simon's clothes, tightening the shorts as much as I can, then folding down at the waistband.

He's sitting with a mug of his own when I come back into the room. "I showered. I hope that's okay."

Looking up at me from his position on the couch, he smiles. "Of course. Do you want to talk about what happened?"

A sigh pushes past my lips. "I lost my place at Swan. It's a long story, but my beneficiary pulled my funding."

His mouth opens, but words fail him. "I know, right? It's been a really crappy couple of days." I laugh. Otherwise, I may cry and go on a killing spree—starting at Swan.

"I'm sorry this shit has been happening to you. What will you do now?" His fingers drum on his mug.

Sighing, I sip my coffee, curling my legs underneath me on the armchair. "I guess I'll have to go back home to the farm, save up some money, try to get into a production company."

"Is dancing something you've always wanted to do?"

His question really hits me, like a force sucking the oxygen out of the room.

I'm a great dancer, worked my ass off to be great, but it was Mom's dream, Mom's passion, Mom's ambition.

"Did I say something wrong?" he asks, studying me.

"No," I shake my head, the towel coming loose and falling to the arm of the chair. "It's just...I don't actually know. It was something thrust upon me. I never had a choice. I can't remember a time when I wasn't a dancer. It's consumed my life."

"Maybe this is a blessing in disguise. You could figure it out, find what you love and want to do."

Luca Leto.

I shiver at the thought.

"Are you cold?" Simon asks, interpreting my reaction incorrectly. "I'll get you some sleeping stuff. You can crash here tonight and figure things out once you've had a good night's sleep."

I reach for his hand as he passes, squeezing it. "Thanks, Si. You've been too good to me."

"There's no such thing as too good, Alyssa. I just think you're used to being treated unfairly." He pulls free, and his bare feet pad across the hard floors until they fade.

I'll need to book a train ticket, suck it up, go home, maybe try to talk dad into selling the farm and salvaging a little money from it.

I grab Simon's laptop and open it up. My lungs seize. There's a page open that flits to a locked screen, but the logo is right there.

"Alyssa," Simon breathes from behind me, dropping the bedding.

"You're a cop?" I whisper, getting to my feet to face him.

"Why did you open that?" He's pale, his hands pulling on tufts of his hair.

"I was going to book a ticket. I lost my phone. Simon, what the hell?" My heart races. What is he doing working at Vino's?

"You can't tell anyone. If Luca finds out about me, he'll have me killed."

Thud. Thud. Thud.

My head spins. I sit, and then stand. There's too much happening. A chime rings out through the apartment, startling us both.

"Are you expecting someone?" I ask, a wave of nausea twisting my gut.

"No," Shaking his head, he runs over to a bag and grabs a gun from it.

What the hell is happening? He places a finger to his lips, and I follow him to the door, my stomach in knots.

Looking through the peephole, he turns to me, eyes wide. "Did you call him?"

"Who?" I ask, holding my hands up.

Tucking the gun behind his back, he unbolts the door and opens it a sliver. "Mr. Leto?"

What the hell? Does he have me bugged? "I'm here for Alyssa," he growls, pushing Simon aside and kicking the door open farther.

Simon flattens himself against the wall, his eyes pleading with mine.

"Get your stuff," Luca barks at me.

"I don't have stuff." I cross my arms, defiant and confused.

"Then let's go." He takes my hand, leading me out of the apartment. I don't want to cause a scene and force Simon to reveal his gun, so I allow him to pull me forward.

Simon reaches for me as I cross the threshold. "Alyssa?"

Luca stops in his tracks, blue fiery eyes cutting to Simon's grasp on me. "You better let go of my fiancée if you want to keep that hand."

I'm released as if my skins made of lava.

Thud. Fiancée?

I glance one last time over my shoulder at Simon before my head is pushed down and I'm guided into a vehicle, Luca slipping in next to me.

"Luca, what's going on?" I pant.

He smells of fresh linen and salt. "My father is deteriorating. I'm not sure how long he has left. We're to be married. It happens soon—as early as next week." He doesn't even look at me while he tells me my fate. "I'll give you what you want, get you back into Swan."

Air whooshes from my lungs. I feel like I had an epiphany tonight in Simon's apartment.

Simon.

My god, he's undercover, it's the only explanation. Spying on Luca?

"What if I changed my mind?" I murmur, looking down at my hands in my lap.

His glare slices into me, making me finch. "Have you?'

"I'm not sure..." Can I really not pursue ballet after everything I've done to get here?

"This was your proposal," he reminds me.

I squirm in my seat. "I know that. I just don't know if I need Swan, if I want to be a part of that place. My mother's dream was for me to be what she couldn't, and for so long, I got that confused with what I wanted."

He grabs my jaw and turns my head to him. It's not a painful grip like the many times before it, more of a caress.

"What is it you want?"

There's a new look in his eyes, one I've never seen.

Soft.

Warm.

Caring.

My heart shudders.

"Freedom, from ever having to settle at that farm, to go back to that life," I say honestly.

"Then you'll have it." He leans in, his lips brushing mine, so delicate, soft, it renders me motionless. "You'll be Mrs. Leto, my queen."

His queen.

CHAPTER THIRTY-FIVE

LUCA

PULLING UP AT THE HOUSE, Alyssa's eyes widen. Her door is opened for her, but she dips her head, looking out at the huge estate before slowly stepping out. "You live here?"

"At the moment, I have lots of property," I tell her, standing beside her, taking her hand in mine.

She flinches in surprise, her eyes dropping to our linked hands.

Observing her dishevelled appearance, my jaw locks.

Her hair is wet, hanging loose down her back. She's wearing an oversized shirt and ridiculous shorts.

Men's clothing, obviously Simon's, and way too big for her.

When I was informed she'd asked to be dropped off at his apartment, the alpha male in me conjured up a hundred excuses to kill him, then I remembered her touching herself, coming undone for me.

Simon is nothing to her. And to me? He's an ant I can stomp on at any given moment.

"It's incredible," she breathes, rubbing her free hand up her arm to ward off a chill.

"Let's go inside before you catch your death."

Showing her around the important rooms—kitchen, my office, the bedroom she'll be sleeping in—*mine*—warms something inside my chest.

Her reactions to the size and wealth of this place reminds me she doesn't come from the same world I do. What I take for granted brings her awe.

"There's so much space," she drawls, stroking her fingers over every surface.

"I'll have the maid make you some space in the closet for now. Eventually, we'll have your own built."

She giggles, looking down her body, "Yes, please make space for all my designer outfits."

I stalk her, grasping the neck of the tee and tearing it down the middle.

She squeaks in surprise, and my greedy gaze devours her creamy flesh. "You'll never wear another man's clothes, do you hear me?" I caress a hand down the front of her stomach. "Only what's mine touches your skin."

She quirks a brow, her breathing becoming heavy. "Can I wear my own clothes?"

Smirking, I lick my lips, loving the way her eyes lazily drop there. "I suppose, when I'm not fucking you, you can."

Her audible gasp makes my cock pulse. "Now, get some sleep. I have business to take care of."

"It's so late," she murmurs.

"That when the villains come out to play, little ballerina."

I close the door, locking her inside.

I don't want her wandering around before I've informed everyone of the new resident.

THE BLAYDON BROTHERS don't look as smug suspended from the ceiling of the warehouse, stripped naked, their arms pulled taunt at the wrists.

They're hollering behind gags as I approach.

"Good job," I tell Marcello. He stands by, head to toe in plastic overalls, ready to get started.

Thomas wheels in a monitor and parks it so the brothers can get a front row seat.

The screen comes to life with a few clicks of a laptop.

"I offered you boys something I rarely give anyone," I tell them, taking a seat on the metal chair placed out for my arrival.

"An olive branch—and you snapped and tried to stick it up my ass."

They both wriggle and grunt. Marcello chuckles darkly.

"You thought this was a game?" I mock. "You lost the moment you opened your cunty mouth to me," I growl, flexing my jaw.

I signal for Thomas to do his thing, and the monitor flickers before a video of fire billowing high from a house appears on the screen.

It cuts to another house going up in flames. "

Boom," I jeer.

More squeals cry out from behind their gags. "Every family member who shares your name," I inform them.

Another house comes on the screen, and the elder brother cries out recognizing it as his, his wife in bed inside.

"You have a sister, if I'm not mistaken?" I pose it as a question, but it's not.

Thomas disappears and returns moments later, the girl in tow. "She was hard to track down. At school out of town, using her mother's surname," I tut, tilting my head. "You see, I have power and influence everywhere. You should have done your homework, educated yourselves about the players on the board."

Reaching up, I take a strand of her hair in my hand. "Sweet sixteen, a ripe age. I think we'll keep this one," I utter.

Thomas forces the girl to her knees in front of me, tears streaming down her pretty face, her bottom lip trembling.

"What do you think, Marcello?"

He walks over to me and grabs a fistful of the girl's hair. He yanks her back to her feet, her lungs releasing a pained scream.

"Oh, a screamer," he groans, licking the tears from her cheek. "Doesn't your father like them pretty and loud?" he taunts.

The girl's bladder empties down her jeans.

"He does. She can be his new pet," I drool. Thomas retrieves a shipping crate and bundles her inside.

"Please," she screams, slamming her hands against the wood as he closes the lid. "I'm nothing like them."

I nod in agreement. "She's right about that. She's getting to live—at least until we tire of her." The words stir something in them both. Their last-ditch effort to get free is futile, but it humors me all the same.

Thomas wheels the girl away as Marcello steps forward, his knife in hand, the plastic overalls crunching with his movement. "Who's first?" The corner of his lips tilt up into a sinister smile.

"The mouthy one." I jerk my head to the younger of the two.

Marcello wastes no more time. The fear in the room is palpable. They know they won't be leaving here breathing.

With a twitch of his wrist, Marcello lurches forward, stabbing the man deep in his groin. The wriggling from seconds before comes to a halt as pain takes over, shocking his system.

The tearing of skin is unique to the ear and sends his brother into a fit of hysteria.

Marcello carves through skin and muscle, dragging the blade up the torso. It's harder than it looks, gutting someone.

It takes strength, skill. The wails from the brother watching brings me a sense of closure.

They deserved this.

A splash of organs hitting the floor sends a spray of blood in my direction. I should have worn overalls too.

Stepping back, Marcello admires his work, then hands me the blade.

Taking the knife, I show the older brother the blood dripping from the steel edge before I stab it into his flesh, puncturing a hole just under his ribcage, collapsing his lung.

"You fucked with the wrong man," I tell him, then stab him again, taking care not to hit anything fatal.

"Do you know that a body's cells begin breaking down within hours of death? The pungent stench is vomit inducing if you're not accustom to it. Fluids leak from all orifices. It's a really an unpleasant thing to witness."

He moans behind his gag. I pull it free, listening to his labored breathing. A wheeze catches with every intake of breath.

"Just kill me. Kill me," he begs.

Shoving the gag back into his mouth, I tut, "I plan to kill you—just slow. Your belly and lungs are going to fill up with blood. It's excruciatingly painful. And while you're dying, I want you to smell your brother rotting beside you while knowing we're defiling your little sister."

His muffled cries feed the demon in me. Handing Marcello back the knife, I dust my hands off—another suit for the fire.

CHAPTER THIRTY-SIX

Alyssa

EVERY PART of me feels revived when I wake up in a bed that could fit ten people. The sheets crisp and soft, and there are a mountain of pillows to choose from. It's heaven against my naked skin.

A clicking sound alerts me to someone unlatching the bedroom door.

Pulling the covers up my body, my cheeks heat when a woman enters with a pile of clothing. "Good morning, madam," she says to me, giving a slight bow of her head.

"I was asked to bring these to you and inform you breakfast is being served in the dining room."

"Thank you." I don't know what else to say. It doesn't feel real.

When she leaves the room, I wrap the sheet around my body and go to the pile she left just inside a walk-in closet.

The space is bigger than my room at the farm and Swan put together.

Rows of designer suits hang neatly on what looks like a motorised rack.

Picking up the clothes left for me my eyes enlarge, the price tags dangling from them with numbers that make my eyes water.

A giddy excitement bubbles my stomach, I hold up the underwear to my body, checking myself out in the full-length mirror consuming the back wall. I could get used to this treatment.

Grabbing up the pant suit I head to the shower.

Once I'm washed and dressed, I make my way downstairs, perplexed to see so much activity in the house, such a contrast to last night.

Men I recognize as Luca's security loiter by the front door. What looks like medical personnel bring in equipment from outside.

Attentively coming down the stairs, a nervous fluttering vibrates in my chest, a startled squeak leaves my lungs when the woman who brought my clothes steps out of the shadows at the bottom, "Madam." She greets me.

Was she waiting there that whole time for me?

"I'll show you to the dining room."

"You can call me Alyssa," I inform her, and her head bobs in acknowledgment.

Walking through the house in daylight is like a different experience, the grand entry ways and dark wood floors, high hanging chandeliers all look like something from a castle not a house.

My mother would have been in her element here, she'd love the royal feel it gives off.

Entering the dining room, butterflies dance inside me, the aroma of cooked meats filter into my nose.

There's a long cherry wood table dominating the centre of the space, with high back chairs. My eyes track to Luca who is sat next to an older man at the head of the table, both eating and talking to each other.

My stomach growls, reminding me I'm starving, his eyes turn to mine. "There you are." Luca grins when he sees me, and a blush crawls up my neck from his predatory gaze.

"Come, Alyssa." He stands, taking my hand and propping me in front of the older gentlemen.

His worn, weathered face holds a fraction of resemblance to Luca. "This is my father."

"It's a pleasure, sir," I say, offering my hand. There's something in his eyes that brings out the submissive in me, he commands the room, including his son.

He reaches for me, taking my hand and gesturing for me to twirl.

"Good hips for bearing children," he announces, like he's sampling cattle.

"Amongst other things," Marcello chimes in, entering the room with the swagger of a film star. "I hope it's okay if I join you?" He holds his hands out, waiting for the invitation.

"Our table is your table, brother." Another voice joins the gathering. My lips part when he comes into view. It's the man from the benefit.

Didn't he say he was Marcello's brother?

"Antonio, shouldn't you be sleeping off a hangover somewhere?" Luca's father grumbles, coughing, his chest rattling, like mother's used to.

Pulling out a chair for me next to his, Luca instructs me to sit with a tilt of his chin. A waiter comes over to pour me a glass of water, and I immediately gobble it up, suddenly parched.

"I'm glad you're all here," Luca announces as everyone takes their seats, helping themselves to the food laid out before us.

"That's a first," Antonio snorts, his eyes studying me, a knowing smirk hooking his lips.

"Alyssa and I are getting married," he declares, making me almost choke on my drink, tears spring to my eyes as I cough.

"Seems like that's news to her and us." Marcello raises a brow, placing a piece of bacon into his mouth.

"Mother's money was well spent it would seem." Antonio chuckles, pushing food around his plate. Luca tenses beside me, and a crimson tinge heats my cheeks.

"What does that mean?" Luca's father asks, his voice weak. He cradles a bandaged wrist.

"Alyssa is a ballerina, right?" Antonio asks, summoning a waiter over with the crook of his finger. "Bring me something stronger."

"It's nine a.m.," Luca bellows, slamming his fist into the table, making the plates jump and drinks spill. "Don't bring him a damn thing," he orders, turning to his father. "Alyssa takes ballet at Swan academy. I met her there when delivering a check in mother's name." He narrows his eyes on Antonio, and it hits me that they're the ones who are brothers, not Marcello.

"Your mother was fond of that place," their father muses. "She thought dancers held a grace lost to most people." He closes his eyes briefly. When they open, there's a sadness there. "Luca is to be married here at the house as soon as possible, and you'll keep your mouth closed, Antonio. You're a disappointment to me."

The room falls silent, a heavy fog closing in, thickening the air.

"Well, congratulations to the happy couple." Marcello raises a glass of water. Not waiting for anyone to chink his glass, he places it back down and fills his plate with eggs. "I'm famished."

"Eat," Luca tells me, placing some bacon and eggs on my plate. My ribcage is tight, the realization of what I agreed to, who I'm marrying, and the extension of that becoming a weight on my chest.

WE'RE IN ANOTHER OFFICE, this one bigger and more homely than the one at Vino's. The décor is old fashioned but it works, large leather chairs sit in front of a roaring fireplace, a mammoth cherry wood desk with the man I agreed to marry sat behind it is the focus of the room.

"Come closer." He summons me with a crook of his fingers, a man enters behind me, placing a briefcase on the desk, and opening it up.

"I'll be outside when you need me, Sir." He bows his head to Luca, smiling at me as he passes me.

"Pick one," Luca tells me, gesturing into the briefcase getting up from his chair and leaning his ass against the lip of the table.

Walking to his desk, my heart thunders in my chest.

They're beautiful, dazzling giant rocks standing on small rings of gold.

"Lu-uca..." I stutter, my eyes bulging at the beauty before me. Something like this must cost a fortune.

"I can't choose," I say, biting my lip to cause pain, helping me stay grounded,

"Then have them all." He smirks, looking them over.

"No, I couldn't." I place a hand to my chest, willing my over-beating heart to steady. "You pick one for me. Isn't that how it's normally done?"

Chuckling, his rich sexy tone warms me in places I want to be touched.

"There's nothing normal about us, Alyssa." He skims his hand over the options, stopping to pick up a platinum band, a singular stone oval shaped standing on a claw in the centre, it's stunning.

"This one," he tells me, taking my hand and slipping the ring over my finger.

It's dizzying, the moment overwhelming me. "I'll have him resize it today."

Thud.

"This is happening so fast." I murmur, looking the ring over, unsure if I'm dreaming all this.

Taking my jaw in his fingers, the pad of his thumb strokes my bottom lip. "This has to happen fast. I'm not sure how long my father has left."

Thud.

"What happens to his assets if you don't marry? Will he really not pass everything down to you out of spite?"

An amused laugh rattles his chest. "It's nothing like that, little dancer. I want him to feel content, comforted knowing I married, that I have a plan and what I've created for our name is safe."

I don't understand what he means by most of that, but now is not the time to unpack it.

"Is there anyone you need to inform about our engagement?" he asks, leaning over his desk and writing something on a form.

"I suppose my dad." I shrug, my eyes still glued to the ring on my finger.

"Very well. I'll have him notified today. A planner will be here this afternoon. Go over anything you want input on with her."

My heart keeps racing. I'm going to have a heart attack.

"I think I should go to Swan and collect some things today. Maybe speak with Michael and see if there are any options for me there."

His head snaps up, eyes narrowing, "I thought you said you didn't want to attend Swan any longer—that it was your mother's dream, not yours."

Pacing the carpet in front of his desk, I rub my hands down the side of my body, "I know what I said, but I think I should still talk to him. Dance has been a part of me since before I can remember, I still feel like a dancer at my core. Maybe I could still train with him, see how I feel. Speak with them about how the girls are treated. The night of the benefit, when I was told you pulled my funding, I was offered up to a rich pervert like a cheap meal."

"Wait, what? Is that why your dress was torn?" His anger is palpable, veins bulging in his neck.

"It's okay, Luca. He didn't get to do anything, I stabbed him."

"You what?" he gasps, amusement coloring his tone.

Shrugging, I stroke the diamond. "Only in the hand, he had it coming."

"What do you want to do?" He asks leaning back against the desk, his hands resting beside his hips gripping the lip.

It's sexy, there's something so intoxicating about him it makes me weak.

"Is wishing the founders dead and taking over the school myself too much?" I jest sighing, "Maybe I can talk with my choreographer and go from there?"

"I'll have them brought to the house," he decides.

I stop pacing and chuckle. "Luca, you can't just have people brought to me like slaves. I can go to the academy to see him."

"I'd prefer you didn't leave this house." It's not a request. His tone implies it's an order.

"Am I a prisoner?" I scoff, the ring weighing down my finger.

I've irritated him. He folds his arms, dipping his head, narrowing his eyes on me.

"Alyssa, don't make this hard, just do as I ask."

Oh my god, I'm a prisoner.

"I'll have your things brought here. And if you want to see this Michelle—"

"It's Michael," I correct.

"Right, then they'll be brought here too."

THE VOICES all blend together as people speak to me about flowers and color schemes, dresses. A wedding as soon as next week being planned.

Can you even get a license in that time?

This is Luca Leto. He can get anything he wants.

"What do you think about this one?" a woman asks. I think she said her name was Sarah. There's a dress on her screen.

It's beautiful.

They all are.

"That's fine," I push away from the table, a headache making itself known.

Pain sits behind my eyes. I've been listening to these people plan all day long. In truth, I don't care about how any of it looks, what individual flowers are called, what colors they come in or what they blend well with.

"I'm going to leave it up to you, just let me know if you need to me to try anything on," I tell them.

I need some air.

Heading toward the front door, I almost crash into a wall of muscle when one of Luca's men steps forward. "Sorry, miss. Can't let you pass."

A laugh bubbles up my throat. "Don't be stupid. Let me by, I need some air," I state.

"Orders." He shakes his head no.

"Let me fucking by." I attempt to move around him, but he's gigantic and cuts me off easily.

"I'm afraid you need to take this up with the boss."

White hot fury drenches me. "You should be afraid," I snap. The rebellious entity inside me rushes to the forefront of my mind. I want to take his gun and shoot him in his kneecap.

Try stopping me when you're hopping, asshole.

Instead, I cross my arms and ask, "Where is he?"

Marching to his office, I don't knock. Instead, I barge in, slamming the door behind me.

"Have you told your men not to let me leave?" I'm breathless, the anger making me so mad, I'm becoming emotional. Tears spring to my eyes.

"Good afternoon, fiancée." He throws a pen down, leaning back in his chair, hands clasping behind his head, completely at ease. He looks so royal, important, and masculine, I hate how my body still reacts to his.

"Luca, I won't be your prisoner. I'm going to go out of my damn mind." My pitch is high. I'm spiralling, tangled up inside, and can't handle it.

"Calm down, Alyssa."

"Don't tell me to calm down," I snap, pointing my finger at him. "You're the reason I'm losing it."

"You're not losing it." The chair creaks as he gets up to come over to where I'm pacing. Grabbing my wrists to halt my movement, he leans in. "You're not losing it," he repeats.

"Don't tell me what I'm doing." I pull myself free from his grasp and turn to leave.

He's on me in a heartbeat, clasping the back of my neck and spinning me back to face him.

I lose my sanity when his rough kiss punishes my lips. His free hand pushes into my hair, gripping tightly, anchoring me to him.

The flick of his tongue on mine weakens my body.

My nipples pebble against the fabric of my shirt. An ache in my lower belly pulls at my core.

Breaking away from me, his eyes focus on mine, a glaze of lust shining in them. "You need me to fuck this anxiety, pent-up anger, and horniness out of you, little dancer?"

Thud. Thud. Thud.

I can't speak, so I just nod. Yes. God yes.

"Undo my slacks and take my cock in your hand," he orders.

My stomach flutters, heat surging through me.

Biting my lip, I reach for his belt and yank it open. My fingers jitter with anticipation.

His thumb skims my jaw line, tugging over my bottom lip to free it from my teeth.

I undo his slacks and free his cock. It's heavy length slaps against my palm, and a moan creeps out from both our lips.

Taking the opportunity of my mouth parting, he slips his thumb inside, touching over my tongue. I collapse my lips around him, sucking.

Embracing his length firmly in my hand, I stroke upward, my thumb caressing over the fat mushroom head.

Precum escapes, coating his tip.

"Strip and put your hands on the desk," he orders.

Doing as I'm told, I make a scene of relieving myself of the clothes I'm wearing. With slow, sensual movements, I tease my skin, dragging the fabric down my body.

His electric blues watch as he uncuffs his sleeves and rolls them up his arm.

I want him to touch me everywhere, show me how much he wants me.

Leaving my heels on, I strut to the table and lean my palms against the wood, my ass prone in offering.

Stalking me, drinking me in, his foot kicks at my ankles, widening my legs.

"I'm going to make you sweat for me, baby." He slaps a heavy palm to my bare ass cheek, igniting the bruised flesh in an intoxicating burn.

Hands skim down my body. A tremor shudders through my veins. Fingers swipe through my folds, pushing into my needy hole. The wetness guides him in with ease, gripping tight.

"Don't tease me, Luca," I cry out. There's been too much build up. I just want him to fuck me. We've fought it long enough.

"Tell me what you want?"

"Your fat cock. Bring the pain, Luca," I pant. "I can take it."

His hands grip my shoulders. The thick head of his cock pushes against my pussy lips, forcing his entry, hard, punishing, perfect.

My lungs squeeze out a groan when he thrusts forward, filling me up, stretching me out.

"Take all of me, baby," he groans.

My head tilts back when he fucks me. Bucking his hips, I push my ass back, meeting him with every thrust forward, his girth and length a beautiful agony.

"I've wanted inside you for so fucking long." He wraps a fist in my hair, his other hand gripping my hip painfully.

My hands give out. Manoeuvring me to lay flat across his desk, my hips hit the lip. He doesn't stop his assault, giving me everything I need.

Curling my spine, his hand tugs on my hair, tilting my head back farther. "You're fucking perfect, little dancer," he growls, pistoling his hips.

A warm heat builds at my core, rippling through me like a tidal wave of euphoria.

"You're making me come," I cry out, my legs shaking, a sheen of sweat breaking out over my skin, goosebumps raising.

"Come on my cock. Soak me in you," he grinds out, his cock pulsing inside me, filling my womb.

CHAPTER THIRTY-SEVEN

Luca

FINALLY, being inside her feels too good. Her warm, wet cunt is so inviting, my cock never wants to leave.

It's not enough. It will never be enough. I want to take her again, make her sore, tire her out so she needs to sleep for a week until I get my ring on her finger.

I can't believe I nearly let her go. I pull out of her reluctantly, our juices mixing and dripping down her legs.

She takes her time, gathering her wits and steadying herself.

Grabbing up her panties, I wipe my cock with them and then stuff them into my slacks. Putting my cock away, I admire her flushed, naked skin, her body a piece of art.

"Do you feel better?" I quirk a brow, smirking at her mussed hair and dazed eyes.

"For now," she breathes, slipping her pants up her legs. "I'm going to shower," she adds, pulling her shirt over her body.

I swallow back my groan, my cock jerking in my slacks, like a beacon wanting to follow its new owner.

MORELS HOVERS NEAR MY DESK, his hands fidgety. "Can you stop jittering?" I fume, looking over the folder he handed me a couple seconds ago.

"I'm trying to quit smoking. It's a nightmare." He blows out a breath before chewing on his nail.

"What is this I'm looking at?" I sigh, exasperated.

"The person who killed your mother must have known her. There were no bullets fired from her security team, no defensive wounds on her. She trusted the person—knew them. Same with Serena. This car was picked up on street cameras within a three-mile radius of both sites at the time of the killings."

"Whose car is it?"

"I don't know yet. The plates are fake, which is a huge red flag."

"So, what do you know? Because it appears you're no closer to finding this prick than you were months ago."

Crossing his arms he scratches his chin, "It takes time."

Slamming the folder closed, I point to the door. "Get the fuck out of my house and don't come back until you have real answers."

Taking back the folder, he tucks it under his arm and goes to leave, stopping at the door. "Eddie's body washed up," he says without looking back at me.

Spinning my chair in the opposite direction to him, I growl, "Eddie who?"

Thomas enters as Morels exits. "Sir." He bows his head.

Thomas has worked for me for a long time. He's loyal and worth every penny I pay him. There's a mutual respect we have for each other that comes from monsters recognizing the darkness in each other. I trust him with my life and the tasks I hand over to him.

"I want you to deep clean everyone on our books, even those

who share my blood. I want to know any detail, no matter how small, that raises a flag. I'm done waiting for this asshole to strike again, I'm coming for him."

Violent intent hums in the air between us, both ready to take apart this fucker.

"I understand, I'll get it done. What do you plan for the Blaydon girl?"

She's a loose end, "I haven't decided yet." I hadn't thought about her. It was more of a tactic to make her brother think I'd be doing those things I told him I would be.

He doesn't need to know my father couldn't get it up nowadays and the only girl I want to destroy sexually is waiting upstairs.

"May I keep her?" he asks, looking me directly in the eye. It's not something many can do. I'm not sure what Thomas's kinks are, but if he wanted this small thing, he can have it.

"As long as she doesn't become a problem for me down the line." She's seen too much, including my face.

"That won't be a problem, sir."

Another problem solved. I dismiss him and power down the computer.

Enough business for one day.

Alyssa is laying with one leg hooked over the covers, her naked body summoning me to take her again.

Peeling my clothes from my body, I crawl in behind her.

She's warm to touch, perfect. How the fuck did I get this lucky? She stirs in her sleep, groaning and pushing her ass into my cock.

My teeth bite down on her shoulder, and a small gasp flees her lips. Palming one of her tits, I grind my cock up the crease of her ass, pinching her nipple, caressing, guiding her onto her back. Her thigh's part, my name murmuring from her mouth.

"Lift your knees, baby. I'm going to eat your pretty cunt until you're weak."

CHAPTER THIRTY-EIGHT

Alyssa

LAYING on his chest is bliss. Many lonely nights, I thought about nothing but being in his arms, but my mind didn't do the real thing justice.

His naked body is toned, strong. He holds onto me, allowing me a sliver of affection after fucking me into almost unconsciousness.

"I saw that detective here earlier," I tell him, stroking my fingers over his pec. "Do you not mind him showing up here?"

I'd come to tell Luca thank you for my things earlier, including my missing cell phone that was in the bedroom waiting for me with my belongings from Swan after dinner.

I didn't want to disturb him when I saw Morels entering his office, so I came back to the room.

My head bobs with his chuckle. "I'm not a fan of the law, but it can be useful to have them on your payroll," he tells me, his honesty both surprising me and warming me.

I like that he trusts me with valuable information.

Simon pops in my mind, a knot forming in my stomach.

"Are you not worried he'll be found out to be dirty and use what he knows against you to save himself?"

His finger hooks under my chin, tilting it up so our eyes meet. "All secrets get found out eventually, little dancer. If and when he becomes a problem, he will be dealt with." His lips press to mine. "Now, sleep."

His breathing evens out after a few minutes, but I can't sleep. The thought of Simon being dealt with leaves an icky stirring in my stomach.

I have to do something.

*

I'M UP BEFORE DAWN, trying to be as quiet as possible moving through the closet, slipping on a pair of leggings and a hoodie.

Holding my breath I take another look at Luca, feeling my chest expand with the vision of him, naked the sheet resting over his lower half. His chest rises and falls in a peaceful rhythm.

Dragging down the door handle, I wince when the door squeaks open, he doesn't move so I make my move, sneaking out and gently closing the door behind me.

I wait for a couple of seconds just outside the room to be sure he doesn't stir, before moving toward the stairs taking them two at a time.

There are men stationed at the front door again, so I nip into Luca's office and unlock the window, climbing through.

The small drop to the ground is easy, the flower bed losing a couple of heads under my feet.

Racing across the green my heart races a little. There are men outside the house walking the perimeter, but the estate is huge. It doesn't take much for me to slip into the brush and sneak off the property.

Walking takes me an hour. The sun is just kissing the horizon when I knock on Simon's door, waking him up.

He appears dishevelled, surprise enlarging his eyes. Fear pales his skin as he takes me in.

His eyes scan the street again. "I'm alone," I tell him. "Are you going to let me in?"

Moving to the side so I can pass him, the door latches closed and bolts into place.

"I've been going crazy," he says, pushing his hand through his hair, his bare feet padding across the floor. "What the hell was that with Leto?"

Sucking in a deep breath I shrug my shoulders, "You have to quit." I tell him, getting straight to the point.

"What?"

"You're compromised. Your cover is blown. You have to quit." Folding my arms, I hold my position, trying to remember the Simon I know is a façade, a character he's playing.

"Did you tell him?" he asks. Frantic, he rushes over to the kitchen window and peers out through the blinds.

"No, Simon—or whatever the hell your name is." I throw a hand up. "But I will if you don't quit. Now. Today."

Coming back to where I'm stood, he asks, "Is it true what he said, about you being his fiancée?" He places his hands on his hips.

He doesn't even look old enough to be an undercover cop. Don't you need experience for this kind of work?

"It complicated, and frankly, none of your damn business." I tire of this conversation, knowing it's going to take me an hour to get back and Luca will be awake by now.

"You're ruining my career threatening me like this."

A twinge pulls at my heart. Isn't he trying to destroy Luca? If he's undercover, it's to get dirt.

"It's not a threat, Si. I'm going to be his wife, you're the threat. This is your only warning."

CHAPTER THIRTY-NINE

Luca

ADJUSTING TO THE LIGHT, I seek out the clock. It reads six a.m. I haven't slept that good in a long time.

Reaching out, I stroke the empty sheet, and my chest tightens. It's irrational, but the fear of something happening to her is becoming more dominant inside me.

Slipping into a pair of lounge pants, I listen for the shower, but don't hear anything. "Alyssa?" I call, barging into the bathroom, I'm greeted with silence. It's empty.

Where are you?

Racing through the house, I search every room, becoming more frantic with each one that comes up empty.

"Sir?" A maid asks, as I spin on the spot in the foyer trying to think where to search next.

"Where is Alyssa?" I bellow to the men guarding the front door.

"We haven't seen her, sir. She didn't leave the house." They look between themselves, their hands out like beggars.

"Then where the hell is she?" I bellow. "Find her."

Placing a hand over my erratic heartbeat, I go to my office and slam the door, bringing up the tracking app I have on her phone.

The little dot pings in this room.

My eyes search the space seeing she left her phone on a chair by the window—the open window. She left me. My thoughts race. Where would she go?

Simon.

Swan.

Farm.

I take the stairs two at a time and throw clothes on. She will be coming home today, whether she wants to or not.

How can you share what we have and then run?

Gathering everyone in my office, I begin dishing out orders on who will look where when fingers appear over the window ledge, all eyes draw there.

Her beautiful face appears through the gap, her lips popping open, forming an O when she sees everyone looking at her. Rushing over to her, I lift her inside, planting her on her feet.

"Leave us," I command.

When the last person leaves and the door softly clicks shut, I pull her into my embrace, cradling her head. She's wearing a hooded sweatshirt dressed all in black, like a robber.

She's lucky one of my men didn't shoot her on sight.

Pulling her away from me, I grip her upper arms. "Where the hell have you been?"

"I needed air. I told you I can't be a prisoner, Luca. You didn't listen." She's so fucking beautiful, it's making me crazy.

"There's a reason I don't want you going anywhere alone. Can't you just do as you're told?" I snap, the last hour of not knowing where she was leaving me exhausted.

"Because I'm not a damn child, Luca. I'm an equal."

Throwing myself in the chair I found her phone in, I quirk a brow. "Sneaking out of here through a window is very childlike."

Folding her arms, she purses her lips. "You gave me no choice."

Leaning forward, I grab her wrist, pulling her onto my lap.

She makes a little squealing sound that awakens my cock. "You won't like the consequences if you give me no choice," I warn her, grasping her face and crushing my lips to hers.

When I break away, she's breathless, her eyes brimming with lust.

"No choice to do what?" she breathes, her chest raising and falling rapidly, her need growing. She's insatiable.

"Need to keep you safe." I run the pad of my thumb down her jaw line, drinking her in.

The overwhelming need to touch her has my hand moving down her body. Slipping into the waistband of her pants, her body jerks when I make contact with her bare pussy.

My fingers part her lips to find her clit. Applying pressure, I circle the little bundle of nerves with the pads of my fingers, feeding from her reactions. I increase speed, my cock screaming to be inside her.

A beautiful pink tinge blushes over her cheeks, her moans growing.

"Put your fingers inside me," she begs, but I don't give into her.

"You don't get to give orders. You're a bad girl."

Biting her lips, she tries tilting her hips to get my hand closer to her greedy hole.

A cell phone begins ringing on my desk, stealing the moment.

"That's mine," she says, not taking her eyes off me. Her nimble fingers wrap around my wrist, urging me not to stop.

Pulling my hand free from her pants, she gasps, "No," making me chuckle.

Slipping her off my lap, I smack her ass and get up, walking to where the phone rings again. Hannah's name lights up the screen.

"Are you going to answer it?" I tease, bringing my fingers to my lips and sucking her scent from them.

"Am I allowed?" she mocks, coming over and answering the call.

Gone is the glow of arousal. Her face creases in concern. "It's okay. I'm coming over right now. Send me your address."

She ends the call and looks up at me, shaking her head. "I'm sorry, Luca. I need to go to her."

"No," I growl.

Placing her hands on her hips, she shakes her head stubbornly. "I can either leave through the door or another window, but I'm leaving." She attempts to storm toward the window, but I'm on her in a heartbeat.

"Where?" I growl.

"Where what?"

"Where do you need to go?"

Relief washes over her features. Letting out a breath, she says, "Hannah's. She thinks she's having a miscarriage."

Hannah's pregnant?

CHAPTER FORTY

Alyssa

JUMPING FROM THE CAR, I attempt to run up Hannah's garden path, but Luca grabs my arm. "Let me go first." His cautious eyes are everywhere, as if waiting for someone to jump out on us.

The door handle gives way under his hand, opening up into her house. Faint crying can be heard from inside.

Pushing past him, I rush toward the sound, finding Hannah sitting in a bathtub, the water pink.

Luca closes the bathroom door to give us privacy. "I'm sorry. I didn't know who else to call." She sobs.

"Don't be sorry." I stroke down her hair, dipping my hand in to pull the plug. "We should get you to the hospital."

Her head bounces in agreement.

Searching the bathroom I find a stack of towels, pulling one free and wrapping it around her body, I guide her to her room. "I'm going to find you something to wear." I tell her. Moving to her closet, finding a dresser with yoga pants and a sweater inside.

Helping her put clothes on, I bite my lip, giving her a sanitary pad to line her underwear with.

"He did this to me, killed our baby." She sniffles, swiping her eyes as fresh tears leak from them.

"Who?" I huddle around her, giving her a safe space. Her lips tremble. As they open, so does the bedroom door.

"I've called ahead. They're waiting for her arrival." Luca nods his head. Hannah's nails pinch into my skin.

"It's okay," I promise her. "I'm going to come with you, okay?" Nodding her head, she allows me to help her out to the car.

Her head remains bowed, her hands clenched in her lap.

Luca's eyes watch me the entire journey to the hospital.

"You don't have to stay," I tell him once we're inside.

It's a private part of the hospital Hannah is taken to, curtesy of Luca.

The nurses usher her down a corridor in a wheelchair.

"If you're staying, I stay."

AFTER A FEW RESTLESS hours of waiting, a nurse appears in the doorway of the waiting area. "You can come see her now, one at a time." She informs us.

Luca, squeezes my shoulders gently nudging me forward to follow the nurse.

She guides me to a room opening the door for me to enter.

Hannah's eyes map my entrance, color returning to her cheeks, monitors beep next to her bed, tubes in her hand. "Hey?" I smile, coming around the bed to take her free hand.

"Hey," she croaks, her throat sore from crying. "Where's Luca?" she asks, looking toward the door.

"He's outside. We didn't want to overwhelm you with visitors. Is there anyone I can call for you?"

A gentle shake of her head causes a tear to fall. "No, I don't want anyone else to know."

Her words from the house have played on my mind since she spoke them. "Hannah, who were you talking about at the house? What did the father do?"

Squeezing my hand, she shakes her head again. "Nothing. I wasn't thinking right."

"Does he know you're here?"

"Alyssa," she says, pleading, "please just leave it. I'm tired now. I think I'm going to sleep."

I take the hint when she releases my hand and turns her head to look in the opposite direction. "Okay. I can bring you some of your things later?"

"No, it's fine. Thank you for coming to help me. I'm grateful you came."

I don't want to leave her, but being here is clearly causing her stress.

Walking to the door, a sigh leaves my lungs. "I'm here if you need anything. What you tell me won't go any further than us two," I assure her.

Opening the door, I'm just stepping out when she calls "Alyssa."

I turn back, her brows pinched. "I warned you about those men. Please get away from them."

Thud. Thud. Thud.

"YOU'RE QUIET," Luca says on the drive back to the house.

"It's been an unsettling day," I defend, watching the world pass by through the window. My life is so different now compared to only months ago.

I feel older, awake.

"Did you know Hannah was pregnant?" he asks, studying me.

"No." I turn to him. "Did you?"

Blanching, he glowers. "No, we're not friends, Alyssa. She's an employee." He checks his phone, then asks. "Who is Clint?"

THUD.

CLINT'S NAME on his lips makes my stomach turn. "Why do you ask?" I sound defensive to my own ears.

"He's at my house demanding to see you." My mind fogs, his words taking their time to penetrate my brain.

Clint's here.

At the house?

"I've seen his number on your phone. Always calling, texting. Who is he?"

He sounds calm, but his words and the look in his eyes are anything but. "He's a friend from back home."

"A friend isn't that persistent, little dancer. Do better with your lies."

Narrowing my gaze, I square my shoulders. "He's a friend from back home," I state once more.

Moving so fast, I gasp in shock when he pushes his body against the side of mine, his hands grasping his favorite spot on my jaw line.

"Has this friend been inside your body?"

My breathing is rapid, his hold making my pussy throb with need. I like when his aggression bleeds through into action.

"Once," I pant, biting down on his thumb when he pushes it into my mouth. He doesn't even flinch.

"You don't understand how addicting you are, do you?" he growls, removing himself from next to me.

The cold rush of his departure leaves me wanting.

"I've known him nearly my entire life, Luca. He declared his love for me and was hurt when I didn't feel the same way. It was a pity fuck, and barely that. It was over in seconds and not memorable."

"He remembers," he barks at me as the car comes to a stop.

Following him out of the car, my stomach churns to see Clint, here, in this space.

He jumps up from the steps of the house, attempting to jog to me, but a massive giant of a man grabs him by the shirt, halting his movements.

"Let me go." He struggles, but it's pathetic. "Alyssa?"

Luca's demeanor must read danger because he stops wriggling and pales slightly at Luca's approach. "How did you get this address?"

"Your father got an invitation to come here. Something about a wedding. Alyssa, what the hell is going on?" He talks over Luca's shoulder, directing his questions to me.

"Can you let him go?" I snap, smacking the hands away holding him in place. Once released, he grabs my hand, pulling me a few feet away. Luca's eyes are deadly, his jaw ticking with annoyance.

"What are you doing here?" I fume, tugging from his grasp.

His eyes widen. "What are you doing here?" His floppy blond hair covers his eyes before he swipes it away.

"Is my father coming?"

"No. He sent me here to see what the hell is going on." I know my father doesn't care about me, but him sending Clint here instead of coming himself stings a little.

"Luca and I are getting married." I shrug.

"That's crazy talk. Go get your stuff. I'm taking you home." A gulp bobs his throat when the barrel of Luca's gun pushes against his temple.

"This is her home, little boy. Now, Alyssa, do you want him here for the wedding?"

The pocket of guilt I hadn't felt in a while opens up. "No," I whisper.

"Alyssa?" My name is a plea on his lips, but him being here only reminds me of why I'm doing this. I can't go back to that mundane existence.

"I love you," he croaks, wincing when the gun digs in further.

"Love isn't allowing the other person to feel guilty for not loving you back, Clint. That night in the field wasn't right. You knew that and still took what you wanted selfishly."

Reaching up, I tug Luca's reluctant arm down, rubbing my hand up his back to try to calm him down. "You're not wanted here. I'm happy and marrying Luca."

Clint's face is ashen, his chest vibrating. "It's time to leave," Luca warns him.

The security giant steps up to take Clint in hand, but he jerks out of reach, sneering, "I'm going. You're not who I thought you were."

Sad thing is, he's no doubt known that for a while, he was just too consumed with his own fairy tale and greed, he willingly overlooked it.

"WHERE ARE YOU GOING?" Luca asks me once inside the house. I'm already up three of the stairs, heading to our bedroom.

"I want to take a nap."

I WAKE up to a dark room. The night has taken over the day. I try to move, but I'm restrained.

Fear bubbles up my throat. The blanket is pulled away from my body, a lamp switching on near a table at the foot of the bed.

Luca's dominant structure looms near the mattress, a sexy smirk on his lips. I'm naked and spread-eagle, leather cuffs wrapped around each of my ankles and wrists, the restraints disappearing beneath the bed.

How asleep was I? I look to the clock. It's reads three a.m. I slept for so long.

"I have some work to do, which means I'll be leaving the house. I can't have you climbing out windows."

"Luca," I warn. "Don't you dare leave me cuffed to your damn bed."

Licking his lips, his eyes devour the offering between my legs, his hard cock perfectly outlined along the crotch of his slacks.

A vibrating noise sounds through the room, his hand rising up to show me a little device shaped like a U.

"I'll only be an hour." He drags the silicone toy up my legs and over my mound.

"Luca." I gasp as he swipes it through my folds, the vibrations dancing over my clit. Pushing one side up inside me, my body jostles, the entry slow and deliberately teasing.

The curl of the toy rests the second part between my lips, the end vibrating over my clit, the sensation stealing my breath.

My pussy throbs around the toy, desperate for movement.

My nipples pucker, wanting attention.

"Be a good girl while I'm gone," he taunts.

"Luca!" I scream out when the bastard leaves the room, locking me inside.

CHAPTER FORTY-ONE

Luca

PEOPLE FILL THE HOUSE, preparing for the wedding. Usually, it would be a grand affair with family from all over coming to pay their respects, but I don't want to wait any longer, so while Alyssa slept, I made arrangements for it to happen in two days' time, close family members only.

All that matters is she and I are there, and my father.

I conclude my business involving Swan Academy and am back at the house in just over an hour.

Peeling off my tie, I leisurely take the steps to our room, unlocking the door. Alyssa's body wriggles on the mattress, a beautiful sheen glistening over her skin.

"You bastard." She mutters, her eyes closing, toes curling. It's a glorious sight.

Peeling my shirt off in deliberate movements, I jerk my belt open and slip it free, letting the leather kiss the air. Folding it in two, I snap it closed. Her body lifts from the bed, her perfect tits jiggling with the movement.

"How bad have you been?"

"Real bad," she cries out, her limbs pulling on the restraints, marking her in red welts.

I lash the belt over her flesh, the end hitting her nipple. The sound makes me painfully stiff. She cries out. A red stripe over her creamy flesh makes my balls heavy.

"I said I've been bad," she groans.

Swiping out again, a second lash paints her flesh. Another, and another, until she's sobbing.

"Fuck me, Luca. Make me scream."

Dropping my slacks, I crawl between her legs, pulling the vibrating toy from her cunt, juices dripping over the silicone head.

"You're so wet, little dancer. I'm going to drink you down like a fine whiskey." I lick out, tasting.

My fat tongue traces up her folds, flicking over her sensitive clit before licking, biting, and kissing up her torso. I caress my tongue over her marks. Reaching her nipple, I take it between my teeth, applying a little pressure then licking.

The toy still vibrates in my hand. I dance it across her other nipple, her juices dampening the puckered bud. Moving my mouth there, I suck the scent from her skin. My cock lining up with her greedy hole, I push inside her, teasing her with a couple inches.

She tries bucking her hips to force me deeper, but her restraints prevent her.

"I'm going to kill you for this," she cries.

"Not if I kill you first," I tease, pistoling my hips to the hilt, filling her up, stealing her breath.

I wrap my hand around her throat, applying pressure. Fucking her rough and hard, I knock the headboard against the wall. My other hand fists her hair, forcing her face to me as I power into her, her cunt squeezing my cock, her body jerking as she runs out of air.

I release the pressure, and she gasps for air. Her body shudders under me, her scream of release music to my ears, sending me over the edge.

WATER POURS down on us as Alyssa lathers me in soap. "The wedding is going to be in two days," I inform her, her hands slowing their movements.

"That soon?" she murmurs.

"Are you having second thoughts?" I'm a bastard who will keep her even if she says yes.

"I just wanted something different when I proposed the wedding. Something has changed inside me now."

I push her against the tiled wall, taking in my finger marks on her neck. She's like a painting, new brush strokes every time we touch.

"I'll give you whatever it is you want. I've already made arrangements to pay off your family farm's debt. If Swan is what you want, I'll give you it. If you trust me, I'll give you the world."

Her breathing becomes heavy as my hands slide down her body. "What if I wanted to work at Vino's still?"

"You were fired from Vino's," I tease, lifting her body and lowering her onto my cock. She winces, slowing my movements. "Are you sore?"

"Blissfully so. Don't stop." She kisses my bottom lip, lowering her hips until she's seated on me.

"I could be manager," she croons, tilting her head back, allowing me access to her neck. I suck her there, lapping her flesh.

"We have a manager."

"Co-manager." She does this tilt thing with her hips and clenches her core muscles. Sliding up my shaft, she rotates on the tip of my cock. It's sensational and nearly makes me come the second she does it.

Willing my mind to think of other things to make me last, I say, "How about owner?"

All those businesses will go into her name once we're married.

"Owner?" She moans. "I like that." She twists her hips, and my cock fills her womb.

LYING IN BED, I have breakfast brought to the room. I don't want to leave this room today. "Tell me something I don't know about you," I tell her.

A shadow passes over her face, haunted for a second before it passes. "I'm double jointed." She pops a grape into her mouth, making a show of bursting it between her teeth.

"Aren't all ballerinas?"

"Tell me something about you." She forks a piece of mango and holds it out to me in offering.

"Apparently my mother had an affair with Marcello's father." Her mouth drops open.

"Luca, does Marcello know?"

Shaking my head, I swig from a glass of orange juice. "I didn't know until recently. It's not something I want him to know.

"You love him."

"He's my brother, more so than Antonio. He's been a loyal friend and a worthy number two."

"Why are you both single?" She studies me like there must be something wrong with us.

"I'm not single," I jerk my chin to the ring on her finger. "And Marcello lost the woman he loved. Annemarie was it for him. What he will never understand or know is that she loved my stupid brother. Fuck knows why. If anything should ever happen to me, he will take care of you, marry you."

"Inherit me?" She chuckles, her brow crinkling.

"Antonio doesn't deserve you, so yes." She waves me off like it's comical. Maybe it is.

"Antonio seems immature compared to you and Marcello."

I don't think I've ever spoken so openly with someone in my life, not even Marcello. She brings me a sense of peace and freedom I've never had before.

"Antonio never had to grow up. He had everything done for him, given to him—even his wife. He took her death hard, blames a lot of his idiocy on me. He'll grow out of it."

I fucking hope.

CHAPTER FORTY-TWO

Alyssa

THE DAYS HAVE PASSED SO quick, I selfishly wish time would stand still.

I feel closer to Luca. Over the last couple days, he's been attentive, showing me a side of him I didn't know existed.

He brings something out in me. Like he's the sunrise, I awaken in his glow.

My dress is fastened, hair neatly placed, flowers weaved through it. Slipping into my shoes, I walk through the house in a haze.

Static energy hums through me. The racing of my overbeating heart forces the blood to rush to my head. It's floating, trying to flee. My neck acts as a balloon string, tethering it to my body.

Is it supposed to feel this way, soul changing?

Maintaining an even breath, I attempt to fade out the people all staring at me, curiosity alight within their eyes. I focus on the man at the end of the aisle.

His tense jaw and penetrative gaze sends a rush of fear and

delight flooding through my nervous system. My hands tremble, making my small bouquet quake in my hold.

Just breathe, I will myself.

Everything appears out of focus, like I'm looking at my life through a blurred lens.

Just a couple more steps.

The pounding of my heart becomes louder with each step I take closer to him—the man I promised so much to for what feels like too little now. Did I get anything in writing?

Thud, Thud. Thud.

His fiery blue eyes narrow on me in warning, saying *don't fucking run*. If I bolt now, would he chase me down?

Yes, run...

They say before you die, your life flashes before your eyes. This feels like death. I see everything I've done up to this point, but nothing beyond it.

I thought I understood what it meant when I agreed to this, but now, it's not about gaining material things.

I love him.

The realization almost buckles me, hitting me with the force of a freight train.

I love him.

My knees lock as I reach him, and he offers his hand for me to take. Without it, I think I may trip. My legs don't feel like my own. They're stuffed with Jell-O.

My feet are crammed into six hundred-dollar stilettos. The white gown I'm wearing clings to my curves, suffocating me beneath it. The lace around my neck is a noose.

Am I making a mistake? It was different before when it was just an arrangement, but now, knowing my heart is invested...

This is it. I turn to face him, the sound of my blood gushing in my ears like the sea's tide crashing against the shoreline.

The world fades away as he stares at me, those incredible blue eyes with flecks of darker shades alert and blazing as they consume me.

With just a look, he renders me weak. I'm not sure if I flourish under his gaze or wane, but I crave that look from him, a flower seeking the sun.

His large palm extends out to cup my cheek, stealing what's left of my erratic breath. Heat spreads up my spine, blooming over my neck as he leans toward me.

His breath warms over my ear, causing a fresh wave of goosebumps to prickle my skin.

His words send a whirl of nervous butterflies to take flight within me. "This is your last chance to flee, my beautiful dancer. Once you say, 'I do'—you're mine. There's no going back."

Thud. Thud. Thud.

This is it...

My stomach churns. I look back up the aisle, then to him, knowing the words coming to my lips.

I do.

THE HOUSE HAS BEEN full of people all day and night, all of them wanting time with Luca and I.

The white dress adds to my fraudulent appearance. This feels like I'm living outside my body. Should I not tell him the game has changed—that my feelings are warping, growing?

My eyes track the room, looking for Luca. He's cornered by a woman, talking a mile a minute.

"That is my mother. Prepare to be inundated with lunch date offers. She always wanted a daughter to spoil." Marcello grins, wrapping an arm around my shoulder.

"You look like a deer in the headlights." He chuckles, handing me his glass of amber liquid.

"Here. Drink this."

"I don't know anyone here. It makes me feel out of place, like I don't belong here." I exhale, tipping back the burning amber.

Squeezing my shoulder, he releases me. "It's a tough room, but you do belong, Alyssa. I've never met a woman like you before or seen Luca come alive the way he does in your presence."

The words make my chest bloom, the swirling of affection clenching my stomach. "I fear I don't know much about his world, only that it's dangerous." The liquid fire warms in my stomach.

"It is," he agrees, looking around the room. "But you're safe with us—you're one of us, now and always. That's what it meant when you married him today."

I blush, chancing a glimpse up at him through my lashes. "Luca said something about that. If something happened to him, I'd be married to you."

His grin is blinding. Such a handsome man. How could any woman want Antonio over him?

"It's an old tradition, but it's effective in ensuring assets and children remain safe and with their family."

"What if the woman doesn't want to re-marry?" I scoff.

He winks at me. "I think you'd be okay with it. Unless you'd prefer that idiot." He winces, looking over at Antonio.

He's being a drunken fool, making a scene with one of the waitresses.

Our eyes meet, and he leers, licking his lips. Marcello rolls his eyes, turning to face me. "I have to take my mother home." Kissing my cheek, he adds, "Try to relax and enjoy the night."

I miss his company when he leaves. He's become a friend, and I need those. Not one person here is for here for me.

"Sister," Antonio croons, opening his arms out wide as he moves toward me. Another man beside him is just as intoxicated. "This is my friend, Carlos."

"I don't care," I state, gathering my dress. Repulsion knots my stomach when the friend's eyes ogle my chest. I attempt to turn away and disappear into another room, When I do, they follow me.

"I like your dress," the friend says, running his gaze over my body like a snake would a mouse. Only...I'm no mouse. I'm a queen. *So why do I feel cornered?*

Antonio drops into a chair at the table set up for us to have dinner, fancy china and silverware all neatly placed as if serving royals.

"She could wear a sack and pull it off. That's the benefit of a ballerina's body." Antonio grins. I sense Luca's approach, silent, deadly, mine.

"I thought we were supposed to fuck the ballerinas, not marry them," the friend drools.

I shrink inside. The night Jewel's father tried to attack me rushes to the forefront of my mind.

Bastard.

My palm hitting his cheek sends a clap sound ringing through the room. "Bitch," he groans as Antonio breaks out into a boisterous laugh.

My body visibly shakes as I try to gain control of myself.

Luca moves through the room, reaches for a silver dinner knife, and wraps his arm around the friend's head from behind. Pinning him against his body, he stabs the knife into his neck without missing a beat.

"What did you say to my wife?" he growls as my lungs empty.

"Luca, don't..." Antonio shouts, his chair scooting out behind him.

It's too late. Luca drags the knife across his throat, roughly tearing.

Blood squirts from the wound, the red, warm spray hitting my face. Mist coats my wedding gown. My brain takes a second to register what's happening.

The blade glints under the chandelier light. Once he pulls it free, the gruesome fleshy slice from ear to ear pours a river of blood down the friend's body, soaking the floor.

My head whooshes with the pulse thumping in my chest. He releases his body, and it hits the ground by my feet with a heavy thud.

This is who I married.

A killer.

A monster.

A dark king.

CHAPTER FORTY-THREE

Luca

I'D TAKEN my eyes of Alyssa for a few seconds while Marcello relieved me of his mother's gushing. I search the room, but she's nowhere. My heart kicks up, pounding violently. It's been doing that lot lately—because of her.

My father summons me with a crook of his finger. "I'm retiring for the night. You made me happy today," he tells me, patting my arm, gesturing for Edward to come and help him to his room.

As soon as he leaves, I go in search of my bride. It doesn't take me long to track her down. My spine bristles at the sound of my brother and his worthless friend's voice taunting.

Who the fuck do they think they are?

Adrenaline pumps through my veins as I silently move through the dining hall, the table set for a feast I had planned for a few of us tonight.

Alyssa doesn't know anyone here, so I didn't want to prolong her discomfort and planned to have everyone leave before our meal.

My beast rears up within me, taking over as I reach for a knife and grip the bastard in my hold, slicing through his neck, the knife made for slicing through cooked meat, not raw, living flesh.

It takes some carving, but I manage, cutting from one ear to the next. Alyssa's beautiful face becomes painted in blood, her eyes wide, mouth parted as I release the body and he falls at her feet.

Dammit. She's going to run.

"You motherfucker," Antonio bellows, coming around the table and shoving me. Turning on her heel, Alyssa rushes out of the room, and I give chase, ignoring my brother's hollering.

"Alyssa!" I call out, chasing her up the stairs into our room.

She races through to the bathroom, stopping at the mirror. Her fingers move to the blood stains decorating her creamy skin. She wipes, smearing them down her cheeks.

"I'm sorry you had to see that. This is who I am, Alyssa," I breath, her eyes flitting to mine through the mirror. "This is who you married, baby," I tell her, the blood soaking through my suit, my hands sticky, dripping.

If she wants out, she can't have it. There's no way I can let her go now. I fucking love her.

"I couldn't let him speak to you that way. You're mine." I exhale, my chest tightening. "And I'm yours. Can you love a monster?" I ask, my fists clenching.

She turns to face me, her brow crashing. Swallowing, she says, "You're not a monster—you're a king." She launches herself at me, grasping my face. "A dark king."

The lust in her eyes makes my cock stiffen. She isn't afraid or horrified. She's saturated with need.

The animal in me awakens the animal in her. My body takes over, a desperate need to be inside her.

"Fuck me, Luca. Fuck your queen," she pants, nipping at my lips. Grabbing my tie, she pulls me to her, her ass hitting the counter.

Frantic fingers unbuckle my belt. Unzipping my slacks, she releases my cock as I gather her dress up around her waist, tearing her panties from her.

Lifting her ass, I impale her on my cock, her scream echoing around the room, making me growl in response. "Harder," she cries, jamming her hips down on me as I thrust up.

The smeared blood on her face, painted in her hair, acts as her crown...my dark fucking queen.

AFTER SHOWERING, fucking her again, I take our clothes to my office throwing them on the fire.

It's a shame to watch her dress burn but necessary, maybe in the future we can have a second wedding, invite everyone to witness who she belongs to.

"Sir," Marcos enters my office. "The dining room mess is cleared."

There will be no signs of the slaughter that happened here tonight.

"Thank you, Marcos, where is my brother?"

Clearing his throat, he jerks his head to my drinks cabinet.

"Antonio got lost in a bottle of vodka and crashed in the study, Sir." Antonio will act like a prick for some time before he gets over what happened, but deep down, he knows that motherfucker was a waste of life and had it coming for a long time.

"Keep someone stationed at the door to keep an eye on him." I tell him, following him out of the office.

"Good night, Sir, and congratulations." He tells me as I ascend the stairs.

Entering our bedroom, I curl up next to Alyssa's sated sleeping form, never feeling so content in my entire life.

Alyssa's soft moan makes me smile. I wish I could see inside her head, see what she's dreaming about. To be sleeping so soundly after what she witnessed makes me think it wasn't the first time.

She's witnessed death before.

Snuggling into the heat of my body, her hair tickles over my chest. I move her curtain of hair from her face so I can look at her. The wedding band circles her finger. It's the sexiest thing I've ever seen.

It's crazy how you can avoid something, not want it, or think it will happen for you, but when it does, it's everything. She's changing me.

Her phone beeps on the bedside table, an incoming message.

I pick it up, checking to see if it's that weasel, Clint. It's from Hannah.

Simon quit. Said he's moving away and you're marrying Luca.

Please tell me that's not true.

Don't do anything until I can speak with you.

I'm home now. I want to talk to you.

Please, Alyssa.

Hovering my finger over the call button, I almost drop the phone when a fist pounds the bedroom door. "Luca, it's your father."

CHAPTER FORTY-FOUR

Alyssa

LIGHT FLOODS THE ROOM. A pounding on the door rouses me from sleep, my body sore from Luca's fucking tonight. The sight of the blood, his power, sent my libido into overdrive.

"What's happening?" I ask him. He's throwing on clothes, chucking a shirt at me.

"My father," is all he says. By the look on his face, I know it's not good news.

Rushing to put our clothes on I follow him across the house to a separate wing. There's a gathering outside his father's bedroom, a nurse standing with her head bowed.

"He was gone when I came in to give him his medication, sir. I'm sorry."

Thud.

Marcello steps around the nurse, planting his hand on Luca's shoulder. "He didn't suffer. He went in his sleep to be with your mother," he tells him, slapping down before releasing him.

Luca opens the door and steps forward. With my hand

clutched in his, I have no choice but to follow him inside the room. It smells of illness and old people.

The old man doesn't look like someone who ruled the criminal world like Simon suggested. His frail skin drooping over bone, his eyes wide open, staring up at the ceiling...he looks like Mother did. My stomach stirs.

Guilt. Guilt. Guilt.

Brushing his hand over his father's face, he closes his eyes. His grip tightens on me. "He got to see us marry. He can rest now," Luca says, his voice strained.

When we leave the room, Antonio is standing next to Marcello, swaying slightly on his feet. "So, he's dead then?" He juts his chin out to his brother.

"All life is temporary, brother. He lived longer than most," Luca tells him. A moment passes between them, and then we're moving, Luca dragging me back to our room.

"You can get some more sleep," he tells me, going to the closet to pick out a suit.

"What are you going to do?" I ask, leaning against the doorframe, watching his muscles flex as he changes from a t-shirt to a button down.

"Preparations."

"Luca," I walk over to him, stroking my palm up his back, "you don't have to do that right now."

Turning, he clasps my cheeks, kissing me hard and punishing. "I need to keep myself busy," he breaths as he breaks away.

I leave him to finish getting ready. Checking my phone, I see a message from Hannah.

Simon quit. Said he's moving away and you're marrying Luca.

Please tell me that's not true.

Don't do anything until I can speak with you.

I'm home now. I want to talk to you.
Please, Alyssa.

I WAIT for Luca to leave the room and call her. "Alyssa," she breathes down the line. "I've been worried about you."

I check the clock. It's six a.m. "What's going on, Hannah?"

"Simon quit. Do you know anything about that?"

Walking the room, I recall our conversation. Does she know who he is? "Why would I?"

She sighs. "I don't know. I think he liked you and was upset. He said you're marrying Luca?"

"Married," I correct.

The silence hangs between us. "I'm coming over," she tells me, ending the call. I stare at my phone not sure if she hung up or lost connection.

Blowing out a breath I go to the closet and pull out a pretty white summer dress the wedding dress designer brought over for me to wear last night for the reception, I brush my hair and teeth, then go down in search for some food.

My stomach growls, empty from missing out on dinner last night.

There's no sign of a murder.

The dining room is cleared and spotless, breakfast being brought through and set out.

"Madam, can I get you something?" the girl who refuses to use my given name asks me.

"I was just coming to look for some breakfast," I tell her, and she gestures for me to sit.

"I can bring you anything you want. We have Mr. Leto's favorite prepared."

"He's spoiled." Marcello chuckles, coming to join me at the table. "I heard last night turned into quite the event after I left."

My hand goes to my face, the phantom spray warming my cheeks.

"You could say I got to know my husband a little better." I shrug, reaching for a strawberry and popping it into my mouth.

"And?"

A warmth blooms in my stomach, "I'm still here." I return his answering smile.

The girl brings a tray of coffee just as Antonio walks in, grabbing a cup and sitting. He eyeballs me over the rim of his mug, his gaze flicking to the space a few feet away where he's friend died.

"I'm sorry about your father." I try to be civil, but he scoots out of his chair, taking the coffee pot with him.

"You should stay away from him. At least until we get him sober." Marcello scoffs.

The smell of bacon wafts in with another waiter. This place is like a hotel. My stomach growls in approval when I shovel a mountain of it onto my plate.

"Hungry?" Marcello asks.

"Ravenous." I sigh, biting into the first piece. "Were you close with Luca's dad?"

He re-fills our mugs and helps himself to some bacon and eggs. "I spent most of my time here growing up. My father died when I was a teenager, so I needed a strong father figure, and he was that for me."

"Will Luca be, okay?" I ask, worried about how this may affect him.

Placing his hand on top of mine, he nods. "His father's death was expected. It's easier when you've had time to come to terms with it."

I know that all too well.

"Alyssa, there you are." Luca frowns, coming to where I'm sitting, and taking my hand. "I need you in my office. Marcello, you too."

Grabbing a couple of pieces of bacon, I allow Luca to pull me from my seat and through the house to his office.

There's a man inside wearing a suit that rivals Luca's. His hair is neatly styled, and he wears a cocksure smile, just like Marcello's.

"Robert," Marcello greets him with a handshake. "A little early for business, no?"

"Not when your client is Luca Leto." The man tilts his head. "I have the documents ready to be signed and filed."

"Is now the time?" Marcello looks between Robert and Luca.

"Yes." Luca nods firmly.

"What's going on?" I ask, the bacon turning sour in my stomach.

"Come sit down. I just need you to sign some papers. We're moving some of our assets into your name, like we spoke about."

I don't argue. He's having a rough day and it can only be a good thing that I'm becoming a business owner with a flick of my wrist. "Remember to sign in your new name."

My eyes trace over the paper, seeing Mrs. Alyssa Leto for the first time.

Thud.

I sign where Robert points to, a sticker in place to guide me to the next page. When he moves onto a second document, I look up at him. "Really?"

"I want it in paper, Alyssa, I need to know you'll be taken care of," Luca urges. I look over to Marcello. He raises his brows to make light of the moment.

I scribble my name and watch Marcello sign where his is printed. Agreeing to marry me if anything should happen to Luca is morbid and unfair.

What happens if Marcello meets the love of his life and can't marry her on the off-chance Luca dies and he has to marry me?

Cupping my cheeks, Luca brings his lips to mine, tasting,

biting, sending my pulse racing. "I'm not going anywhere, but thank you for indulging me."

A knock on the door breaks our moment. Marcello opens it to one of the workers announcing Hannah's here to see me.

"Take my office. I need to get some food and deal with some things. Promise me you won't leave this house, Alyssa."

I don't like having to promise him that, but I can't bring myself to piss him off or make him worry on the day his father died. "Promise me," he says again, his voice firmer.

"I promise."

His eyes close briefly. "Good girl."

Hannah is shown in. She doesn't look like her usual well-put-together self, which is understandable with what she's been through.

She closes the door once we're alone, her movements awkward, nervous.

"It's not a good time to be telling me I shouldn't marry Luca, Hannah," I warn her, holding up my hand, his ring firmly in place.

"I know." She swallows. "But I need you to know if something happens to me..."

"What?" I go to her, taking her arms in my hands. "Why would something happen to you?" She's unstable, a crazed look in her eyes, bags sitting beneath them.

"Can we sit down?" she asks, her lips trembling.

"Sure," I guide her to the big leather armchairs, allowing her to sit down while I crouch next to her.

"A while back, we had a peeping Tom in my area. I got scared when one of my neighbors said this man broke into someone's house and stole their underwear." She sniffles, playing with the cuff of her sweater.

"Did something happen?" If that pervert did something to her...

"No," she shakes her head. "But because of that, I got some

cameras. Just ones you link to your cell phone. Inexpensive, but effective."

"Okay..."

"I captured the baby's father putting pills in my drink the day of the miscarriage." Her voice breaks, sweat beading her forehead.

"Hannah," I breathe, "can't you take it to the police or Luca?" I say before thinking it through.

Maybe it's something I can bring up to him. Scum who could do that to her don't deserve to be walking the earth. Maybe I should deal with him for her.

I could do it.

She springs forward, startling me. Her small hands grab my face. "You can't tell Luca any of this, what I'm going to show you..."

"Okay, okay. It's okay." I pull her hands free and place them in her lap.

"That wasn't the first time I got him on film." She panics, her skin paling. "The night of Serena's murder..."

Her body begins to shake, fear silencing her for a moment before she continues. "He asked to use my car. Not my main car, the one I inherited from my father a few years back. It's old. The plates aren't even real. It was used for a movie. I drove it over here to show you."

This is crazy. She's terrified, and I don't know what I'm supposed to do with this information.

"Hannah," I stand when she moves to pull something from her purse. Her phone.

"Who is this man?" I ask her. The tension has given me a stomach-ache.

The office door opens with a loud bang, crashing against the wall. Antonio waltzes in like he owns the place.

Hannah startles, almost dropping her phone. "I have to go," she announces, ducking her head and rushing past him.

What the hell?

"Was it something I said?" he calls after her, kicking the door closed. "Where's Luca?" He stalks toward me, and I back behind Luca's desk, remembering the gun he keeps there.

I won't use it, but it's comforting knowing it's there.

"Getting breakfast, why don't you join him—soak up some of that alcohol?" I mock.

"You've made yourself right at home, haven't you? Funny how he has a thing for dancers—pole or otherwise. Both bought and paid for," he spits, venom crawling across the room, trying to poison me.

"We're nothing alike. Serena was a whore he paid to fuck." I curl my lip.

"Isn't that what you are?"

"Be careful with your words. The last man who spoke to me like that bled out in the dining room. Luca may have my hand in marriage for a price, but the sex I give him for free."

Scoffing, he takes a step toward me again. "You think that makes you special? You're just a product—someone to control and use. He'll tire of fucking you and go back to paying for it."

"You sound hard up, Antonio. What's the matter? No one fucking you even when you offer to pay for it?"

"Bitch," he growls. "My brother said you were feisty. Said you like it rough."

My heart pounds. Luca wouldn't tell him that.

My phone vibrates with an incoming message, drawing his eyes to my pocket.

"Since it's also my money paying for you, maybe I should fuck you too—show you just how rough it can get," he sneers, lurching forward.

I'm quick.

Dropping to grab the gun from under Luca's desk, I aim at him before he reaches me.

"You wouldn't fucking dare." He laughs, taking another step.

I lower the gun to his foot and shoot.

"You don't know me," I remind him as he drops to the ground, wrapping his hands around his bare foot.

"You shot me." He looks up at me astonishment.

Pulling my phone from my pocket, I open Hannah's message while keeping the gun aimed at the prick.

She sent a video.

I click open and take a couple steps away from him to concentrate on what I'm seeing, the door opens, and Marcello enters. Looking to Antonio, he rushes over to him. "What happened?"

"You're right about the bitch being feisty. She fucking shot me." My eyes snap to Marcello.

"You said that?" I glower, the news inciting nausea. I thought he liked me?

"He interprets shit." Marcello rolls his eyes, coming to me and taking the gun.

"What are you watching?" he asks, coming around me to watch over my shoulder.

My breath hitches when his image comes on the screen. He's getting out of a car at Hannah's house and going inside.

The cameras switch to him in her kitchen washing blood from a knife.

"I'm really fucking sorry you had to see that, Alyssa. This is going to pain me a lot more than you," he whispers in my ear.

Just as Luca hurries into the room, shouting, "No!"

Marcello's knife stabs into my back.

Pain, sharp and pulsing, explodes within my flesh, spreading like a wildfire up my back and abdomen.

Shocked eyes of the man who promised me safety will be the last thing I see.

The fire steals my breath. My mouth opens, but only a squeaked, inhuman noise exits.

I'm going to die here.

Warm, crimson coats my clothes, spreading out across my pretty white dress. So much it runs down my leg, pooling at my feet.

I want to scream, call out.

My lungs squeeze. There's no air.

Noise, loud and pulsing, echoes around me.

Roars of anger shatter the air, splintering my mind.

I'm falling, the corners closing in, dark shadows chasing away the light.

Shots are fired.

Pop. Pop. Pop.

The world spins, fading...

How can it end like this?

I was a queen.

His queen.

And his kingdom killed me.

CHAPTER FORTY-FIVE

Luca

"WHAT'S HANNAH DOING HERE?" Marcello asks, following me through to the dining room and taking a seat as we leave Hannah and Alyssa to talk.

"She doesn't want Alyssa to marry me," I grunt, thinking back to her text.

She has a point—I'm a dangerous man—but I have a feeling she doesn't realize Alyssa's a dangerous woman.

She was drawn to the beast inside me because there's one in her too.

"Did you know she was pregnant?"

Almost spitting his coffee, he says, "How do you know that?"

Filling a plate, I shrug. "I took her to the hospital with Alyssa. She was distraught. Did you know?"

Shaking his head, he scratches his jaw. "I didn't. Then again, why would I?" He shifts, and it's the first time I've seen him uncomfortable.

My god.

"Tell me that wasn't your fucking baby." I blow out a breath, losing my appetite.

His throat bobs. "It may have been."

Motherfucker. "When the hell did that start?"

"It's nothing. A couple times when she was working late."

Pushing my plate away, I wipe my mouth and walk from the room, Marcello following behind me. "I think I'm going to wait and speak to Hannah, ask her about the baby," he informs me, jerking a thumb in the direction of my office.

"Fair enough, meet me at your mother's. She's going to help sort arrangements for my father's funeral," I tell him, still in disbelief he was fucking Hannah.

He stalks down the hall in the direction of my office as I summon Thomas, leaving through the front door.

Opening the car door for me, I falter, noticing the other car in the driveway pulling away.

Every nerve ending sizzles, the veins solidifying my blood.

It's the car from the pictures. "Whose car is that?" I ask Thomas, who looks in the direction of my stare.

"The blonde lady, Hannah, arrived in it, sir."

No fucking way.

My legs take off running. I race through the house, crashing through the door to my office, my eyes taking in the scene.

"No!" I cry out, water filling my eyes as Marcello stands behind Alyssa, her body jarring forward, a gasp fleeing her lips as a crimson stain spreads across her abdomen.

Her eyes spring wide, looking at me to save her. Her phone clatters to the ground.

My gun is pulled in seconds, but she's still in his hold. He has a gun in his hand, his arm wrapped around her shoulder, aiming at someone on the floor beside them.

Antonio.

"Why?" I roar.

"The fact that you don't know shows what a self-involved prick you are. How about Annemarie?" He rubs the gun against Alyssa's cheek.

She's fading, her back slouching against him, blood dripping down her leg. "I asked you to step in to keep that wedding from happening."

"Annemarie didn't fucking love you!" Antonio screams from his position on the carpet. He's bleeding from the foot.

Marcello growls, aiming the gun. He shoots into Antonio's shoulder, jerking him backward, a painful grunt slipping from his lips.

"Everything okay in there, sir?" Thomas asks through the door.

"Tell him yes or Alyssa gets another hole," Marcello warns through gritted teeth.

"Yes. Fine. Leave me," I bark, turning my attention back to Marcello. "I went to Annemarie. She didn't want to be with you, Marcello. I'm fucking sorry, but she didn't want it."

"Liar," he spits out. "That was my kid in her belly."

"No!" Antonio cries.

"That's why she killed herself," I breathe, my insides churning, my soul weakening with every passing second of Alyssa still bleeding out right in front of me.

This is karma. All those people I've killed in front of their loved ones... Fuck, I can't breathe.

This can't be happening. It was Marcello this whole time.

"You're lying."

"She left a note. I didn't want Antonio or you dealing with the pain, so I didn't let it be known. I hid it from you both."

"I don't believe you," he roars, Alyssa choking in his hold.

Fuck. Fuck. Fuck. I've never felt so helpless in all my life.

"Did you kill our mother?" Antonio asks, my head whirling. She was his aunt.

He loved her.

He couldn't

"After you told me what he heard our mother's talking about, I confronted my mom. She killed my father in his sleep because your mother couldn't keep his dick out of her whore cunt," he sneers.

Alyssa groans, tears streaming down her cheeks, her breathing becoming labored, her legs giving out.

He fucking drops her to the ground, his gun aimed at me.

"I had fun killing Serena too, but you didn't really feel her death—not like I did with Annemarie. I planned for you to want Hannah, marry her, then leave crumbs for you to think it was Antonio doing the killing, have you tear each other down, and then little ol' me, the one always second, always in the shadow of Luca Leto, would take it all. But you never liked Hannah, so when Alyssa took your interest, everything was still going to work out exactly how I planned, only Hannah went and ruined every-thing," he tuts, nudging Alyssa's legs.

"I was looking forward to having that beauty in my bed."

We both fire at the same time, my bullets making purchase as two of his pierce my skin, burrowing into my arm and shoulder.

We fall to the ground, guns still aimed. I pull myself behind an armchair while he props himself up behind my desk.

I need to get to Alyssa.

Pulling out my phone, I bring up Thomas's number and text.

It's Marcello.

Two seconds go by, and the door opens.

Shots ring out, and I'm on my feet, moving through the room, around the desk, my gun to Marcello's head while he's distracted with Thomas coming through the door.

"It's over," I announce, pulling the trigger, the shot loud, turning my stomach.

His body slumps over, limp and it fucking hurts seeing him like that, my insides churn, my head pounding.

I drop the gun and cradle Alyssa up into my arms, her body floppy as I lift her, ignoring the screaming of my own wounds, she's so fucking pale.

"Get the nurse and car ready," I bellow, rushing through the house, a flurry of feet moving opening doors for me. Thomas follows me out, Antonio over his shoulder.

Getting into the car, I lay her over my lap, touching two fingers to her neck. A faint pulse thumps against my skin.

One of my father's nurses jumps in with us, her face paling.

Lifting Alyssa's dress, an oozing red slash pumps her life from her. "We need to apply pressure to her wound," the woman says, ripping a piece of her shirt and pushing down on the slit.

I gather the dress up and hold it to the wound on her back. "Please, baby. Please be okay." There's so much fucking blood.

She's as pale as milk. Not conscious. I can't lose her.

Her blood drenches me, a warm river soaking into my slacks.

My worst fear is coming to fruition.

Tears blur my vision as the nurse begins pumping her chest, blowing into her mouth,

I'm dying.

She's going cold in my arms.

I can't breathe.

Please don't leave me.

CHAPTER FORTY-SIX

Alyssa

EVERYTHING HURTS AND FEELS STIFF. My throat is dry. My eyes attempt to open, peeling like skin from a burn. Light intrudes, blinding me.

"Luca, she's waking up." Is that Hannah's voice?

"Baby?" Luca...

Memories of what happened assault my mind. Tears leak free. "It was Marcello," I choke out, my voice not sounding like my own.

"It's over. I'm so sorry. I'm so damn sorry, Alyssa."

His hand wraps around mine, his head resting against my forehead.

The beautiful blue of his eyes come into focus. "Luca," I breathe out, grateful to see him. "Why?" I ask, remembering them exchanging words.

I couldn't focus on them.

"It's a long story. None of that matters. You're okay—we're okay—that's all that matters."

The door to the left opens, and a man enters. "She's awake?" I know that voice.

"Dad?" I croak.

"You're awake." He sounds relieved.

"You came?"

"Of course I came." He strokes my hair from my forehead. "You're a lucky girl. You'll still dance," he informs me, but it doesn't bring me comfort. Just knowing I'm alive is enough.

"If you want to," Luca adds for him. "Only if you want to dance."

"I love you," I tell him, brave and truthful. His lips part, his face contorting in pain, relief, joy.

"I love you too." He chuckles, bringing his lips to my head. "God, I fucking love you too." My chest expands, my head feeling free.

"You do?" I cry, my stomach twinging, bringing pain. I embrace it, anchor it inside me so I don't forget this moment.

"You're hurt?" I announce, noticing the sling on his arm.

"It's nothing," he tells me.

Hannah comes into focus at the end of the bed. "I'm so sorry, Alyssa. I should have gone to Luca...I was just so scared..." she cries, her hands covering her mouth.

"It's okay," I tell her. "Can someone please bring me a drink."

A round of laughs ring out, then movement. The nurses come in. They sit me up, check my monitors, and finally offer me a cup of water, placing a straw to my lips.

When she pulls it away, I remember something and announce, "I shot your brother in the foot."

My dad looks to Luca, then back to me. "Were you aiming for the foot?" he asks, and it makes me smile.

"Yes."

"Did he deserve it?" Luca adds.

"Yes. He's an asshole," I breathe out, getting tired again. "But he is your brother."

"You need to rest. We will rebuild from this. No one will ever hurt you again."

"Or you," I tell him, clutching his hand. "I'll protect you and love you for infinity and then more," I whisper, my eyes getting drowsy as he says, "And then more."

EPILOGUE

Luca

THE DRIVE IS LONG. I could have just let Thomas come, but there are some things you have to deal with yourself in person, and this is one of those things.

Looking out the window, I enjoy watching the change in scenery, thinking of my beautiful queen at home planning what she intends to do with the gift I gave her as a late wedding present.

It took some bribery and a lot of money, but Swan academy is now hers to do with as she pleases. No more whoring out their dancers to perverted old cunts.

I open my notebook on my phone, adding the name of the man who tried to buy her to my list. I may even invite Alyssa along for that one.

Her wound healed beautifully. A two-inch scar on her back and six inches on her front from the small operation to stop the bleeding.

My injury healed without issue, but Antonio had to have physiotherapy, which he got while doing a rehab treatment plan.

I gave him Annemarie's letter, her confession to being pregnant with Marcello's baby, her shame and fear that Marcello would never allow them to be happy together. She was right, he wouldn't have.

Marcello's injuries should have been fatal, but the bullet to the head lodged in part of the brain we don't use. It left him in a coma.

The doctors suggested we harvest his organs and donate them, but I like the idea of him lying there alive but dead in a sense.

He doesn't deserve closure. He doesn't deserve death. Let him suffer. He'd hate being there wasting away.

I pull out my phone as we draw close to our destination and text my wife.

Let's have a nice dinner tonight.

A celebration for ridding the world of another cunt. The dots appear, then her text.

I want you for dinner. To feel your cock hitting the back of my throat as I gag around your fat girth. Feed me, my king.

"We're here, sir," Thomas informs me.

Adjusting my cock, I say, "Let's make this quick, Thomas. My wife's hungry."

Stepping out, Thomas checks his phone again. The scan of the house from above shows the one occupant.

"Just him, sir."

"Good," I grin, flexing my shoulders.

"Do you want a particular weapon? I brought a kit," Thomas tells me, gesturing to the trunk.

"No. For this one, I'll use my hands."

Walking to the door, I rap my knuckles, waiting for the surprised face opening the door.

"Hello, Clint," I growl. Covering his mouth with my hand, I back him inside the house and kick the door closed.

THE END...

ABOUT THE AUTHOR

Ker Dukey is an international bestselling author based in the United Kingdom.

Genres include:

Dark Romance, Psychological Thriller, New Adult Romance, Romantic Suspense, MC romance and Mafia Romance. Ker, is an international bestselling author, with over thirty titles published. Her titles have held multiple #1 bestseller banners and have had rights sold to numerous countries.

In addition to being an author, Ker is an annoying wife and a mother of three children + one dog (who thinks he's human.) She has a passion for reading and binge-watching crime documentaries.

Find her on social media, where she loves interacting with her readers.

WWW.KERDUKEYAUTHOR.COM

ACKNOWLEDGEMENTS

Thank you to all for coming on this journey, I loved Luca and loved Alyssa even more. There's something empowering about a leading lady with a back bone.

Big thank you as always to the people who make it happen:

My editor, Word nerd editing.

My proof queen AND beautiful friend, Teresa Nicholson, thank you.

BLOGGERS! My rockstars, thank you for everything you do.

Candi Kane for a great PA service.

K Webster & Kirsty Moseley my sister's from different misters. I adore you guys. Thank you for always being my cheerleaders.

My Hubby and amazing kids who put up with me zoning out when a story consumes me and gives up precious mum/wife time when I need to work stupid hours.

I love you all.

BOOK LIST.

Titles by Ker Dukey

Empathy Series:

Empathy

Desolate

Vacant

Deadly

The Broken Series:

The Broken

The Broken Parts of Us

The Broken Tethers That Bind Us

The Broken Forever

The Men by Numbers Series:

Ten

Six

Drawn to You Duet:

Drawn to You

Lines Drawn

Standalone Novels:

My Soul Keeper

Lost

I See You

The Beats in Rift

Devil

Dukey's Dark Delight titles. (Bite sized dark reads)

Stalk Her

Muse

Heart Thief

Royal Bastards MC series.

Animal

Rage

Carnage Pre-order

Co-Written with D. Sidebottom

The Deception Series:

FaCade

Cadence

Beneath Innocence

The Lilith's Army MC Series:

Taking Avery

Finding Rhiannon

Co-Written with K Webster

The Pretty Little Dolls Series:

Pretty Stolen Dolls

Pretty Lost Dolls

Pretty New Doll

Pretty Broken Dolls

The V Games Series:

Vlad

Ven

Vas

KKinky Reads Collection:

Share Me

Choke Me

Daddy Me

Watch Me

Hurt Me

Play Me

Joint Series

Four Fathers Series:

Blackstone by J.D. Hollyfield

Kingston by Dani René

Pearson by K Webster

Wheeler by Ker Dukey

Four Sons Series:

Nixon by Ker Dukey

Hayden by J.D Hollyfield

Brock by Dani René

Camden by K Webster

The Elite Seven Series:

Lust – Ker Dukey

Pride – J.D. Hollyfield

Wrath – Claire C. Riley

Envy – M.N. Forgy

Gluttony – K Webster

Sloth – Giana Darling

Greed – Ker Dukey & K Webster

Titles found on Amazon.